GUARDIAN OF THE DARK SLAP

TALES FROM THE DARK PAST
BOOK FIVE

HELEN SUSAN SWIFT

For The One I Love

PRELUDE

GALIPOLLI, SUMMER 1915

Gunfire lit the horizon, with the nonstop flashes destroying the sanctuary of the dark. Lieutenant Thomas Armstrong of the King's Own Scottish Borderers crouched in the trench, feeling the ground tremble under his feet as the first shells exploded around him. The noise was so continuous that he could not distinguish any single sound and could hardly hear the man beside him speaking.

"Sir!" Sergeant Kilner mouthed the word. "We've lost Number One Section. A Turkish shell landed directly on top of them."

Thomas nodded. "Thank you, Sergeant!" He flinched as a shell exploded twenty yards away, sending a shower of earth and small stones to patter on his helmet and shoulders.

The bombardment continued, with explosions all around the British and Anzac trenches, blasting dirt, stones, and fragments of men into the air. It rose to a crescendo and stopped abruptly at dawn, leaving men stunned, gasping for air, and scrabbling for cover in the bottom of shallow trenches.

The Turks will attack any moment now, Thomas realised. He forced himself to stand upright and peer over the dust-hazed landscape towards the Turkish positions. A glitter in the distance warned of a moving mass of men carrying rifles with fixed bayonets.

"Here they come, boys! Stand to!"

Whistles sounded along the length of the British trenches, and men emerged from cover, adjusting their helmets, checking their rifles, and staring into the rising sun.

The Turks advanced as bravely as always, a mass of men in dark khaki uniforms cheering as they ran forward. The officers led from the front, resolute in their determination to push the invaders from their land.

The British artillery opened fire, raising fountains of dust among the Turkish infantry, smashing men to a pulp, or sending deadly shrapnel to lacerate frail human bodies. The machine guns came next, the .303 Vickers, renowned for their reliability as they scythed down the advancing men. After a few moments, the Lewis machine guns joined the cacophony, with the riflemen firing last.

"Come on, Borderers!" Thomas shouted. "Show Johnny Turk what we're made of!"

The men aimed and fired, worked the bolts of their Lee-Enfields, held the stocks firm to their shoulders, and fired again. Soon there was no need to aim; the Turks were so close the Borderers fired at the mass of dark khaki, working the rifle bolts frantically.

"Come on, Johnny Turk!" Thomas found himself shouting as he stood in the trench, encouraging his men. "Come and face the Borderers!" He emptied his revolver and paused to reload, pushing the cartridges into their chambers with trembling, dirty fingers. He dropped one cartridge and watched the growing light reflect on the brass as it spiralled, seemingly in slow motion, down to the dust.

Thomas jammed the final cartridge into his revolver and looked up. Despite their losses, the Turks were nearly at the trench, teeth and bayonets gleaming.

"Fire!" Thomas roared. "Send them back to Constantinople, boys!" He squeezed the trigger, saw his bullets knock a Turkish officer sprawling, and then the Borderers were fighting bayonet to bayonet.

A stocky Turk jumped into the trench and lunged at Thomas, who shot him, seeing the man's head shatter under the force of the bullet. Another Turkish soldier took his place, and then another until Thomas had emptied his revolver and was fighting with fists and boots. He saw Wee Willie Scott leap into the air and smash his forehead into a Turk's face as Danny Hunnam fell with a Turkish bayonet in his stomach.

"Fight them!" Thomas shouted and screamed as something long, sharp, and cold snaked into his side. He turned around and saw the swarthy face of a Turkish private, and then somebody cracked a rifle butt on his head, and he crumpled to the ground. Before he passed out, he saw a shadowy figure at the far end of the trench, a tall man dressed like a mediaeval knight.

What the devil is he doing here?

～

"Tom!" The voice came to him from far away. "Tom! Wake up!"

Thomas fought away the memories and opened his eyes. "I had that nightmare again," he said. "What a mazurka!"[1]

"I know," Eleanor told him. "You were shouting in your sleep." Her smile teased him. "Your language was shocking."

Thomas struggled to sit up. "Trench language," he explained. "Not fit for a lady's ears."

"Well," Eleanor said, "I'm no lady, I'm your sister, and I've heard it all before. Get up, wash, and get dressed. We've got a bit of a drive before us."

"It was the war," Thomas explained.

"The war ended three years ago," Eleanor reminded sternly. "It's time you forgot about it."

"It's in my mind all the time," Thomas said.

"That's why we're moving to somewhere quiet." Eleanor dragged the covers from the bed. "New beginning and no old memories. Come on!" She slapped his leg and pulled his arm. "Up!"

Thomas frowned. "This dream was a little different," he said. "I thought I saw a knight in armour in the trench."

Eleanor shook her head. "Were there not angels and archers at Mons? Maybe there's a connection."

"I was dreaming of Gallipoli," Thomas said, shrugged, and slid out of bed. "Come on, sister-of-mine. We have a longish drive ahead of us."

"I think I already said that," Eleanor told him.

CHAPTER 1

THE HOTEL LOOKED unprepossessing as Thomas pulled the dark green Crossley to a halt outside the front door. Two storeys high, with the whitewash peeling off the outside wall and the sign, Wardlaw Inn, creaking in the wind, it would not have appealed to him before the war. Now, in the aftermath of four years of bloody slaughter, appearance meant nothing, he had discarded luxury, and even comfort was not supremely important.

"Are you ready?" Eleanor asked brightly.

Thomas nodded to her with his eyes dull. "I'm ready." He glanced along the street, seeking inspiration.

The village of Newbigging was quiet, with the drizzling rain dampening the autumnal dust on the pavement and weeping from a neglected gutter above the inn's signboard. Nobody walked the street, while a solitary farm cart rumbled slowly along the road. The driver stared at the Crossley as he passed, saying nothing. He managed a reluctant nod in response to Eleanor's cheery hail.

An aroma of dampness greeted them as they pushed open the inn's front door. There was no reception desk, merely a small table with a vase of wilting flowers and a brass handbell. Eleanor rang the bell, the sound breaking the sombre silence of the inn. When nobody appeared, she rang again.

"I heard you the first time." The man was in his late middle age, with a bald head and a limp. "What do you want?"

"We've booked in for the week," Eleanor said. "Thomas Armstrong and Eleanor Machrie." She waited for his comment.

"That will be two single rooms," the man said after a short pause.

"Or a twin," Eleanor said with a smile. "We're brother and sister."

Eleanor expected his downward glance to check if she was wearing a wedding ring. "My husband died at Ypres," she said.

The man grunted, eyeing Eleanor sourly. 'Twin," he said. "First floor. Room number three. Where's your luggage?"

"In the car," Eleanor told him. "My brother will bring it in."

The man nodded. "Dinner's six till eight. Breakfast's seven till eight."

"Thank you, Mister..." Eleanor waited for the man to give his name.

"Johnston," he said grudgingly. Turning away without another word, he slouched through a half-glazed door.

"Twin," Eleanor confirmed. "First floor. Number three. Could you fetch the bags, Tom?"

She waited for Thomas to return and climbed up the creaking steps to the first floor, past the panelled walls with their faded pictures of Walter Scott, Robert Burns, and the ubiquitous Landseer print of a stag at bay.

The room was decorated in similar taste, with a once-good-quality but now worn rug on the ground above varnished floor-boards, two iron beds, and pictures of Edinburgh Castle and the Eildon Hills on the wall. Eleanor half expected to see a portrait of Queen Victoria, dead these last twenty years, frowning down on them.

"How are the beds, Thomas?"

She heard the ominous creak of springs as Thomas sat on the nearest.

"Good," he said.

Eleanor tested the second bed and nodded when she found it better than she had feared. "Here we are, then."

"Here we are," Thomas agreed.

"Tomorrow is the big day."

Thomas nodded, sitting on the bed, staring at the wall with his mind elsewhere.

"You unpack while I look at the view." Stepping to the window, Eleanor stared up the street. She gave a wry smile, thinking they must have arrived at the busy period, for now, half an hour later, nothing at all stirred in the village. Newbigging was dead. She counted three shops: a baker, a butcher and one with the name Elliot in faded gold letters against a brown background. Eleanor presumed the locals would know what Elliot's sold, while any visitors would have to guess.

Eleanor knew the layout of this village, although she had never been here in her life. It was similar to a score of other eighteenth-century planned settlements in Scotland, with two streets intersecting at right angles in a reasonably large market square, where the Inn, the church, and the shops were situated. Simple, robust, and practical, it allowed nothing for the local geography.

"This place doesn't belong," Eleanor observed.

"Why not?" Thomas joined her at the window.

"It's too manufactured. Somebody has deliberately placed

it here." Knowing Thomas would not understand her reasoning, Eleanor looked beyond the houses to the distant hills. Long, grey-green, and gently curved, they had endured tens of thousands of years of history. "I prefer organic growth."

"Oh." When Thomas said no more, Eleanor knew she had lost him.

"Best get changed," Eleanor said. "We'll be late for dinner." She watched him out of the corner of her eye, wincing at his clumsiness. "Let me help you."

"I know how to dress!" Thomas said.

"Of course you do," Eleanor said, fighting her pain. When Thomas thought he had finished, she adjusted his tie, brushed down his shoulders, and headed downstairs.

Although Eleanor and Thomas were the only guests in the inn, there were two other couples for dinner. One pair had evidently been married for many years, as they communicated with hardly a word while still managing to make themselves understood. The other couple had apparently never seen strangers before, to judge by the interest they took in the new guests. When the man bent forward to murmur something to his companion, Eleanor saw Thomas tense, with his right fist clenching around his knife.

"No, Thomas." Eleanor shook her head. "It doesn't matter." Turning around in her seat, she returned their scrutiny, giving them stare for stare until they dropped their eyes. Eleanor continued to watch them as they ate.

"Is everything all right?" The waitress was blonde-haired and cheerful, a breath of fresh air in that room of gloom.

"Fine, thank you," Eleanor assured her. As she looked willing to help, Eleanor continued. "Are you local to the area?"

When the waitress smiled, her freckles merged, so half her face was one mass of ginger. "I've lived here all my life," she said. "As has my family as long as time."

"That's good." Eleanor gave her an encouraging smile. "You'll know your way around, then."

"As well as anybody," the waitress replied.

"Do you know a house called Anton's Walls?" Eleanor asked. "It's a strange name, but I know it's somewhere nearby. I didn't see it on the Bartholomew's map."

"I ken it fine." The waitress's smile broadened. "It's empty, though. Old Jock Armstrong died over a year ago if you were looking for him."

"I was not," Eleanor said. "Could you tell me how to get there, please?"

Pulling up a chair, the waitress sat beside Thomas. "Are you walking? There's no' a bus service that way. Maybe you can hire a chaise from Geordie Rutherford's in the village."

"We have a car," Eleanor said. "It's parked in the street outside."

"Oh!" The waitress shook her head. "I wondered who owned the Crossley! I should have known it would be yours!" She treated Thomas to a smile.

"Is there a road to Anton's Walls?"

"There's a bit of one," the waitress told me. "A country road, as we call it, not a metalled road."

Eleanor nodded. She had expected nothing else. "It'll be a quiet place, then."

"Aye, it's quiet," the girl said. "There's nothing much there except the moor. Not even sheep, since old Jock Armstrong died." She glanced at Thomas, sitting quietly at Eleanor's side. "Maybe Old Jock's ghost."

"That won't bother us," Thomas said quickly.

A rough voice broke in. "What do you want to go to Anton's for?"

Eleanor had not seen the elderly man arrive. He stood

beside the table, dressed in faded working clothes and smelling of damp soil and tobacco.

"There's nothing there for toonies and stooriefeet. Anton's is in the middle of a wilderness. Why would anybody want to build a house there?" The man's voice was harsh, like gravel dragged under a gate, and a mass of wrinkles hid his eyes.

"It may be a wilderness now," Eleanor suggested. "It might not have been a couple of hundred years ago. The population has shifted. Back then, there might have been hundreds of little farms, each with a family running it." She turned to Thomas. "Get the map out, Tom. This lady might point out where Anton's Walls is."

"My name's Sharon," the girl volunteered.

"Deepsyke's always been a muir," the old man grumbled.

When Eleanor spread the map over the table, Sharon bent across with her long hair brushing against Thomas. "I've never seen it like that before," she said. "Look at all the names written down." She traced her finger over the linen-backed paper. "Hawkshaw, Wolf Rig, Wardlaw, Bareback Knowe, Hangingshaw, Dod's Bog, Bareback Cleuch, Dundreich, Deepsyke Moor – they've spelt it wrong. It should be muir, not moor."

Eleanor allowed Sharon a few moments to peruse the map. "Could you show us where Anton's Walls is please?"

"Here." Without hesitation, Sharon stabbed a finger down. "Right in the middle of Deepsyke Muir."

The name sent a shiver through Eleanor as if the bleakness of the moor had entered her soul. "A syke is a burn [1] in boggy ground, isn't it? Is Deepsyke Muir as bleak as it sounds?"

"Aye." The old man breathed out stale tobacco fumes. "There's naething there but bogland and dark water."

"It's not that bad." Sharon shook her head. "Don't listen to Martin here. He likes to see the dark in everything!" Her eyes laughed at the elderly man. "Don't you, Martin? Deepsyke

Muir is a lovely place when the sun shines. You'll hear the lave-rocks singing, the whaups calling, [2] and the bees searching for heather honey."

"You'll hear the hoolet too," Old Martin croaked. "Dinnae forget the hoolet."

"Exactly," Sharon said. "You'll hear the hoolets too. That's the owls," she explained for the benefit of city-bred people who did not know what a hoolet was.

"There's nothing there except moss, heather, and peat holes deep enough to suck you down forever," Martin said. "You'd best get back to Glasgow or wherever you belong."

"Edinburgh," Eleanor told him, smiling.

"Aye." Martin stepped back. "Edinburgh." He repeated the name as if it were a curse. "You'd best get back where you belong. There's nothing for you in Anton's Wa's except hard-ship and misery."

"We've seen that." Thomas looked up with a dark light at the back of his eyes. "We've seen hardship and misery." Reaching out, he gripped Martin's wrist. Eleanor saw life spark into Thomas's face for a second, and then it died away again as he released Martin and slumped in his chair.

Sharon looked from Eleanor to Thomas and back with a question in her eyes. Eleanor diverted her attention. "I heard that the house was named after somebody called Anthony. Is that correct?"

"Aye," Martin answered first. "Jock's great-great-great-grandfather, Anthony Armstrong, built the place. He gave it some fancy name that nobody heeded. Everybody called it Anthony's Walls, which became Anton's Wa's, although the stooriefeet call it Anton's Walls." His glare at Thomas conveyed his contempt for stooriefeet as he called incomers to the area. [3]

"Are you a local historian?" Eleanor asked politely.

Martin favoured her with a dark glower. "No."

"Martin knows everything about the Wardlaw Valley," Sharon said. "Or he thinks he does. Isn't that right, Martin? You've been here so long you probably lived through it all,"

"I know enough." Martin spoke without looking directly at her.

Sensing a little tension, Eleanor took the map and carefully crunched it into a hideous mess on the table. Absently, Thomas sorted it out, folded it neatly and replaced it inside his jacket.

"Thank you, Tom," Eleanor said.

"Sharon!" The voice was sharp as Johnston stood in the doorway. "Your job is to serve the guests, not gossip to them."

"Excuse me, please." Sharon stood, bobbed in an old-fashioned little curtsey, and scurried away. Eleanor looked at Thomas hopefully, but he did not watch her hips swaying in their black-and-white uniform. Instead, he stared straight ahead, with his eyes seeing events that happened years before.

Eleanor hid her disappointment and masked her pain behind a bright smile.

With lunch over, Thomas and Eleanor walked around the village. It did not take long as there was not much to see, just two streets, a handful of small shops and the war memorial. Eleanor knew these structures were springing up throughout the country in tribute to the tens of thousands of dead Scotland lost in the Great War. She thought the monument at Newbigging was too elaborate for such a small place until she saw the number of names inscribed underneath the figure of a soldier with his head bowed and rifle reversed.

Eleanor read the names. Armstrongs, Johnstons, Elliots, Croziers, Grahams, and others. All the old Borders surnames, all dying a long way from their homes in the war to end all wars.

Thomas put out a finger, tracing one of the names. "I was

with him when he died." He spoke quietly. "Davie Graham. A Turkish sniper got him at Gallipoli. He'd only taken three steps from the boat."

"Poor lad," Eleanor commented.

"Aye, he was seventeen years and two days old."

Eleanor listened as Thomas relived his war, his finger following the names of men, tracing the letters as his memories traced their lives and deaths.

"Shuggie Elliot. He died at Ypres; the gas got him. Nice lad, Shug." Before Eleanor could stop him, Thomas stepped back, snapped to attention, and saluted. Although they were deep in the Scottish Borders, Eleanor knew Thomas had never left the war. When he looked at her, she wondered what he saw and what images were in his mind.

"Rest easy, lads," Thomas said. "We'll never forget you."

"Can you hear that?" Eleanor lifted a finger. "I hear music. It sounds like some old French song." She frowned, for the music was familiar, although she could not say from where. She began to sing, softly intoning the words.

"Ce fut en mai
Au douz tens gai
Que la saisons est bele,
Main me levai."

Eleanor stopped, shrugging. "I don't remember where that came from. Do you know it, Tom?"

When Thomas shook his head, Eleanor saw the light die from his eyes again.

"It's a French song," Eleanor prompted without success.

"I can hear music, right enough," Thomas said, "but not French music."

Eleanor nodded. The French words had faded, and the sounds of somebody singing came from a small house at the very edge of the village. Looking older than the rest of the street, the building was thatched, with tiny, deep-set windows and an open door. "We'll stand outside and listen," Eleanor said. "I'm sure nobody will mind."

Laughter punctuated the music, with light female voices joining the deep male and the clink of bottles or glasses. Only then did Eleanor see the sign hanging above the door with the name Dryfe Arms in faded black letters on a plain white background.

"It's a bit of a hole in the wall," she said, "but shall we go in?"

Thomas nodded and stepped through the door. Eleanor followed him to find the place crowded. The music stopped as soon as they entered, and a score of men and women turned to stare at them as if they were aliens. One broad-shouldered man brooding in a corner fixed them with a malevolent glower and ignored Thomas's cheerful greeting. As Eleanor wondered if they should leave again, Thomas stepped up to the shirt-sleeved barman.

"What do you have?" Thomas glanced over the meagre display behind the bar.

The barman frowned. "Beer or whisky."

"Do you have any wine for my sister?"

"Beer or whisky."

"One pint of Youngers then, and a small whisky with water."

After Thomas found two seats at a small round table, most of the clientele stopped staring at them and resumed their previous occupations. Only the broad-shouldered man continued with his pointed glare.

"He's a cheery fellow," Thomas said.

Eleanor nodded, leaned back, and listened to the music. It was rough and ready, without any sophistication but with plenty of energy as men and woman in shabby working clothes banged their feet on the ground and sang lustily. Some of the songs were new to Eleanor, others she recognised, although the words and tunes differed in detail.

Eleanor saw old Martin in the crowd. He fixed her with a very intense look, shook his head, looked away for a moment, and then returned to his scrutiny. His neighbour, a burly man in late middle age, ran his gaze down her body from head to foot and back and favoured her with a nod.

Eleanor nodded back, smiling.

After half an hour and two more whiskies, Eleanor was irritated by the broad-shouldered man's staring. Aware that every eye was on her, she walked across to him, weaving past the tables and chairs.

"It's ages since I saw you! You look so different like that." Treating the man to her best smile, she touched his shoulder. "We'll meet again soon, shall we?"

The man started, lifted a dirty red hat, and stormed out of the inn without saying a word. Eleanor returned to Thomas, who stared ahead of him. Eleanor did not think he had noticed.

Old Martin gave Eleanor a slight nod that could have signified approval. He stepped over to her. "That man was Wally Nixon, the factor," he croaked. "An ill man to cross." He lowered his voice to a harsh whisper. "You did well, my friend. Now listen to my song and pay heed."

Eleanor nodded. She felt something had changed, as if she had stepped through a hidden doorway. Brushing away the French song that whispered in her ears, she tried to concentrate on Martin, knowing something significant was about to happen.

CHAPTER 2

LEAVING ELEANOR, old Martin returned to his table and remained standing.

"You all know me. I'm Martin Crozier, so haud your tongues when I'm singing the *Twa Corbies*." He began to sing in his weary old voice, with the room obediently quiet. He fixed Eleanor with a stare as if to ensure she was paying attention.

The *Twa Corbies* is a five-stanza Border ballad where two corbies – crows – talk about a dead knight lying behind a dyke. Sung properly, it carries an air of tragedy, of the desolation of loss and the ever-present sadness of the old Border. Eleanor had heard others singing it and had been disappointed, for although they were undoubtedly melodious, they failed to capture the horror of the crows pecking the "bonny blue een" from the abandoned knight.

From a grumpy old man, Martin Crozier became the object of everybody's attention. He sang in a voice rusty with age but with such power and feeling that Eleanor had to listen.

"As I was walking all alane,
I heard twa corbies makin' a mane,"

Martin's broad Border accent seemed to heighten the meaning of the words, so as Eleanor sat in that room, reeking of strong tobacco smoke, she was mentally transported back in time to the old border of peel towers and raiding armies.

"The tane unto t'other say,

Where sall we gan and dine today?"

Eleanor could see the two black crows sitting on the grey-green turf of the dyke, searching for food in a devastated countryside. Martin's cracked voice portrayed the essence of those days in a song where every word carried menace. The crows spoke of "a new-slain knight" and the chilling message that,

"His lady's ta'en another mate

So we may mak our dinner sweet."

Eleanor imagined that unfortunate young knight, with his blood still congealing on his battered body, while his girl rode away with a new lover, and one crow sat "on his white hause-bane" while the other picked "out his bonny blue" eyes.

Martin's eyes seemed to fix on Eleanor as he sang as if he were conveying some special message to her.

"O'er his white banes, when they are bare

The wind sall blaw for evermair."

When Martin intoned the final, hopeless words, Helen envisaged the knight lying abandoned on the ground. She looked around, expecting rapturous applause, but realised the audience had lost interest. Martin had an audience of one. Eleanor had never been prone to follow the crowd in anything, so she stood up and clapped, wondering if anybody else had the good manners to join in. When Thomas followed her example, Eleanor blessed his kind heart, but nobody else moved. In that whole room, not one other person understood Martin's message.

After a few moments, Martin ordered the barman to refill

his pewter mug with Youngers beer and sat beside Eleanor. "You're in the wrong place." He ignored Thomas.

"Where should I be?"

"You understood the *Twa Corbies*," Martin accused.

"I did." Eleanor nodded. "You sang it well."

"What's your name?"

"Eleanor," she said.

"Not your first name." Martin sounded irritated. "What's your real name?"

"I'm Eleanor Machrie," Eleanor said.

"Mrs Machrie?" Martin glanced at Thomas, who stared straight ahead with his mouth slowly working as he shouted silent orders to long-dead men.

"Mrs Machrie," Eleanor confirmed.

"That's not the name I want," Martin said. "What's your family name?" He leaned across the table, so his face was closer to Eleanor's. "Where are you from, Mrs Machrie?"

"My family name?" Eleanor knew she should have been offended by Martin's persistent questioning but still felt the power of his song. "My maiden name was Armstrong," she said.

Martin's smile was unexpected and took twenty years from his age. "A Border name, that's why."

"I don't understand," Eleanor said. "That's why what?"

"That's why you can understand," Martin explained in his cracked voice. "You belong."

"This place is not very welcoming," Eleanor complained. "I don't think the people want me to belong."

"People are transient," Martin said. "And belonging is not about being welcome. It's about blood." Standing up, he drained his tankard in a single noisy draft, wiped the froth from his half-shaven chin and looked at Eleanor through red-rimmed eyes.

"Your blood is from here. You can hear the message in the wind and feel the spirit of the hills."

Eleanor stared at him, suddenly uncomfortable. "Who are you, Mr Crozier?"

Martin ignored her question. "You don't want to belong here, Eleanor Armstrong. For the love of God, don't go to Anton's Walls, or you'll never want to leave. Go back to Edinburgh and take that damaged man with you."

"What?" Eleanor asked, but Martin was already loping away, shouldering aside a much larger man as he pushed through the door. A blast of cold air entered the room, causing Eleanor to shiver.

A woman pushed the door firmly shut.

"Did you hear that, Thomas?" But Thomas was shaking, dodging shells that had exploded six years before. Eleanor sighed. "Come on, Tom. It's time we were back. We have another long day tomorrow."

The crows flapped away, circled the village, and landed in front of the Wardlaw Inn. Not understanding the crows' significance, she paid them no heed as she guided Thomas away from the Dryfe Arms.

Eleanor lay in her bed until Thomas fell asleep. She listened to him fidgeting and wondered what he was dreaming.

Oh, God, if there is a god. Grant me the strength to help my brother through his trauma. She closed her eyes, seeing again the wounded men waiting outside the hospital, some with hideous injuries and smelled the mixture of fear, raw blood, and powerful disinfectant.

Reaching into the bag at the bottom of her bed, she stealthily removed the small silver hip flask, unscrewed the stopper and placed it to her lips. She fought the shaking. *Keep me from weakness, Lord, so that I can help my brother through his pain. The* whisky was welcome as it exploded in her stomach. She drank more, draining the flask dry, and closed her eyes, grasping at sleep as a relief from her worry.

Later that night, something woke Eleanor. Opening her eyes with a start, she looked around the unfamiliar room, unsure where she was. She sat up in bed, checked Thomas, pulled the tangled covers over his twisted, sweat-sodden body, and stood up with her head full of strange fancies. That song from the previous night still rampaged through her brain, while she could feel old Martin's eyes still scrutinising her as he asked his strange questions and gave his weird pronouncements.

"Your blood is from here. You can hear the message of the wind and feel the spirit of the hills." *What on earth had that meant?*

Stumbling to the window, Eleanor looked outside. Newbigging was quiet under pale stars, with the street lights flickering on the uniform architecture, yet something nagged at the back of her mind.

Eleanor heard an owl hoot once, twice, and a third time, the sound somehow melancholy in that sleeping village. The hoolet, she thought, with a wry smile, and shook her head. Eleanor did not know how long she watched the horseman before his presence registered in her tired brain. Perhaps because he looked so natural in the Borders, or maybe because she was still half asleep, he was quarter way up the street before Eleanor realised she was staring at him.

He rode past slowly, unhurried, with the hooves of his horse making little sound, yet although Eleanor looked directly at him, she could not describe anything about him until he lifted his head and looked at her.

Eleanor would swear that it was old Martin Crozier astride that horse in the small hours of the morning, except in the half-light, he looked straight-backed and younger, with a long cloak descending from his shoulders and a bulky bag hanging from his saddle. He gave her one long, searching look and then he was gone, leaving her unsettled without any reason. After all, there was no reason why Martin should not ride his horse any time he liked. Eleanor watched him cross the central square and past St Bride's Church. When she looked away, Martin vanished, although Eleanor had not seen him turn into a side street.

Eleanor's uneasiness continued as a pair of crows landed opposite the hotel, dark bodies highlighted by the street lamps.

CHAPTER 3

Dawn can be spectacular in the Scottish Borders, with a deep orange glow highlighting the long smooth curves of the hills and spreading up the sweet valleys. It is an ethereal time of great peace, as if the growing light disguises the history of dispossession, invasion and sordid deeds. Thomas was usually awake before dawn as if to prepare for an expected attack, and Eleanor joined him at the side of the window.

"Good morning, Thomas," Eleanor said.

"Good morning." He looked at her with his eyes slowly clearing. "What are you doing here, Eleanor?"

"We're looking at Anton's Walls today," she reminded.

Thomas nodded, rational again, and the shadows were absent from his eyes. "We'll start immediately after breakfast."

Eleanor listened as the plaintive cry of sheep rose from the green slopes around the village and wished that she could have her brother and husband back from the war. Instead, she put on her brightest smile.

"That's the spirit!" Eleanor said.

The waitress who served them was the same red-haired girl

who had been so helpful the previous evening, and she greeted them cheerfully.

"Are you off to Anton's Walls today, then?"

"We are, Sharon," Eleanor said.

Sharon glanced out the window. "It's a pity about the weather," she said. "You won't see the moor at its best."

Eleanor looked outside, where the pink dawn had evolved into thin greyness. "It's not too bad."

"It will rain before nine o'clock," Sharon said cheerfully. "You'd best take your coat and hat."

Thanking her for the advice, Eleanor added. "We take the road northeast, don't we? And then turn left."

"That's right, take the hill road up towards Hawick for three miles or so and look for a track on the left. You won't see it from the road, but there's an ancient standing stone a hundred yards from the turn-off. There might be a signpost, but it's probably fallen now." Sharon shook her head so her dark blonde hair cascaded around her shoulders. When Eleanor studied her, she saw the waitress was not as young as she had thought, for there were little lines around her eyes and mouth. Eleanor would have judged her age as mid-twenties.

"Deepsyke Muir is not level; it undulates up and down." Sharon waved her hand up and down to demonstrate what she meant by undulates. "After rain, the down bits get wet. You'll have to watch for the bogland because the floods get deep. When you pass the highest point, Deepsyke Head, there's a nasty dip that fills in bad weather; that's the ford over the Deep Syke, and Anton's is straight ahead down the track."

"Thank you." Thomas surprised Eleanor by speaking. "How far down the track?"

Sharon screwed up her face. "About a mile from the black road. You'll be driving in your Crossley, won't you?"

"That's correct." Thomas replied first again.

"The new model?" Sharon asked.

"That's right." Eleanor felt a surge of joy at the light in Thomas's eyes as he pursued his favourite subject of anything mechanical. "The 19.6."

"The 19.6 is famous for its hill climbing." Sharon was so enthusiastic Eleanor wondered if she was going to ask to join them. "A Crossley will manage the track better than most, but even then, you'll have to be wary of the Deep Syke if it's swollen with rain."

Eleanor said nothing as Thomas replied again. "I didn't see that name on the Bartholomew."

"I doubt it's marked," Sharon said. "The track goes right across, or rather, right through." She smiled. "You'll see the ruins of Blackhouse Tower as well." She leaned against Thomas, much to Eleanor's delight.

Thomas smiled. "Thank you for your help, Sharon."

Eleanor thought her brother was about to say more when a door banged shut somewhere in the hotel, and he started. She saw the light vanish from his eyes as though somebody had drawn a shutter, and he sank back down on his chair. Eleanor put her hand over his as he reached for a knife.

"Thank you, Sharon." Eleanor diverted attention from Thomas's reaction. "Now we know exactly where to go. Onto the Hawick road and watch for a track on the left."

"That's right," Sharon said. She put a hand on the back of Thomas's chair. "It would be good to see Anton's occupied again. Deepsyke Muir can be a lonely place."

"We want somewhere quiet," Eleanor said with a telling glance at Thomas. "The quieter, the better."

"You could not find anything quieter," Sharon said before she hurried away in response to another customer.

Thomas mustered a weak smile. "Did you hear that gunshot?"

"It was only somebody banging a door." Eleanor released his hand. "Come on, eat up, Thomas, and we'll get away."

"A door?" Thomas repeated and grinned. "I thought it was a rifle. My nerves must be getting the better of me."

Eleanor nodded. *That's the first time he's admitted his nerves. This place is already working.*

~

Newbigging was awake when they left the inn, with half a dozen locals wandering to the shops, a pair of horse-drawn carts jostling for position in the street and a group of youths examining the Crossley.

"Is this your car, mister?" a broad, open-faced youngster asked Thomas, with something like awe in his voice.

"Yes," Thomas said.

"How fast does it go?" The boy looked as if he was ready to jump in the driving seat to try her out.

"Sixty." Thomas slid into the driving seat. He grinned at the boy. "Sometimes faster if we're heading downhill with a following wind."

"Sixty!" the boy said, with wonder in his voice. He stepped back for a better look.

"Should I not drive?" Eleanor asked.

"I'll drive," Thomas insisted.

Taking a deep breath, Eleanor sat in the front passenger seat, prepared to take over if Thomas's mind retreated into the past. They drove out of the village with the hood down, the sound of the engine drowning out the bleating of sheep and half the local youths watching in envy. The countryside altered as they headed northeast, from well-tended fields to long stretches of pastureland dotted with sheep and the occasional prosperous farm snuggled into the hills. Twice they passed a

21

ruined tower house, the simple defensive structure that had once held the Borders against invasion or reivers.

"This was a contested land," Thomas said, with his eyes alert.

"It was," Eleanor agreed.

It's good to have you back, Thomas. Stay a little longer this time.

When Eleanor saw the great grey-green hump of Deepsyke Head rearing up to their left, they began to look for the turn-off. Heather stretched on either side, rising to distant hills where tendrils of grey mist slithered close to the ground.

"Sharon was right," Eleanor said, checking Thomas's watch. "Here comes the rain."

The first droplets were light, but Eleanor was not fooled. The dampening patter was the harbinger of the remorseless Scottish drizzle that soaks the clothes and creeps insidiously through every possible defence humanity creates.

"Park here for a moment," she said, and Thomas pulled up beside a weeping hawthorn bush. Leaving the Crossley, Eleanor dragged up the hood, knowing it would only give a limited cover.

"The rain is very atmospheric," she said brightly. "Look for this side track. It can't be far away now. Sharon said it's near an old standing stone."

"That will help," Thomas said, smiling. "There must be a thousand stones here."

After a few miles, Eleanor realised they must have passed the track as the heather moor gave way to fields of sheep and grey-stone farm steadings. She smiled when she saw a pair of crows in the middle of the road, remembering Martin's song the previous night.

"We'll have to go back," she said.

Thomas performed a three-point turn in an already-spreading puddle and returned slowly along the narrow road as the rain steadily increased.

"There!" Eleanor nearly shouted the word. "There's something! Is that not a standing stone?"

Nine feet tall, the stone thrust skyward beside the road, so prominent that Eleanor wondered how she had missed it when they drove past.

"It looks like one," Thomas agreed.

Gorse bushes had grown tall on either side of the track's opening, obscuring it from view, while a half-rotted wooden signpost leaned at a drunken angle behind a spreading elder tree. Years of Border weather and human neglect had almost obliterated the words, with just enough remaining to make out what had once been written.

Anton's Walls.

"That's us," Eleanor said as excitement surged through her body. She saw the hoodie crows rise slowly from beside the signpost and again remembered the song from the previous night.

"As I was walking all alane,

I heard twa corbies making a mane,"

Shrugging away the words, she looked at their route.

Despite her desire to retain optimism, the sight was not prepossessing. There seemed more puddle than track, with brown mud between the dark water and boulders thrusting through tufts of coarse grass.

"Do you want me to drive?"

"I do not." Thomas bristled at this assault on his driving skills, selected first gear and eased the Crossley onto the track. The hoodie crows returned to their previous position, with their predatory eyes watching the car's progress.

Thomas was an experienced driver, so they bumped, splashed, and jolted up the track as the rain grew heavier and the puddles correspondingly deeper. Eleanor held on tight to the door handle as they lurched into one particularly deep flood where a rock rattled off the exhaust, and Thomas took three attempts at reversing before they struggled free.

"Are you sure you're all right to drive?" Eleanor asked, looking at the deteriorating track ahead. She wondered who had been here previously and why. Suddenly she understood why people avoided this route, but despite the dreariness, she felt an attraction to the area.

Thomas glanced at Eleanor. "Do you want to carry on?"

Eleanor nodded, for she felt quite comfortable in this waste of mud, heather, and water. After another ten minutes and another two hundred yards, they drove down a dip and arrived at a stretch of water and mud that extended across the path and deep into the moor on either side. Eleanor saw patches of bog cotton and reeds bowing to the persistent rain.

"Welcome to desolation," Thomas said.

"The Deep Syke," Eleanor said. Although she had never been here before, she knew she was correct.

"Hold on, sister-of-mine!"

Thomas eased them down until the nose of the Crossley touched the flood.

"That flood could be deep." Thomas had to raise his voice above the constant hammer of the rain. "I'll go out and test the depth."

Eleanor watched as Thomas stepped outside, lifted a stick from the moor and began to probe into the puddle. After a few moments, he returned and gunned the engine.

"It's not as bad as I feared. Hold on tight!"

Eleanor took a deep breath as Thomas drove slowly into the bog, with the engine alternatively screaming as they stuck on the soft mire beneath the water, then roaring as they lurched free. Rocking from side to side, Eleanor gasped as they plunged nose-first into a sea of mud that half-covered the windshield.

Thomas was tight-lipped as he negotiated their way through what seemed like a small loch and up a ridge to higher ground. "Look to your right!"

Eleanor did so. On the map, the name Blackhouse Tower was prominent, as if there was a splendid mediaeval castle amid the wasteland. However, the reality could hardly have been more different.

Situated on an outcrop of black rock, bare stone fangs thrust skyward from a raised green mound of turf, with the tumbled boulders of an outer wall half merged with the surrounding moor. Even from the track, Eleanor could sense an atmosphere of gloom rather than romance. For all her imagination, she could not envisage knights in armour and ladies fair riding around the walls or peering from the topmost parapets.

"Well, that's a place to give the old romantic poets pause," Thomas said. "Not even Sir Walter Scott could make a cheerful story out of that."

Eleanor agreed and wondered if the hoodie crows perched on the topmost stone fragments had followed them up the track or if they were entirely different birds.

"Ce fut en mai

Au douz tens gai."

The French words drifted into Eleanor's head as if carried on the wind. She smiled, knowing they were familiar as if she had sung them in happier days before the Great War.

Earlier than that, something told her, and she shook her head. She would not have known the song when she was a child before the war.

"What are you smiling at?" Thomas asked good-humouredly. "And what song is that?"

"The French song that came to me yesterday," Eleanor told him. "I can't get it out of my head."

Thomas grunted. "As long it's not that dirge about the crows," he said. "That was just depressing."

They drove on, with the rain still falling but the road higher and drier as they steered towards a belt of trees. They passed the shell of a building on the left, and then came a sharp bend, a sudden dip to yet another flood, and a steep rise to a fairly substantial house.

"This must be it," Eleanor said doubtfully as Thomas switched off the engine beside the house. "There's nothing else here." Without the reassuring sound of the engine, the moor suddenly seemed a lonely place. The sound of rain on the car sounded as loud as hoof beats on a hard road.

Eleanor had not expected anything grand, but perhaps a name board would have helped. Anton's Walls stood alone amid the moor, with a semi-tumbled drystane wall as a boundary for the extensive garden.

"So this is Anton's Walls," Eleanor said to break the silence.

"This is Anton's Walls," Thomas agreed.

Standing four-square and uncompromising against the elements, Anton's Walls boasted a central doorway with a window at each side, three windows on the upper storey and a slate roof from which the rain wept like the tears of God.

CHAPTER 4

"I LIKE IT HERE," Eleanor said, surprising herself as the atmosphere wrapped around her like a gauntlet. Somewhere in the moor, a whaup whistled, its call melancholic yet strangely beautiful.

"It's rather austere." Thomas examined the property they had never seen before.

Anton's Walls made no compromises to the terrain or the weather. The house stood solid and defiant, glaring over the moor from its wide dark eyes as if saying. "Here I am and damn you. Do your worst, for I am not moving."

"Whoever built this place had an eye for territory," Thomas said with complete lucidity. "The path is muddy, but the moss on either side is impassable. Anton's Wall's guards the pass or the slap [1] as they call it."

"The pass?" Eleanor asked.

"Can't you see?" Thomas swept his arm around the moor. "The track is the only east-west route from Liddesdale to that gap in the hills." He pointed to a ridge they could dimly see through the rain.

Eleanor nodded. "I'll take your word for it." She tried to understand.

"Anton's Walls stands like a sentinel over the slap, the pass. Not like Blackhouse Tower," Thomas continued. "Somebody built it too far from the track." He shrugged. "Unless it was purely defensive and used the moorland as a moat." He stopped as if afraid he had said too much.

"Carry on," Eleanor encouraged.

Thomas shook his head as the light died from his eyes. "Shall we go inside?" he suggested and forced a grin. "After all, we do own the damned place."

"Yes," Eleanor said. "We'll look inside."

Fishing in her handbag, she located the key and handed it to Thomas. "There we go."

Thomas looked at the key for a few seconds as if unsure what to do.

"Look, the rain is easing," Eleanor said. The batter of rain on the car's roof had faded to a more gentle patter. "The house is welcoming us."

More than the house welcomed them, for a stray shaft of sunlight pierced the gloom to brighten one small square of the moor. Eleanor checked for crows and was strangely disappointed when there were none.

"Ladies first," Thomas said, handing Eleanor the key. She smiled, inserted it into the lock, and it turned easily. The door creaked slightly when Thomas pushed it open, and they stepped inside.

Eleanor always experienced a slight thrill when entering an unfamiliar house, and Anton's Walls was no exception. She felt a difference in the atmosphere the instant she stepped over the threshold, as if entering a place that had once been familiar.

Anton's Walls was a typical eighteenth-century farmhouse, square, solid, and unpretentious. The front door led into a short hall from which four doors opened, one each for the kitchen, living room, storeroom, and a small room of indeterminate use. A flight of stone stairs led to four bedrooms, and another flight led down to the dark basement.

"This is nice," Eleanor said, although she did not understand the shiver that ran through her as she stooped to pick up the bundle of letters that had piled up behind the door. "What do you think, Thomas?"

Thomas looked around without any change of expression, saying nothing. Eleanor realised he had slipped away from her again.

Somebody had stripped Anton's Walls of everything portable, presumably after Jock Armstrong had died. The pine-panelled doors and the floorboards were in place, but that was about all. There was no carpet or other floor covering, no blinds or curtains to shield the windows, and, as they shortly discovered, no fittings except a Belfast sink in the kitchen.

"At least there is a WC!" Eleanor said when necessity compelled her to check.

"Is the water on?" Thomas came to himself.

Eleanor brushed away the cobwebs and pulled the chain. "No."

"There'll be a stop tap somewhere." Thomas looked under the kitchen sink, shook his head and disappeared outside. A few moments later, Eleanor heard the thunder of the water tank filling.

"Thank you, Thomas!" She knew she could rely on Thomas if she needed anything practical.

A few moments later, they began to inspect the house. There were cobwebs everywhere and spiders running from the intruders, but Eleanor could see no sign of mice or rats. Nor could she see any trace of rot or dampness on the walls or ceilings, despite a year's worth of Border weather.

"As far as I can see, the house is structurally sound," Thomas said.

"That's good." For some reason Eleanor could not explain, she was positively enthusiastic about Anton's Walls. She already felt as if she belonged as that old French song echoed in her head. "The windows don't leak, either."

"The woodwork needs a coat of paint," Thomas said. "And there's a bit rot on the outside windows, but I'll soon sort that out. I'll check the attic to see if the roof leaks." He studied the ceilings for a few moments. "There's no sign of damp patches that I can see. Whoever lived here last took pretty good care of the place."

"That would be Old Jock Armstrong," Eleanor said. "Our great-uncle or something."

"Certainly something," Thomas agreed.

There was no ladder to get into the attic, but Thomas was athletic and hauled himself up through the hatch without difficulty.

"There are a few loose slates," he shouted, "but nothing I can't fix with a hammer and nails!"

The cellar was next as they searched for any traces of rising damp. There was nothing as modern as electricity, but they had expected that and brought oil lamps and fuel. Eleanor lit the wick and adjusted the flame until the glow pushed away the dark, revealing harsh whinstone walls and a stone-slabbed floor, with a single small window hard against the ceiling.

"It's as dry as a desert in midsummer," Thomas said as Eleanor bounced the lantern light around. "Interesting stones, though." He took the lantern from Eleanor and focussed the light on the wall. "Look at this, sister-of-mine."

Eleanor had no interest in looking at stones in a wall and told Thomas what she thought of his suggestion.

"They're dressed stone," Thomas said, "with a mason's mark of a double V with a line above."

"Is that significant?" Eleanor felt a flicker of interest.

"It is highly unusual for a simple farmhouse," Thomas said, and for a few moments, Eleanor had her brother back, complete in body and mind. "This is a late eighteenth-century farmhouse built during the agricultural revolution. Scores were built across Scotland, and I have never seen one with a mason's mark or using dressed stone." He paused for a while as he examined the deeply chiselled carving. "If a mason wished to leave his mark, why in the basement, the least visited part of the house?" He grinned at his sister. "We have a mystery here, Eleanor."

"I don't mind a mystery," Eleanor encouraged him, hoping to dispel the war damage in his mind.

"We'll have time to solve it here," Thomas said. "I can't see you throwing wild parties or dancing through the wee small hours."

Eleanor laughed. "Nor can I, Tom." She led the way back upstairs.

The rain began again a few moments later, hammering down from low, bruised clouds as if each drop was intent on destroying everything it hit.

"If this continues," Thomas looked at the heavy sky, "the track will be impassable. We'd better head back."

Eleanor agreed, although she was reluctant to leave Anton's Walls. "We don't want to be stranded here."

"I thought you liked the place." Thomas looked sideways at her, his eyes already shading again.

"I like it fine, but I don't want to stay overnight in a stone shell when a comfortable bed is waiting for me in the hotel."

"We'd best get moving then," Thomas told her.

They were fortunate that Anton's Walls stood on a slight rise, so the car was above the floods, but the moment they descended onto the track, Eleanor realised they had spent too long inside the house. Puddles that had been extensive were now stupendous, and the deeper pools had expanded into lochans, some complete with seagulls or ducks.

"We'll be lucky to get back," Thomas said as the Crossley slewed sideways on deep mud, and it took all his skill to bring us back onto the track. Eleanor grunted as they thumped into yet another hidden pothole.

They lurched, splashed, jolted, and complained for another few hundred yards before the Crossley finally plunged into the Deep Syke, a morass deeper than even its powerful engine could manage. Thomas swore, worked the gears, cursed and eventually, after ten minutes, while his language grew steadily more coarse, he gave up.

"Sorry about the trench language," Thomas belatedly apologised. "I was getting a bit frustrated."

"I should think you're sorry!" Eleanor said primly, then nudged him with her elbow to show there were no hard feelings.

Thomas smiled. "We'll have to push."

Eleanor glanced outside at the deep, muddy flood. "You first," she invited.

Thomas gave his old pre-war, characteristic smile and stepped outside, with the water reaching well past his knees. "This would be easier if there were two of us."

Sighing, Eleanor joined him, hating the feel of cold water clasping at her calves as she lifted her skirt and tied it between her legs.

They pushed, shoved, and swore, trying everything they could to escape the expanding flood.

"It's no good," Eleanor said. "We may as well try to lift the vehicle bodily for all the good we're doing."

The Crossley remained static as Eleanor's temper, never the sweetest, rose by the minute.

"We're getting nowhere." Eleanor looked around at the bleak countryside. "Maybe some farmer will pass and tow us out."

Thomas grunted. Eleanor knew how much he hated to ask for help. "There are no farms here," Thomas told her. "We'll have one more attempt."

"One more or twenty more," Eleanor said. "It will do no good. The car is well and truly stuck." She glared at Thomas as if he had personally brought the rain and planted Anton's Walls at the end of a pot-holed track.

"I'll go for help," Thomas said.

About to agree, Eleanor wondered if Thomas could manage. She was apprehensive that he might drift away inside his head and return to the war. The doctor had warned her anything could trigger his mind, from a sudden sound to a smell or the sight of a gun, and she was scared to leave him alone for any length of time.

"We passed a farmhouse down the road a bit," Thomas said. "We can ask for help there. They'll have horses to drag us out."

Eleanor looked down the track, now gloomy with falling night. She could not see any lights where the farmhouse might be. "We can try," she said doubtfully.

"You stay here if you like," Thomas suggested, "in case somebody comes along."

"Who's going to come along here?" Eleanor asked as the strain on her nerves began to tell. "There's nowhere to go except Anton's Walls!"

"Come with me, then," Thomas said. "Or sit in the car out of the rain."

They waded through the flood and onto the track, which

was now like a small river. Fortunately, Thomas had remembered to bring the lantern, so they blundered from the least wet part of the track as the rain slashed into their faces and the gusting wind tried to push them into the moor. Outside the beam of the lantern, they could see nothing but blackness.

"Where the devil was that farm?" Eleanor was wet, tired, miserable and becoming more bad-tempered by the minute.

"Along here." Thomas seemed to be enjoying himself, although Eleanor was unsure if he knew where he was. "It was off to the left as we drove up, so it must be on the right now." He peered into the driving rain. "We can cut across the moor and cut off the corner."

"Don't be bloody silly." Eleanor employed some trench language of her own. "We'd fall in a bog and drown." She searched for a dry piece of ground to place her feet. "I can't see any lights," she said. "Surely they'll have lights of some sort."

"Maybe we've missed it."

After half an hour, Eleanor had enough of walking through a torrent. "Let's go back to the car," she said. "We'll spend the night there and find the farm in the morning."

"There's a light!" Thomas said. "Back there!"

Eleanor had never been so excited at seeing a light before. She looked up, with the water running from her head and down her nose. "Where?" She saw it, a faint, wavering yellow gleam. "It's miles away!"

"It's not from the farm," Thomas said. "I think that's coming from Anton's Walls."

"The house is empty," Eleanor snapped. "We've just left the bloody place!"

"Maybe somebody's gone in for shelter," Thomas suggested. "What do you think?"

"I think I'd rather be anywhere than standing here in the

rain," Eleanor snarled. "If there's a light, there's a person, and they might help us."

They returned up that track faster than they had walked down, less heedful of puddles as they were already wet, hurrying to reach the light before it disappeared.

"Can you hear that?" Thomas asked. "Music. I think I heard music."

The sound was faint, so Eleanor thought it might have been the wind playing through the strands of a post-and-wire fence, but the harder she listened, the more she realised that Thomas was correct. It was music, a stringed instrument of some sort.

"A harp," Thomas said. "I think that's a harp."

"I didn't think anybody still played the harp," Eleanor said, cringing before the near-horizontal rain. "It can't be from Anton's Walls. There was no harp in the house, and nobody's passed us."

"Maybe there's another road," Thomas said. "One that's not on the map."

"Or one we missed," Eleanor said. They hurried, with the harp music drawing them toward Anton's Walls. "Who would carry a harp to a house in the middle of nowhere?" she asked.

The music grew louder as they approached Anton's Walls, passing their car with hardly a glance and nearly running the final quarter mile in their eagerness to reach sanctuary. As they neared the house, they saw the light originated from the northmost side.

"That's strange," Thomas said.

"This whole thing is strange." Eleanor jumped over a puddle, slipped, nearly fell, and righted herself.

'Hello there!" Thomas shouted as they approached the front door. "Hello!"

They did not expect a reply. "Get the key ready," Eleanor reminded.

"There's no vehicle here," Thomas said. "The musician must have walked."

"His car must be round the back." Eleanor shivered as the wind altered direction to blow from the north. "Unless they walked over the moor."

Anton's Walls looked even darker this time, despite the glow of Eleanor's lantern. They both shouted. "Hallo!" when they re-entered the house, but only echoes replied.

Thomas swore when the crow fluttered past, with its outstretched wings brushing Eleanor's hat and its beak slightly open.

"How did that get in?" Eleanor asked.

"There must be an open window somewhere," Thomas dismissed the incident. "Listen!"

The music was quite distinct, coming from the cellar where Thomas had found the carved stone, although they heard no voices.

"They can't hear us," Thomas said.

They thundered down the stairs to the cellar door, which was firmly closed. Thomas knocked loudly, and they pushed in.

The cellar was in darkness, with no harp, harper, or sound of any kind.

"That's queer," Eleanor said as Thomas probed the darkness with his lantern.

"But interesting," Thomas said.

Eleanor felt the hairs on the back of her neck rise as something cold ran up from the base of her spine. "I saw a light from here," Eleanor said, "and we both heard the harp."

"We must have been mistaken," Thomas said. "The wind perhaps, and the reflection of the moon on glass. Something like that."

"There is no moon," Eleanor said, "and we both heard harp music."

"It must have come from somewhere else, then." Thomas returned up the stairs. "Now we have to decide what we are doing?"

"Well," Eleanor said, "I'm not walking back to Newbigging. We'll just have to stay here the night."

"I agree," Thomas said. "It's not great, but better than nothing. At least it's dry."

Eleanor could not help the shiver that ran through her, but she blamed it on the chill weather.

CHAPTER 5

"Choose a room," Thomas said, "and I'll get a fire going in the fireplace." He grinned at Eleanor, enjoying this small adventure far more than she was. Despite the damp chill, Eleanor was glad to see the old Thomas back.

"This room." Eleanor selected the living room and helped Thomas scour the place for wood. Although Anton's Walls was empty, Old Jock had used one of the outhouses as a wood store, and they transported armfuls of logs to the main house.

"They're surprisingly dry," Thomas said. "Whoever built this house did a good job."

They used straw to start the fire and, within ten minutes, had some warmth spreading into the room. Brother and sister, they had no embarrassment in stripping to dry their wet clothes.

"Somebody needs to sweep the chimney," Thomas said as the wind roared in the lum and blew down smoke and soot. He smiled. "That's another job I can do later."

Eleanor returned the smile, still wondering about the harp music and the disappearing light.

"We'll sleep here tonight," Thomas said. "It's the warmest room. Tomorrow we'll try the car again." He built the fire high, with the heat seeping through the house.

Despite her tiredness after the day's adventures, Eleanor slept fitfully. She woke during the night, eyed her brother, told herself he was too handsome to remain single and vowed to find him a suitable woman.

That was a strange thought, she told herself, rose and walked around the house. The French song was in her head, mingling with the strains of the harp in a discordant, nerve-jangling medley. She found herself in the basement, smiled and returned to the living room.

When Eleanor woke, she knew something was wrong. She lay still, curled on the dirty floorboards with the embers of the fire a memory of past warmth and Thomas's steady breathing a reassurance that he was at peace, at least for the present. A light glimmered against the dirty glass of the windows. After a few dazed moments, Eleanor realised the light originated outside. "Thomas!"

She might as well have tried to awaken Ben Nevis. Since he had returned from the war, Thomas's sleeping had been disrupted, but now that Eleanor needed him awake, he was dead to the world. Sighing, she pushed herself upright and stepped to the window. There was neither moon nor stars, but she saw a flaring light deep in the moor.

Poachers? Eleanor wondered and shook her head. Poachers would hardly advertise their presence with lights. *Perhaps the farmhouse is on fire?*

No. The farmhouse lies in the opposite direction. There was nothing that way except endless miles of moorland and the derelict Blackhouse Tower. Eleanor shivered and forced rational thoughts into her sleep-hazed mind. She knew many men had returned from the Great War unable to settle down to a civilian routine. Maybe one of them had taken shelter in the old tower house. She watched the light for a few moments with a hundred thoughts chasing through her head. *At least the rain has stopped.*

The light bobbed across the moor, throwing a yellow circle on the treacherous moss, and then it stood still, close to the house. For a moment, Eleanor thought she saw a figure behind the light but shook her head in disbelief. She must have been imagining things, for the man she saw was wearing armour. He had a flowing surcoat on top, with a coat of arms of horizontal red stripes on a white background, with a diagonal red line from top right to bottom left.

Nonsense. I must still be asleep. Eleanor rubbed her eyes, and the knight was gone, with the light withdrawing to a distant ridge. Shaking her head, she returned to her uncomfortable bed.

∽

"We'll have to lay pipes here." Thomas was always at his best when discussing practical matters and ushered Eleanor into the cellar to explain his plans. "Old Jock must have had a water supply, or there would be none in the taps, and the toilet would not flush. We'll tap into it and run pipes to the kitchen."

Eleanor agreed, not caring about the details but happy to see Thomas more like his old self.

"Jock probably had a private reservoir," Thomas said, "that won't be difficult with all this excess water." He grinned, enjoying wrestling with the practicalities. "There will also be a filtration system, so I'll expand and improve both."

Eleanor nodded absently, content to allow Thomas to take charge of such matters. She thought of the harp music and the knight she had seen the previous night.

"I'll make a hole under the wall and bring in the pipes here." Thomas stamped hard, then looked up, surprised. "Did you hear that?"

"Hear what?" Eleanor wondered if Thomas had heard the harp again.

"Listen!" Thomas stamped his foot again. "Now listen to this." He stepped away and stamped for a third time. "Can you hear the difference?"

Eleanor shrugged. "Your feet made a louder sound over there." She wondered if the knight was related to the harp. *Is somebody playing a trick on us?*

"It's hollow," Thomas said and drifted away, staring at nothing. Eleanor knew he was back in the war, listening for Germans burrowing under the British trenches or Turks creeping up to the allied lines.

"Thomas!" She pushed away her thoughts to bring her brother back to the present. "Let's have a look."

"What?" Thomas stared at her as if she were a stranger.

"You said the floor was hollow," Eleanor reminded him.

"Oh, yes. Let's have a look!"

Time and neglect had spread a layer of dirt on the floor, but they scraped away a few square feet to reveal smooth rectangular slabs.

"That's good workmanship." Thomas admired the level flagstones. "I thought the floor would be earth and rubble." He smiled at Eleanor. "First, we find that stone with the mason's mark, and now we have quality slabs on the floor. There is more to Anton's Walls than I thought."

Eleanor knelt on the floor, not caring about the damage to her skirt. "These slabs are well-fitted," she said. "Do you have a knife?"

Thomas handed over a small pocketknife. "Don't break it," he said. "I carried that from Gallipoli to Amiens."

"I can hardly slide the blade between the slabs," Eleanor said. She brushed away more of the dirt of ages, ignoring an indignant spider. "Look at this, Thomas! There are more carvings here."

"Is it another mason's mark?" Thomas joined her on the ground, scrabbling at the slabs with his fingernails.

"No, I don't think so," Eleanor said, scraping at the ingrained dirt. "It's far bigger and deeper."

"It is," Thomas agreed. After a few minutes, they traced the outline of a cross with some writing underneath. "What the hell is this, sister-of-mine?"

"I don't know. What does it say?" Eleanor was becoming fascinated by this discovery in her new house.

"I can't make it out," Thomas said. "Half the letters are worn away."

"Let me see." Eleanor pushed Thomas aside and traced the letters with her fingers. "I have a more sensitive touch than you. It's P something," she said. "It starts with a P."

Thomas shrugged. "Peter? Paul? Penelope? It could be anything." He placed his lantern on the ground.

"Wait," Eleanor said. "Move that lantern slightly, it's creating shadows around the words."

When Thomas altered the lantern angle, Eleanor found the words easier to read. "Pax," she said. "There are two words, and the first is Pax."

"That's Latin for peace," Thomas reminded.

"Thank you, Thomas," Eleanor said sarcastically. She scraped away more dirt, ignoring the damage to her fingernails, and shifted the lantern slightly. "The second word is also small. Dei? Does that make sense?"

"Dei." Thomas corrected Eleanor's pronunciation. "That's Latin for God. Pax Dei means the Peace of God."

"Of course it does," Eleanor said. "That's a strange thing to carve on the floor of a cellar."

"I doubt anybody carved it in an eighteenth-century farmhouse," Thomas said. "I think these slabs, and the mason's mark, were cannibalised from somewhere and reused to build this farmhouse."

"I'd agree with that," Eleanor said. "Pax Dei. That's a mediaeval term for the Church's protection." She did not know from where her knowledge came. "I think the Church attempted to limit violence to women and civilians and install rules into warfare."

Thomas's mouth twisted. "It didn't work."

Eleanor did not pursue the subject as Thomas's eyes darkened with memory.

"Hey!" She nudged him. "Stay with me, Tom!"

"I'm here." Thomas dragged himself back to the present and banged his boot on the carved slap. "This is the hollow section of the floor. I wonder if the builder put that particular slab on top as a marker." He grinned at Eleanor, momentarily returning to the schoolboy she had known before he went to war. "I want to see what's beneath."

Eleanor's initial reaction was to ask why, but she was enjoying seeing the old, pre-war Thomas again. She was unsure if she wanted to cry or laugh.

"Come on then, Tom. Let's destroy our new house before we've even moved in!"

They tried to lift the carved slab without success. "This thing's bloody heavy!" Thomas said as it slid through his fingers to land with a meaty thump on the ground.

"Try again," Eleanor insisted.

By their third attempt, Eleanor's fingers were bleeding, and she had broken three nails. "We'll need tools," she decided.

"You're quite right, sister-of-mine," Thomas agreed. "Let's

see what we can find." He placed a single finger on Eleanor's arm. "Take care."

"I'll be fine," Eleanor told him. She smiled, already feeling comfortable in Anton's Walls, despite the harp music, unexpected carvings, and mediaeval knights.

They knew somebody had stripped the main house, so they concentrated on the outbuildings. There were four, the log store and three others.

"We were fortunate that the house is part of a farm steading," Thomas said as he entered a building roofed with corrugated iron. "Look what we have here!"

Eleanor had never seen anybody so excited about finding a collection of ancient tools. They were so old that rust had welded them into one red mass.

"We're in heaven, sister-of-mine. Stand back." Thomas scooped the bundle up, poised and threw them down with some force. Most of the tools disintegrated, leaving only two intact. One was a pointed spade, and the other a four-pronged pitchfork.

Thomas lifted the pitchfork. "That will do," he said and handed Eleanor the spade. "Come on, Eleanor."

Eleanor hurried in Thomas's wake, eager to see what the carved slab was hiding.

Even with the tools, they struggled to lift the slab, breaking two prongs of the fork and bending the shovel before they succeeded.

As the light in the cellar increased, Eleanor saw the carving more clearly. "That's not a cross," she observed. "It's the left side of a sword."

"So it is," Thomas said, with minimal interest. "The slab's coming." With a grunting, straining effort, he lifted the great slab on its side and eased it upward. "Wait!" Thomas held the fork with one hand and balanced the slab with the other. "I'll swivel this to the side. Keep back in case I drop it on your toes."

"Dear God," Eleanor said as Thomas balanced the slab against the wall. "It's a grave!"

They looked down on a skeleton with a long, rusted sword at his side. The man's legs were crossed at the ankles, and fragments of cloth were still attached to the body. What might have once been chain mail sat in a brown smudge beside the corpse.

"It's a knight," Eleanor said. She felt a chill down her back.

"How do you know that?" Thomas asked.

"Who else would be buried with a sword? These things were too expensive for an ordinary man to afford."

Thomas nodded. "Maybe he was from Blackhouse Tower."

"Maybe he was," Eleanor agreed, "but why bury the man here? He was a crusader, too."

Thomas shook his head. "What makes you think that?"

"People have buried him with his legs crossed," Eleanor told him. "If they're crossed at the ankles, he's been on one crusade. If they were crossed at the knees, it would be two crusades, and if crossed at the thighs, three crusades." She looked at the grave. "His feet are pointing east as well, in anticipation of Christ coming from that direction."

Thomas looked at Eleanor strangely. "From where did you get that information?"

Eleanor frowned. "I can't remember," she confessed. "I must have read it somewhere, but for the life of me, I can't remember where or when." She shrugged. "My mind seems to retain stupid scraps of information and reject things that matter."

"You're a strange little creature, sister-of-mine," Thomas said, with every expression of affection in his voice.

"Thank you," Eleanor said humbly and touched Thomas's arm before turning to look more closely at the skeleton.

"Who are you?" she asked the knight. "And why are you buried beneath an eighteenth-century farmhouse and not in a church where you belong? You should have a glorious memorial if you are a crusader."

Are you the man I saw last night? The man with the red horizontal bars on his surcoat?

The knight did not reply. He lay there with his skull grinning at Eleanor and his ankles crossed in a heroic statement. Eleanor ran her gaze across his white bones, seeking answers she knew she could never find. "You're a mystery, Sir Knight."

Thomas shifted his stance, with the light from his lantern casting distorting shadows and reflecting from something within the grave.

"What's that there?" Eleanor asked.

"What's what?" Thomas did not press the question. He was not as fascinated as Eleanor was by this knight, yet he felt a shiver of recognition, one warrior acknowledging the presence of another. "What's the matter?"

"I saw something." Eleanor knelt beside the grave and peered closer, not wishing to disturb the dead, yet curious to discover the cause of the flash. "With your permission, Sir Knight," she said and bent closer to the skeleton. The reflection came again as if the knight had deliberately lifted his hand to catch the light.

"It's a ring," Eleanor said. "Do you think the knight would mind if I borrowed it?"

"Take it," Thomas gave careless permission, gesturing to the knight. "He's dead. He doesn't care one way or the other."

The words of the *Twa Corbies* returned to Eleanor.

"Mony a one for him makes mane
But nane sall ken where he is gane
O'er his white banes when they are bare,
The wind sall blaw for ever mair."

"Is that correct, Sir Knight?" Eleanor asked. "I can see the white bones, but does nobody know where you have gone?"

The knight remained mute, grinning at Eleanor in a silent message. She stared into his empty eye sockets, seeking something, but she did not know what.

"He won't reply," Thomas said. "Dead people can't talk."

"Sometimes the dead tell us more than the living," Eleanor replied quietly. "With your permission, Sir Knight," she said and slipped the ring from the skeleton's bony finger. It was heavy gold, with an inscription on the front. "I'll find out who you are," she promised, "and let the world know where you lie."

"But nane shall ken where he is gane."

"To whom are you talking?" Thomas asked, gently mocking. "The dead can't hear you."

On Thomas's words, Eleanor heard, faintly but without doubt, the notes of a harp or perhaps the sound of the wind playing through the rib cage of a dead man's skeleton.

"Perhaps they can hear me," she said. "Or perhaps I can hear them."

Thomas's crazed laugh was born in the slaughter fields of Flanders and Gallipoli, yet Eleanor knew it belonged on this turbulent frontier.

The ring was heavy and surprisingly warm as it lay in the palm of Eleanor's hand. She heard the music once more and noticed the square of silk lying against the knight's shoulder, embroidered with the crusader's cross. It was the only fragment of material to have survived the long passage of centuries, a brave statement of intent.

"You were going on crusade, not coming back," Eleanor said in another flash of insight. "From where? And how did you end up here, only a few miles from the English Border?"

The knight did not reply, although Eleanor sensed a story between the harp and the crusader's cross. "Who are you, my silent friend?" It was suddenly important that she found out what had happened.

"Let me see the ring." Thomas held out his hand. "It might be worth something."

Eleanor passed it over obediently, with the knight a sightless witness.

"It's a gold signet ring," Thomas said at once. "With a coat of arms inscribed, a unicorn above a sword." He grinned. "We can sell it for a good price."

"I'm not going to sell it." Eleanor lifted her chin stubbornly.

"No?" Thomas shook his head, smiling faintly. "Then what do you intend to do with it? The money could be useful in making Anton's Walls habitable."

Eleanor snatched back the ring in sudden anger. "I'm going to find out who my knight was."

Thomas snorted. "You're doolally [1], Eleanor. How do you intend to do that?"

"With this!" She held up the ring safely away from Thomas's grasp. "You said yourself that it has a coat of arms. If I identify which family it belongs to, I'll look for a crusader knight, and that will be him."

Thomas shrugged and shook his head. "If you like, Eleanor." He glanced back into the grave. "Was that sword not rusted?"

"Of course, it's rusted," Eleanor replied. "It's been buried for hundreds of years, for goodness' sake!"

"Look." Thomas nodded to the knight's sword. Thirty-two inches long, it lay at his side, requiring some serious cleaning but intact, with the steel of the blade reflecting the light and the wheel pommel bright above a worn leather hilt. "I could have sworn the blade was rusted to hell."

"So could I," Eleanor said. "It must have been a trick of the light." She shook her head, smiling. "How did that survive the passage of time?"

Stooping, Thomas lifted the sword. "It's heavy," he said and wrapped his hands around the hilt. "It's much heavier than I expected. It feels right, though; it is beautifully balanced."

Eleanor watched her brother swing the centuries-old weapon, his face taut with concentration. "You'd better put it back."

"Why?" Thomas swung again, with the blade hissing through the air. "He doesn't need it."

Suddenly they were children again, playing in the back garden in Edinburgh's New Town, with blackbirds' songs sweetening the air. Eleanor saw Thomas as a young boy, dreaming of a future in a solicitors' office. King Edward was on the throne, the world appeared stable, and nobody dreamed of the horrors of industrialised warfare that waited beyond time's horizon.

Dear God, what evil demon created war to destroy so many people?

The harp music returned, and Eleanor looked at the ring in her hand, wondering if there was a connection. "Come on, Thomas. We'd better see if we can return to the inn."

Thomas nodded. "I'll leave the sword here," he said, "and replace the stone." It was easier sliding the grave cover back into place than it had been to lift it.

"Sleep easy, Sir Knight," Eleanor said to the silent grave. She turned to leave the cellar with the harp music predominant, but the old French love song seeping into her mind.

"Ce fut en mai
Au douz tens gai
Que la saisons est bele."
"It happened in May, when skies are gay
And green the plains and mountains,
At break of day I rose to play."

CHAPTER 6

A COMBINATION of weak autumn sunshine and a southerly breeze dried the track sufficiently to allow them to leave Anton's Walls. Thomas drove slowly, with Eleanor lost in thought as the Crossley bumped and jolted over the ruts. Blackhouse Tower was as gaunt as she remembered, with the crow back in residence, watching them leave as it had watched them arrive. His companion was at the opening of the track, standing as if he had never moved, and the intervening time had not elapsed.

Everything seemed as before, and Eleanor wondered if she had ever imagined the knight on the moor or discovered the grave beneath the cellar. She fondled the ring, knowing that her life had changed, although she was unsure how.

Sharon greeted them with a smile as they stepped into the inn. "I was getting worried about you two," she said. "Did you find Anton's Walls?"

"We did," Eleanor said, "and the rain kept us there overnight."

"Ah." Sharon nodded her understanding. "The track

flooded. Deepsyke Muir is bad for that. I should have warned you." She edged closer, tossing back her long hair. "How did you like Anton's?"

"We liked it fine," Eleanor said as Thomas responded with a smile. Eleanor saw his eyes light up when Sharon spoke to him. *Well now*, she thought, *it seems the Borders is good for you, my suffering brother. I'll have to encourage this budding romance.*

Martin Crozier entered the inn behind them, removed his hat and nodded to Sharon. "Hello, Sharon."

Sharon bobbed in a slight curtsey, which Eleanor thought strange to such an unprepossessing man as Martin.

"You two will be leaving soon," Martin said to Thomas.

Eleanor shook her head. "No." She was not sure about this man. He seemed determined to force them away, yet without the animosity of others in the village. "We're staying."

Martin grunted, examining her from head to muddy shoes. "Did you meet the guardians? I warned you about them."

"You didn't warn us about anything." Thomas shared Eleanor's distrust as he shifted his stance, easing his left foot forward as if prepared to fend off an attack.

Eleanor had another flash of insight. "The two crows," she said.

Martin nodded, with a faint smile softening the harsh line of his mouth. "Crows have been nesting there for generations. Always two. The twa corbies."

Eleanor looked at the elderly man with his creased, weather-darkened face and hands that curled like claws. "Who are you?" she asked, fully aware that he was revealing very few of the myriad secrets he held. She instinctively knew that he could be a staunch friend or a dangerous enemy, and she was unsure which side was predominant.

Martin held her eyes, looked her up and down again, nodded slowly and walked away without another word.

"Don't worry about Martin." Sharon guessed Eleanor's discomfort. "He's a bit abrupt sometimes, but there's no harm in him." She reached forward and felt Eleanor's coat. "You're soaking wet! And so are you, Mr Armstrong! Here. Let me dry them off for you. We have a big fire in the kitchen, so I'll have them dried in no time!"

"It's all right," Eleanor said. "We'll be fine."

"It's no bother." Sharon seemed determined to make up for Martin's rudeness. "Do you have a change of clothing with you?"

"We have," Eleanor said.

"Then you two change into something dry, and I'll come up and take away the wet clothes."

"Thank you," Thomas favoured Sharon with a rare smile. Eleanor could see that he was quite taken by her, *and why not? She is a very personable young woman, shapely and cheerful.*

The war had aged Thomas, so Eleanor sometimes forgot that he was still in his early twenties, although his eyes could be as old as time. A little gentle flirting would do him a world of good.

"Come on then, Thomas," Eleanor said, noticing Sharon's gaze following them as they mounted the stairs to their room. "Do you like her?"

"I like her fine," Thomas said.

"How fine is fine?"

But Thomas had stopped halfway up the stairs, staring at a blank wall, and Eleanor knew he was back in the war, facing long-gone enemies.

"Come on, Tom," she said, guiding him upstairs.

~

"What's your interest in Anton's Wa's?" Martin asked abruptly, stepping toward them as they sat in the dining room.

"It's our house." Eleanor was equally direct.

"It was never for sale." Martin faced her. "It will fall to the estate."

"It won't," Eleanor told him. "It fell to us." She nodded to her brother. "We share it equally."

"God forbid." Martin nursed a pewter tankard of some dark liquid Eleanor presumed was beer. "Why did it come to you?"

"The previous owner was a distant relative, Mr Crozier," Thomas explained. "We had never met the fellow." He lifted a knife and fork and stared as if he had never seen such items before. "I didn't even know he existed."

"Anton's Walls came out of the blue," Eleanor glanced at Thomas. "We wanted somewhere quiet to help Thomas's recovery from the war, and our solicitor sent us a letter about Anton's Walls."

Martin dragged over a chair and joined them at the table. "Are you two serious about living there?"

"We are," Eleanor said.

Martin sighed. "All I can advise is to be careful. There are stories about that area that would curdle your blood."

"I've seen things that curdled my blood," Thomas told him. "And my sister was an army nurse. Nothing will shock or scare her."

Martin placed his tankard on the white linen tablecloth, leaving a dark ring. He peered at Eleanor. "Are you sure you haven't been here before, Mrs Machrie?"

"Quite sure, Mr Crozier."

Martin shook his head. "I seem to know you, although your face is not familiar. There is something about you."

"Possibly a family resemblance," Eleanor suggested. "If the

previous owner of Anton's Walls was related to us, we might share some looks."

Martin continued to stare at Eleanor. "Maybe it's only that," he said. "I hope so. I hope to God that's all." He stood up without another word and shambled away.

"He's a strange man," Eleanor said, knowing that Martin unsettled her without knowing why.

Thomas nodded. "I wouldn't worry about him. He doesn't like outsiders." He grinned. "You know the local saying: *it's aye been?* These old fogies don't want anything to change or anybody to come into their lives. Martin's scared of change, that's all."

Sharon walked over, smiled at Thomas, and pursed her lips at the dark circle Martin's tankard had left on the tablecloth. "I am sorry about Martin. He's been around forever and wanders in and out as if he owns the place."

"He doesn't bother us," Eleanor replied. "I find him rather interesting."

Sharon tossed back her hair and smiled. "I can ask him to leave you in peace if you like."

"Thank you, but we don't mind," Eleanor said.

"Is there a joiner in the village?" Thomas asked Sharon, who seemed to have made her comfort her personal mission. "We want to make Anton's Walls habitable."

"I'll find you just the man," Sharon promised. Eleanor was delighted when Sharon deliberately brushed her hip against Thomas's shoulder as she cleared away the breakfast dishes. "Rab Powrie is the man for you."

"She likes you." Eleanor hid her smile as Thomas followed Sharon's deliberately emphasised walk.

"Nonsense," Thomas replied. "She's only doing her job."

"Ah," Eleanor said. "And does her job include waggling her bottom?" She laughed at the expression on Thomas's face.

~

Eleanor answered the tap on their room door.

"I'm looking for Mr Thomas Armstrong," the visitor said.

"That's me," Thomas stepped forward.

"I heard that you're looking for a good carpenter." The man was wiry rather than slim, with a ready smile and a large flat cap that he wore at a jaunty angle on his head.

"Carpenters, builders, plumbers, roofers and anything else," Thomas said.

The man thrust out his hand. "I can get you the best of them from all over the Borders. Robert Powrie."

"Thomas Armstrong." They shook hands, holding each other's gaze.

"How soon do you want them?" Powrie asked.

"Now," Thomas replied.

"Leave it to me," Powrie said cheerfully. "Sharon told me you're fixing up Anton's Wa's."

"Yes." Thomas nodded. "It's a house in the middle of the Deepsyke Muir."

"I know Anton's," Powrie said. "I knew the previous owner as well. He was also an Armstrong, Long Jock Armstrong, or Old Jock if you prefer. Were you related?"

Eleanor listened. She had learned that Borderers could be very direct when they wanted to know something.

"Our great uncle," Thomas said, "although we never met." Thomas nodded to Eleanor. "This is my sister, Eleanor Machrie."

Powrie nodded to Eleanor, his eyes brown and friendly in a nut-brown face. Eleanor guessed his age at thirty.

Powrie glanced at the wedding ring on Eleanor's left hand. "Pleased to meet you, Mrs Machrie." He touched a hand to his cap. "My men will be at Anton's Wa's at dawn tomorrow morning at eight sharp."

"I'll meet you there," Thomas said.

Eleanor debated whether she should join Thomas at Anton's Walls or leave him alone. When the army discharged him, the doctor took her aside and warned her that nobody knew much about shell shock. "Your brother might recover in a few weeks, or he might never be fully better again," the doctor told her. "We don't know enough about the condition."

"What should I do for the best?" Eleanor asked.

"We don't know that, either." The doctor looked exhausted. "I think he needs somewhere quiet to recover. Can you find somewhere?"

"I'll try," Eleanor replied, knowing their New Town house could be noisy with nearby neighbours and passing traffic.

The doctor had continued. "I don't think he should be left alone for long, for anything could trigger off the memories."

"I'll stay with him," Eleanor promised.

That had been two years ago, and she'd kept her word. Thomas had made slow and erratic progress, with few good periods and times when he had sunk into depression and memories. After two years in Edinburgh, the solicitor's letter informing them of Anton's Walls had been a Godsend. Now, Eleanor wondered if she could loosen the reins a little, for Anton's Walls had already helped his recovery. Thomas seemed quite happy when she broached the subject.

"Yes, sister-of-mine," Thomas said. "What do you plan?"

"I'm going to trace the coat of arms on this ring." Eleanor displayed the knight's ring. "Or try to, anyway."

"You do that." Thomas was suddenly enthusiastic. "We'll meet up back here at the hotel."

"Give Sharon my best," Eleanor said and was relieved when Thomas laughed.

"I won't be seeing Sharon," he said.

Elliot's, the local shop, was what Eleanor knew as a Johnny A'things. It stocked everything from a needle to a ploughshare with a window display that looked as if nobody had altered it since Queen Victoria planted her plump posterior on the British throne. Overweight, bald and efficient, Archie Elliot showed no surprise when Eleanor asked him for sealing wax, matches, writing paper and the name of a local historian.

"That's a shilling for the sealing wax," he said, "and old Martin Crozier is your man for local history."

"Martin Crozier?" Eleanor could not hide her dismay.

Elliot did not alter his expression. "If there's anything Martin doesn't know about the area, it's because it hasn't happened yet."

Eleanor sighed, for she had hoped to avoid Martin. "Where can I find him?"

Elliot thought for a moment. "Probably at his farm."

"Where is that?"

"Fairhope," Elliot said. "It's about a mile outside Newbigging on the Canonbie road."

"Thank you, Mr Elliot," Eleanor said.

Returning to the hotel, Eleanor melted the sealing wax onto the writing paper and firmly pressed the signet ring into the molten wax. The imprint was as clear as if a craftsman had made the ring the previous day. When Eleanor looked at the impression, something turned inside her. She wondered if the knight had made the exact same imprint and how he had felt when he viewed the result.

Who are you, Sir Knight, and why are you buried under my house?

The coat of arms was straightforward, a rampant unicorn prancing on a single sword. Eleanor knew nothing about heraldry and hoped that Martin Crozier was as good as his reputation suggested. She touched the ring again, wondering about the owner.

Eleanor guessed that Martin worked on the land, and Mr Elliot's directions had been clear. She found the opening to Fairhope without difficulty and walked up the track, thankful the day was dry, if hazy. As was common in the area, a century and more of wheeled traffic had worn two deep grooves on either side of a raised central ridge of grass and weeds. Eleanor had heard that Sir Walter Scott brought the first wheeled vehicle into the valley. If so, then the locals had undoubtedly become adept at anything mechanical. She looked up as a skein of geese flew past, their calls strangely evocative, as if calling to the wandering blood in the people underneath.

Fairhope was well-named. The land was fertile and well-farmed, with drystane dykes in good condition and an occasional plantation as a windbreak. Like so many in the Borders, the farm steading squatted in the shadow of an old peel tower, with the farmhouse another four-square Georgian building.

Fairhope farmhouse could be the twin of Anton's Walls. Perhaps the same man built both.

Eleanor tapped on the door, wondering what reception she would get.

Here we go. Either Mr Crozier will put a flea in my ear, or he'll be very helpful.

A plump young woman answered the door and raised her eyebrows. "Yes?"

"My name is Eleanor Machrie, and I am looking for Mr Martin Crozier," Eleanor said.

"Oh." The woman was dark-haired, neat, and polite. She looked over her shoulder. "Grandad! There's a woman here to see you!"

Martin appeared, munching on a slice of toast. He glared at

Eleanor for a full twenty seconds before asking what she wanted.

"I'm sorry to bother you at home, Mr Crozier, but I am looking for some help with local history."

Martin nodded. "Aye. Who sent you to me?" He bit into his toast.

"The fellow at the shop. Mr Elliot."

"Aye, Archie Elliot. You'd better come in, then. You'll learn nothing standing there." Martin opened the door wider. "This way."

Eleanor followed him through a square hall and into a back room fitted up as a library, with shelves of books, a battered desk, and a leather armchair that Sir Walter Scott might have rejected as being long past its best.

"Ruth!" Martin raised his voice. "Bring in a chair for Mrs Machrie."

The dark-haired girl obeyed with alacrity, smiling at Eleanor as she placed a straight-backed chair opposite the desk. "There we are, Mrs Machrie."

"Thank you."

Martin sat at the desk, swallowed the last of his toast and thrust a pair of spectacles on. "Now," he said. "What do you want to know?"

Sitting at his desk, surrounded by his books, Martin looked a different man from the dirty-fingered singer in the public house. The spectacles seemed to alter his character, so he looked more like a schoolteacher or even a university lecturer.

"I have three questions for you," Eleanor said. "If you don't mind."

"Fire away." Martin gave his distinctive small smile.

"Do the words *pax dei* mean anything to you, Mr Crozier?"

"Peace of God," Martin said at once. "An agreement that protected churches and clergy and tried to protect women, peasants, and civilians. It allowed knights and gentlemen to pursue a blood feud after a murder." He shrugged. "It was a mediaeval attempt to regulate warfare and turn savage knights into Christian warriors."

"That's what I thought," Eleanor said. "I wondered if there might be another local meaning."

"Not that I am aware of," Martin said. "What is your second question?"

"Do you know an old symbol of red horizontal lines on a white background, with a diagonal line from top right to bottom left? A mediaeval knight might have used it."

Martin stiffened. "Maybe," he said. "That sounds like the de Soulis coat of arms." His eyes narrowed. "Why do you ask?"

"It's just something I came across," Eleanor said as if the matter was unimportant.

"I see. What is your third question, Mrs Machrie?"

"I wondered if you recognised this coat of arms, Mr Crozier." Eleanor placed the wax seal on his desk.

Martin grunted. "Martin. Everybody calls me Martin." He examined the seal through a large brass magnifying glass. "I don't know that one. A unicorn and a sword." He looked up sharply. "Where did you get this?"

"It's a coat of arms on a ring I found in Anton's Walls," Eleanor explained.

Martin grunted again and put the magnifying glass down. "It's not local heraldry," he said, fixing Eleanor with a steady stare. "That I know. Make a long arm and fetch me that book, please. The big leather one, with the red cover."

Eleanor handed the book over.

"This is a book of heraldry," Martin explained, turning the pages, and checking the seal Eleanor had given him. "Where in Anton's Walls did you find the ring?" Although the question sounded casual, Eleanor sensed tension behind the words.

"In the cellar," Eleanor told him.

"I see." Martin stopped at a page about halfway through the book. "Here we are." He motioned for Eleanor to join him at the desk. "Douglas of Maintree. That's a minor branch of the Douglas family in Haddingtonshire, east of Edinburgh. The family has been in Scotland since the early twelfth century." He looked up with curiosity on his face. "Are you sure you found that in Anton's Walls?"

"Quite sure," Eleanor confirmed.

Martin leaned back in his seat, examining Eleanor through aged, intelligent eyes. "I wonder how a seal got there."

"It's on a ring." Eleanor handed it to him. "This ring."

Martin grunted when he accepted the ring and held it as if it were the most fragile crystal. "That's old," he said. "I'd guess thirteenth or early fourteenth century. Long before Anton's Walls was built. How did that get there?"

Eleanor wondered what to say, but Martin, in his study, was far removed from Martin in the public house. She saw the intelligence in his eyes. "It was inside a grave," Eleanor said and saw Martin start and quickly recover.

"I don't know of any graves in Anton's Walls."

"In the cellar," Eleanor explained, and watched the emotions play across Martin's face. She saw shock, curiosity, a tinge of fear and then worry.

Martin handed back the ring. "Was there anything else there?"

"Just the grave," Eleanor said, "the skeleton of a knight with a crusader's cross and a sword. He had *pax dei* carved on the grave."

"Dear God, preserve us." The colour had drained from Martin's face. "Mrs Machrie, I'd advise you to return that ring where it belongs, run back to Edinburgh as quickly as possible, and never return to Deepsyke Moor or the Wardlaw Valley."

Eleanor pocketed the ring. "I can't do that," she said calmly. "My husband died in the war, and my brother came home damaged. He has shell shock. We've seen a dozen doctors and the last two recommended that we find a quiet place to allow his mind to heal. That's why we moved here, and I can already see an improvement in him."

Martin shook his head. "He can recover elsewhere, Mrs Machrie. Why the devil do you want to live in that accursed place?"

"It was available," Eleanor said. "Uncle Jock left it to us in his will."

"You've come to the wrong place," Martin said. "There is no peace in Deepsyke Muir and less in Anton's Walls." He leaned across the desk with eyes as intense as any Eleanor had seen. "If you value your soul and your brother's soul, Mrs Machrie, don't return to Anton's Walls. There is a great evil in that area, a great evil indeed."

"Thank you for your advice, Martin," Eleanor told him, "but we have no choice. We must live in Anton's Walls because we have nowhere else to go."

CHAPTER 7

ELEANOR WOKE FEELING tired after a night of terrible dreams. She sat up, trying to erase the vivid memories of a creature with long nails and a mouthful of sharp teeth.

I haven't experienced nightmares like that since I was a little girl. She shivered and pulled her nightdress closer. She must have torn in fighting the monster of her dreams, and blood had dried on her hands.

That was some dream. Eleanor stood up, realising she had dug her nails deep into her palms during the night.

Throwing open the window, she looked outside, half expecting to see a mediaeval knight riding down the street. Instead, a solitary farm cart trundled over the tarmac, with a teenaged farm hand guiding the horse.

That French song returned to Eleanor's mind.

"Ce fut en mai
Au douz tens gai
Que la saisons est bele,
Main me levai."

That farmer's a handsome young lad, Eleanor thought, running her eyes down his body. She looked away, smiling and began to wash.

She walked down to breakfast, heavy-eyed and with the images of the night still racing through her head.

"Whose car is that?"

Eleanor heard the imperious voice as she spoke to Sharon across the breakfast table. She glanced out the half-glazed door to see a heavy Bentley parked immediately behind the Crossley.

"That's Her Ladyship," Sharon nearly whispered the name. "Lady Fiona Cummings. She always parks in front of the hotel when she visits."

Eleanor snorted, out of sorts after her nightmares. "Well, we're here first."

"Her Ladyship won't be pleased." Sharon looked worried.

"Her Ladyship can be as displeased as she likes," Eleanor said and shook her head as the uniformed driver of the Bentley sounded his horn.

"Mrs Machrie," Sharon began, and Eleanor knew the waitress would ask her to move the Crossley for Lady Fiona.

"No," Eleanor said softly, shaking her head. "I am not moving for the whim of anybody." *I met sufficient of that type during the late war to know some are mere bullies. Stand up to them, and they back down.*

"I must attend to my work," Sharon said. She hurried away as the Bentley's chauffeur sounded a more prolonged blast on his horn. Smiling, Eleanor straightened her hat in front of the vestibule mirror and walked out of the inn. Ignoring the chauffeur, she glanced in the rear seat of the Bentley, saw a furious-faced woman sitting upright and walked on.

You'll have to walk, Lady Fiona precious Cummings, because I've as much right to park there as you have.

Eleanor knew Lady Fiona was glaring at her as she strolled down the street. She did not care, for half the population of Newbigging seemed to do likewise. She joked to Thomas about the Newbigging Stare and treated it as a badge of honour, something that set her apart from everybody else.

Stare away, Lady Fiona. I'm back here now, and I'll be damned before I leave. Back here? From where did that come?

~

"The de Soulis family were important in their day," Eleanor said, reading straight from a reference book.

"Which family?" Thomas barely glanced up as he wielded his pliers to create a new fishing fly. He had asked Robert Powrie for advice on the local fishing, and half the tradesmen had chimed in with expert knowledge. Thomas realised that one fisherman instantly recognised another across the Borders.

"The de Soulis family," Eleanor repeated. "They held all sorts of positions in mediaeval Scotland. For example, in 1301, Sir John Soulis was the Guardian of Scotland, probably appointed by King John Balliol. He opposed Edward Plantagenet's invasion that year."

"Well done, Sir John de Soulis," Thomas said without looking up. "What's he got to do with us?"

"I'll come to that," Eleanor told him. "Have patience, brother dear."

"I need it with you," Thomas said, smiling as he twisted a piece of blue cloth around the fly.

"When a truce came in 1304, Sir John Soulis refused to surrender to Plantagenet but accepted permanent exile in France."

Thomas grunted. "Best of luck to him," he said, holding his fly at arm's length.

"They were the good de Soulises." Eleanor read more of her book, placed her forefinger on her place, and tried to attract her brother's attention. "Others were not so good."

Thomas sighed and laid his fly aside. "Go on, Eleanor."

"There was William de Soulis and Hugo de Soulis," Eleanor said. "William signed the Declaration of Independence in 1320, but he turned traitor a few months later. The English king had meddled again and encouraged a plot to kill King Robert the First and put Sir William Soulis on the throne. Anyway, Robert found out and imprisoned de Soulis for life in Dumbarton Castle."

"I'd have hanged a traitor," Thomas said grimly.

Eleanor looked at her brother, realising that war had created a new, brutal side to him. She briefly wondered how many men he had killed, then pushed the thought away.

"That leaves Hugo de Soulis," Thomas reminded. "Was he another traitor?"

"No," Eleanor said. "He was worse."

Thomas lifted his chin. "Nothing is worse than a traitor."

"No?" Eleanor held his gaze for a moment. "Listen to this before you decide. Hugo lived in a place called Caercorbie Castle, which I'd never heard of but was important at the time. Hugo had a nasty habit of kidnapping local children, who nobody ever saw again."

"Why?" Thomas asked abruptly.

"Why do you think?" Eleanor snapped. "He also had a familiar, a horrible fiend called Robin Redcap, who preyed on children, young people, and travellers. He'd lure them into the castle, kill them and drink their blood."

"Bram Stoker would have loved Redcap," Thomas said. "Are you sure this isn't a gothic novel?"

"Quite sure," Eleanor replied. "This redcap thing needed human blood to keep its cap red. Because de Soulis kept it supplied with passing humans and discarded children, Robin Redcap used its supernatural powers to grant him advantages. It ensured that no human could harm de Soulis by rope or steel, which meant nobody could hang or kill him with sword, spear, or axe."

"He was invulnerable, then," Thomas said.

"Maybe so," Eleanor replied.

"What happened to Sir Hugo?" Thomas asked.

"I don't know," Eleanor admitted. "The book doesn't say."

"I doubt we'll ever know," Thomas said. "Now, remind me how this concerns us?"

"It probably doesn't," Eleanor told him about the knight she had seen on the moor. "He had a de Soulis emblem on his surcoat."

"Ah." Thomas nodded sagely. "As well as friendly crows and a skeleton, you dream about a ghostly knight roaming the moor."

"I do," Eleanor said solemnly. "Do you still wish to live at Anton's Walls?"

Thomas's eyes darkened for a moment, and then he smiled. "According to Robert Powrie, this area has some of the best fishing in Scotland and some splendid golf. A thousand ghostly knights could not tear me away."

Eleanor laughed as relief surged through her. "I see you have your priorities right!"

~

"Mrs Machrie?" The man was tall, with basilisk eyes and a face that a mason might have carved from a block of Aberdeenshire granite. He peered at Eleanor down a long, straight nose.

"That's correct," Eleanor agreed. She sat at the breakfast table with a litter of plates and a half-empty teacup before her.

"Is Captain Armstrong available?" The man wore good quality tweeds, with his skin leathered by wind, sun and weather.

"My brother is not here at present," Eleanor instinctively disliked the man, although she did not know why. She had no intention of telling a stranger that Thomas had journeyed to Anton's Walls with Powrie and the tradesmen.

"A pity." The man held out a large hand. "Cummings." He announced the name as if it should mean something. "Sir Hugh Cummings."

"How do you do, Sir Hugh," Eleanor took his hand, feeling the grasp strong and the skin as rough as sandpaper.

"Can we talk?" Cummings asked. "Let's go into the lounge."

The inn had a small lounge, a front room with a dozen easy chairs, a scattering of side tables and a glass-fronted bookcase. A fire smouldered in the grate, with a supply of logs and a scuttle of coal at the side. The room was comfortably Edwardian, with a slightly stuffy atmosphere.

Eleanor selected a chair near the fire and waited for Cummings to sit.

"Now, Mrs Machrie." Cummings spoke with a cultured tone as if he was used to giving commands. "I'd prefer Captain Armstrong to be present, but I am sure you can relay my message to him."

Eleanor nodded without comment.

Cummings' smile seemed friendly. "I believe Captain Armstrong is interested in purchasing the property known as Anton's Walls?"

"We already own the house," Eleanor said bluntly.

"Do you?" Cummings raised his eyebrows in well-feigned surprise, although Eleanor guessed he already knew every detail of the transaction. "In that case, Mrs Machrie, I will make an offer to buy it from Captain Armstrong."

"I will pass on your offer," Eleanor said, "although I don't believe my brother will be interested in selling." She paused for a moment. "Neither am I."

"I will make an excellent offer." Cummings' smile did not falter. "Sufficient to buy you a very substantial house in Edinburgh. I believe that is where you belong?"

Where you belong? Here's another man hinting we should not be here. "We grew up in Edinburgh," Eleanor agreed. "I will pass on your message, Sir Hugh."

Cummings nodded and rang a small bell that sat on the table. When Sharon appeared, he ordered a pot of tea and two cups. "I am sure you can persuade Captain Armstrong to sell."

"I rather like it here," Eleanor countered. "It's peaceful."

"I believe your brother was wounded at the front."

"Three times." Eleanor wondered what else Cummings knew about them. "Once in Gallipoli and twice in France."

"Badly?" Cummings asked with a pretence of sympathy.

"Badly enough," Eleanor replied cautiously. Her initial dislike for this man was growing. His presence made her feel uneasy, yet she could not deny he was handsome and personable.

Ce fut en mai

Au douz tens gai

The words and music drifted into Eleanor's head, and she relaxed a little, aware she knew how to manipulate Sir Hugh.

"There are few medical facilities here," Cummings told her. "The nearest hospital is in Hawick, which is a long journey in winter. Anton's Walls can be lonely if the weather closes in."

"We'll cope." Eleanor produced a bright smile, allowing some warmth to seep toward him. "I was a nurse during the war."

"Oh?" Cummings raised his eyebrows again. "You'll be aware of the dangers, then."

"I am." Eleanor looked up as Sharon brought a small tray with a teapot, two cups, a jug of milk and a bowl of sugar.

"Here we are, Sir Hugh and Mrs Machrie," Sharon said, placing the tray on a side table. "Shall I pour?"

"No, thank you," Cummings said.

"As you wish," Sharon smiled and withdrew.

No curtsey for Sir Hugh Cummings, Sharon, but one for Martin Crozier?

"I am prepared to pay a substantial amount for Anton's Walls," Cummings said. He glanced at the tray as if expecting Eleanor to pour, exerting control. She sat still, smiling, yet not giving him anything.

"I will pass on your message," Eleanor promised.

"Please tell Captain Armstrong that I will double whatever price he paid.," Cummings made no move towards the tray.

"I shall," Eleanor agreed. "We will discuss your kind offer. And now, if you'll excuse me?" She stood up, with Cummings also politely standing.

Eleanor left the room with the tea still in the pot. She knew Cummings watched her and slightly emphasised the swing of her hips, humming that little French tune.

~

Thomas was in a good mood when he returned to the hotel.

"I've never seen men work so hard and quickly," he told Eleanor. "Robert Powrie had them all organised even before I arrived. At the rate they work, we'll have the house ready within the month and maybe even before that."

Eleanor listened to the enthusiasm in his voice, watched the sparkle in his eyes and knew Anton's Walls was working.

He was more vital, more alert, with no trace of the shadows in his eyes.

"How did you get on?" Thomas asked at last.

"A man called Sir Hugh Cummings offered to buy Anton's Walls for a good price," Eleanor told him.

"I hope you told him to bugger off," Thomas said pleasantly.

"I told him we'd discuss his offer," Eleanor replied.

"All right, we've discussed it," Thomas said. "Now he can bugger off. Wait, Cummings? He owns half the land in the area."

Eleanor shrugged. "Probably," she said. "He was arrogant enough."

Thomas gave Eleanor details of the restoration work, delving into technical language that did not interest her. Finally, he grinned. "You never told me what Old Martin said about the ring you found."

"I did," Eleanor told him. "You were tying fishing flies at the time."

"Remind me what he said," Thomas asked.

"Martin Crozier told me the ring belonged to the Douglases of Maintree, from Haddingtonshire."

"Oh?" Thomas tried to look interested. "Did he know why our knight was buried at Anton's Walls?"

"No," Eleanor said.

"Well, that's that, then," Thomas said. "At least you know who he is."

"I want to know more," Eleanor told him.

Thomas shook his head. "How can you find out more about a man who's been dead for centuries?"

"I'm going to Maintree," Eleanor said. She expected laughter, scorn, or anger. Instead, Thomas nodded in apparent enthusiasm.

"Do that!" he said. "Take the Crossley. I'll go out with Robert and the boys."

Eleanor blinked but accepted the offer before Thomas changed his mind.

CHAPTER 8

ELEANOR LEFT EARLY the following day, heading through Hawick and over the long moors and beautiful valleys of the western and central Borders to Haddington. She drove slowly, enjoying the near-sensual power of the Crossley, with the hood down to savour the sensation of the wind flowing around her.

It's been a long time, she thought and laughed. *A long time? It's only been a few days.*

Eleanor was singing as she entered Haddingtonshire, one of the most fertile counties in Scotland. It is a region of small villages, snug farms, and wealthy estates beneath a vast arc of sky. Eleanor drove through the market town of Haddington and found Maintree without difficulty, an eighteenth-century manor house tucked in a bend of the River Tyne. An old, semi-ruined castle perched on the river bank a few hundred yards away. The atmosphere was of comfort and security, radically different from the Borders' underlying tension.

A flag hung limply above Maintree's roof, with the device of a unicorn and sword on a dark green field confirming that Eleanor had come to the correct place.

Here we go, she said and approached the front door. A trim servant answered her knock, and the lady the servant summoned was around forty and friendlier than Eleanor expected.

"I am Eleanor Machrie," Eleanor said and explained the reason for her visit.

"My goodness, that is unexpected." The lady wore a smart tweed suit with an amethyst and pearl brooch catching the light. "Come in, Mrs Machrie." She opened the door wider. "I am Lady Janet Douglas."

The interior of Maintree House was bright and comfortable, with slightly faded grandeur, an array of portraits decorating the walls and priceless, well-worn furniture. A telephone sat in splendour on a separate table. Two golden retrievers bounded forward until Lady Janet ordered them back and ushered Eleanor into a large, airy room with views over the front lawn.

"Sorry about the dogs," Lady Janet said with a smile. "They won't bite, but they think they own the place."

"Dogs don't bother me," Eleanor said as Lady Janet asked her to sit. She handed over the ring.

"Where did you find this, please?" Lady Janet examined the ring with genuine enthusiasm.

"In a farmhouse in the Borders," Eleanor said without going into details.

"How strange," Lady Janet turned the ring this way and that. "It's undoubtedly our coat of arms. I don't know of any quite like it. Excuse me." She left the room for a moment and returned with a heavy brass magnifying glass. "This looks genuine and very old."

"I believe it's mediaeval," Eleanor said. "May I ask, My Lady, did you have ancestors who went on crusade?"

Lady Janet furrowed her brows. "Yes, indeed," she said.

"Why do you ask?"

"It is an aspect of history that interests me," Eleanor hedged her reply.

Lady Janet nodded. "We are very proud of our crusader ancestors."

Eleanor tried to hide her excitement. "Did you have many?"

"Two," Lady Janet said, still examining the ring. "We had two that we know of."

"Did they both return safely, Lady Janet?"

Lady Janet shook her head. "Only one returned to Scotland. Sir William Douglas was out in the Third Crusade. When he came back, the king granted him lands in this area. We remember him as William the Crusader." She smiled as if she had personally known the twelfth-century warrior.

"Your second crusader ancestor was not so fortunate," Eleanor prompted.

"No." Lady Janet shook her head. "We know a lot more about him." She passed back the ring with a regretful smile. "Look after that, please, Mrs Machrie. Such items are rare."

"I will, your Ladyship." Eleanor held the ring tightly, wondering about these brave men who ventured to the ends of their known world to fight for their religion. "Do you have time to tell me about your second crusader, my Lady?"

Lady Janet's smile did not falter. "Come with me, Mrs Machrie." She led Eleanor up a flight of stairs to a large room with a pair of tall, multi-paned windows. The room was empty except for a long table and half a dozen solid wooden chairs that looked as if they'd been there since Malcolm the Destroyer marched his armies south to the Battle of Carham.

"We call this the Crusader Room," Lady Janet explained.

A large picture occupied one wall, showing a young knight

on a grey horse surrounded by a group of people, with a beautiful castle in the background.

"There he is," Lady Janet could not hide her pride. "Sir Andrew Douglas."

Even before Eleanor looked properly, she knew that Sir Andrew was her knight. He sat proudly on his grey palfrey[1], a young man ready to ride on crusade, prepared to battle the Saracens for Jerusalem, ready to face a world of danger to recover the Holy Land for Christianity. Eleanor stepped closer, noting the ring the artist had painted prominently on Sir Andrew's finger and the long sword that hung at his side.

Eleanor touched the ring in her pocket and remembered the sword in Sir Andrew's grave. The hilt looked similar, with the distinctive wheel pommel and the extended cross-guard. She would have sworn in court that her knight's sword was identical to the weapon in the picture. Sir Andrew seemed to be looking directly at her, with his eyes bright blue and his blond hair lapping over his ears.

"What happened to Sir Andrew?" Eleanor asked, although she already knew the answer.

"He died in Outremer," Lady Janet said. "That's the name the crusaders called the Holy Land."

Eleanor nodded, not yet willing to share the truth. "He didn't return to Scotland."

"No." Lady Janet ran an elegant finger across the picture. "I don't know when this picture was painted or who the artist was, but Sir Andrew probably didn't look anything like this fellow."

Eleanor imagined her knight, adding flesh and features to the bones until she could see Sir Andrew on his horse. "I'm not sure," she said. "I think he was very much like that, tall and noble, brave and handsome."

Lady Janet smiled. "I like to think so. We don't know what

happened. The vaguest tales returned to us, telling us he died defeating some great evil."

"Some great evil?" *Was that not the exact phrase that Martin Crozier had used?* Eleanor looked at the picture again, noticing the two black birds flying above the handsome young knight. "Are these birds crows?"

"I don't know," Lady Janet said. "An old family legend says two black birds followed Sir Andrew." She gave a most unladylike shrug. "If that is the case, they've long gone."

"Maybe they looked after him," Eleanor suggested.

"Maybe they did," Lady Janet agreed, and her smile returned. "If so, they've been a long time away from home."

"They have indeed," Eleanor agreed. "When did Sir Andrew leave?"

"Saint Bride's Day. February 1321." Lady Janet smiled. "We still remember, you see. I told you that we know a lot about him." She shook her head. "I have never met anybody from outside the family that cared."

Eleanor allowed her mind to merge with the picture. She felt as if she already knew this knight.

～

Andrew stood naked in a stone chamber with twenty candles casting bright light over his white, well-muscled body. He had the slenderness of youth, with two scars marring the perfection of his skin. One extended from his left shoulder to his elbow, where a training sword had sliced him. The other crossed his ribs, also on the left side. His chin was up, and his clear blue eyes focused ahead.

Andrew's chest was broad and boasted a fuzz of hair, duplicated in the explosion around his groin, where his manhood hung unashamed. His hips were slender, his buttocks and legs shapely, firm, and strong.

"Are you ready, Andrew?" an older man asked.

"I am," Andrew replied firmly. They spoke in Norman-French, as befitted the rituals that made a youth into a knight, the most privileged class in Christendom.

A group of older men stood watching, each wearing a long sword around his waist. All were stern-faced, and most bore some scar of battle, for the year was 1321, and despite a temporary truce, Scotland was at war with her powerful and aggressive neighbour. A long line of servants poured pails of hot water into a bath, causing steam to rise into the chill air. When the tub was nearly full, Andrew stepped in, with two knights pouring ladles of water over his head while a priest intoned a Latin blessing.

Andrew sat still, unsmiling, aware of the significance of every part of this ritual that washed away all his sins and allowed him to enter knighthood as clean in the body as he was in spirit. When the older knights decided they had sufficiently cleansed him, they allowed Andrew to leave the tub and stand dripping wet in the cold chamber.

"Follow me," the priest ordered, leading Andrew to Maintree Castle's chapel. "You know what to do."

"I spend the night in solitary prayer," Andrew said. Still naked, he knelt on the cold stone floor as the smoke from candles and incense perfumed the air. The prayers came naturally to him as he pleaded with God to grant him strength and fortitude. "I wish to be a good knight, to fight for right and battle evil wherever I may find it."

His word echoed around the chapel he had known all his life, a chapel scarred with smoke where an invading English army had put it to the flames.

Andrew ignored the discomfort of his position and the chill

that raised goosebumps on his exposed skin as he passed the lonely night in prayer. He was about to step over the threshold into knighthood, and temporary pain did not matter.

~

"Are you all right, Mrs Machrie?" Lady Janet's voice penetrated Eleanor's thoughts. "You were miles away for a minute."

"Centuries away," Eleanor confirmed. "You had a chapel in the old castle, didn't you?"

"Yes." Lady Janet threw her an inquiring look. "It still stands, or the remains do."

Eleanor realised she had outstayed her welcome. Lady Janet's smile was not as bright, and she fidgeted slightly, glancing at the grandmother clock in the corner of the room.

"Thank you, Lady Janet," Eleanor said. "You've been very helpful."

"If you find out how the ring came to be in the Borders, please let me know," Lady Janet asked.

"I will do that," Eleanor replied. "May I visit the old castle?"

"Of course," the generous Lady Janet said, "although there's nothing much to see."

Lady Janet was correct. The old castle of Maintree was little more than a shell, with local farmers using the building as a quarry for centuries. Eleanor wandered through the ruins, identifying each room as if she had grown up in the place. She could see the lord's bedroom high in the central tower, with his living room and dining hall beneath and pictured her young knight walking across the courtyard. Eleanor could visualise him now, tall, young, and gallant, with his blond hair blowing. In her head, she altered the sound of the wind and nearby

River Tyne to the music of harpers and the soft singing of ladies.

"Ce fut en mai
Au douz tens gai
Que la saisons est bele,
Main me levai."

Eleanor smiled, slightly shocked at the images that sprung into her mind. She walked across the echoing courtyard, hearing hooves ringing from the cobbles and the echo of smiths, farriers and grooms. As Eleanor held the ring in her pocket, she could feel Andrew's presence as the boy gradually grew into a man. She saw him fishing in the River Tyne, as Thomas had fished in the Tweed in the balmy days before the war. She saw him learning to ride on the heather plateau of Lammermuir, and she smiled as she saw him with his first woman.

Still smiling, Eleanor entered the chapel, a small room with a vaulted ceiling and a space at one side where the altar had stood.

She clutched the ring in her hand, imagining the scene as if she were there.

～

The priest stood at the altar, a tall, thin man with a severe expression. His robes brushed the ground as he listened to Andrew's confession and blessed the long sword that lay, enclosed in its sheath, on top of the altar.

When the priest stepped back, an older knight took his place. Stern-eyed, a scar crossed his face from forehead to chin, and one finger was missing. He was one of the men who had supervised Andrew's ritual bathing the previous evening. His companions watched, men wearing silken robes and the swords of knighthood, men hardened and scarred by decades of unrelenting warfare against English invaders and the Scottish traitors who supported them. The knight with the scarred face, Robert Douglas, lifted the sword from the altar, allowed Andrew to touch it, and then fastened the sword belt around Andrew's waist.

"A sword is the mark of a knight," Robert Douglas said solemnly. "A mark of honour and position." Without warning, he backhanded Andrew savagely across the face. Andrew reeled, staggered, and recovered.

"That was the dubbing," Robert Douglas said, ignoring the trickle of blood that dripped from Andrew's broken mouth. "And that was the only blow a knight can accept and not return. You are now a knight, Sir Andrew. Show courage in the face of the enemy."

Andrew nodded, unsheathed his sword, and laid it, the naked blade gleaming in the candlelight, back on the altar. Led by Robert and Andrew, the knights crowded around to pray over the sword, blessing it to fight only for the right. The priest reappeared, splashed holy water on the blade and spoke in Latin and Norman French.

"Bless this sword, that thy servant may henceforth defend churches, widows, orphans and all those who serve God against the cruelty of heretics and infidels. Bless this sword, Holy Lord Almighty, Father, Eternal God. Bless it in the name of the coming of Christ and by the spirit of the Holy Ghost. Bless it to fight all manner of evil, new and old, wherever the bearer, Sir Andrew Douglas, meets it. And may thy servant, armed with thy love, tread all his visible enemies underfoot and Master of Victory, rest protected from attack, physical or spiritual."

As the knights intoned a solemn Amen, the priest quoted a Biblical passage and continued. "Blessed be the Lord God who formeth my hands for battle and fingers for war. In the name of the Trinity!" The priest placed the sword in Andrew's right hand, received it back and slid the weapon into its scabbard.

Andrew drew the sword with a flourish and brandished it three times before returning it to the scabbard.

"Be a soldier of God," the priest said. "Peaceful, courageous, faithful and devoted to God."

"I will!" Andrew promised.

Robert Douglas stepped forward. "St Louis gave us good advice, Andrew. He said that if you hear Christ's faith maligned, defend it by the sword with a good thrust to the belly as far as the sword will go. I'd give that same advice to you concerning any enemy."

Andrew nodded, taking in all the words of his elders. He touched the hilt of his sword, hoping to emulate the deeds of his distant kinsman, Sir James of Douglas, King Robert's captain who defended the Border.

"I will be a knight worthy of my name," Sir Andrew promised.

∾

Eleanor started, unsure how long she had been in her reverie. The sun had moved across the sky, and now the chapel was empty, bare stones shadowing a barren floor. All the men were long-dead shadows, their hopes and dreams blown away with the dust of their bones. She stood where Andrew had stood, wondering what had happened to her young crusader. How had he ended in the Wardlaw Valley rather than fighting for the Cross in Outremer?[2]

I'll find you, Sir Andrew. I'll delve into your story and let the world know.

Eleanor saw the gleam of his bright blue eyes, the sheen of

his blond hair and the play of firm muscle across his chest and shoulders.

Am I falling in lust with a dead man?

As a light rain washed over Maintree Castle, Eleanor realised that the day was already beginning to fade. She had a relatively long drive back to Newbigging, and no desire to chance the winter-dark roads, only to find the hotel's doors closed when she arrived in the dark of early morning.

I'll stay the night here and drive back tomorrow. Thomas won't miss me, and nobody else will care.

Eleanor drove the few miles to the Douglas Arms in Haddington. The receptionist was friendly, the room clean, and the dinner was very welcome.

"I liked the name of this place," Eleanor said to the waiter.

He nodded. "It's very historic," he replied. "Douglas of Maintree owned much of the land around here and set up the hotel for travellers in the seventeenth century."

"Douglas of Maintree?" Eleanor repeated. "Do you know much about them?"

"The Douglas family was powerful round here," the waiter said. "That's about it."

"Thank you," Eleanor said.

The waiter has no knowledge of the crusaders then or of men fighting for their country. We live, die, turn to dust and are forgotten. Well, Sir Andrew, I'll try to revive your memory.

Eleanor set off after breakfast the following morning, heading southward towards Hawick. As she touched the ring in her pocket, she pictured Sir Andrew riding south for Berwick-upon-Tweed, recently recaptured from English occupation. While most knights would ride with an entourage of servants and men at arms, Sir Andrew was nearly alone, venturing on crusade with one squire, a hunting hound, a hawk, and his sword for company. Eleanor could picture his route in her mind, hugging the coastal plain east of the Lammermuir and then south across the Merse to Berwick.

Sir Andrew would sit straight backed in the saddle with his hound running at his heels, his hawk on his arm and his squire a horse length behind. He would ride his palfrey, with the squire leading his charger, his battle horse.

Eleanor did not realise she was following Sir Andrew's route until she glanced at her surroundings. It must have been instinct that guided her, but at eleven that morning, she arrived at the ruins of an ancient abbey, where fruit trees once stood in serried ranks and ivy coated the walls. The atmosphere was mellow, the result of hundreds of years of monks peacefully tending the fields and caring for the sick.

Eleanor killed the engine and looked around her.

"Sir Andrew? Were you here?"

She knew the young knight had visited, for she could sense his presence. She could see him standing by his grey horse, with the abbot and a dozen monks crowding around him. A pair of black crows sat on the abbey walls, watching the proceedings.

The ubiquitous crows. Do they follow Sir Andrew, or are they following me? Eleanor wondered.

The abbot was talking, gesticulating with his hand as the newly created knight listened.

"Why travel all the way to Outremer to fight for the Lord, Sir Knight, when you can correct a great evil here in Scotland?"

Sir Andrew shook his head, smiling. "The war here is nearly finished, good Abbot. We have defeated the English, and my sword will be better fighting to free the Holy Land."

"This evil does not come from England," the abbot declared. "It is a tyrant knight tormenting his people."

Sir Andrew frowned. "Then the people should complain to the earl or the king."

"Are you so soon to renounce your vows of knighthood?"

The abbot took hold of Sir Andrew's horse. "You swore to defend widows, orphans and civilians, and here in Scotland, a knight is torturing and killing civilians he has sworn to protect."

Sir Andrew shook his head. "I have a ship to catch, my good abbot. I cannot waste my sword fighting a petty tyrant when there are great wrongs to right."

"There will be other ships," the abbot reminded.

"I am a man of war, good abbot," Sir Andrew said, "and you a man of peace. Should you encourage me to fight and kill?"

"St Augustine answered that question, Sir Andrew," the abbot said. "Do you remember his words?"

"I do not," Sir Andrew admitted.

The abbot smiled. "What is there to condemn in war? Is it the death of men who must sooner or later die? I declare that this reproach comes from the mouths of cowards and should not be made among truly religious men."

"Did St Augustine say that?" Sir Andrew asked.

"He did," the abbot confirmed. "The fundamental duty of a knight is to wage righteous war. His prime cause is to protect the true faith and ensure the salvation of the innocent."

At that moment, the crows launched themselves from the wall, circled Sir Andrew and flew south and west. Sir Andrew's intended route to Berwick lay south and east. He watched the birds for a few moments.

"Where is this oath-breaking knight, Abbot?"

"At the Castle of Caercorbie," the abbot said. "The Guardian of the Dark Slap from the West Marches of the Border to Galloway."

"I am not familiar with the area," Sir Andrew said. "What is his name?"

"He is Sir Hugo de Soulis."

As the abbot replied, the sky darkened, and a chill fell over the land as if God had lifted his blessing. A murder of crows exploded from the stark woodland to the east of the abbey, rising above the buildings with their harsh, raucous cries.

Sir Andrew touched his hand to the hilt of his sword. "I have sworn an oath to protect the innocent," he said. "I shall ride to Caercorbie after Mass tomorrow."

"God will reward you, Sir Andrew," the abbot told him.

CHAPTER 9

CAERCORBIE? Eleanor recognised the name, although she did not know the location. She frowned, breaking the word into its components. *Caer,* she knew, was a Welsh or Brythonic word, the ancient Celtic language of much of Britain from Dumbarton Rock down to Cornwall. It meant castle. *Corbie* was Scots, meaning a crow, so Caercorbie was the Castle of the Crows.

Eleanor shook her head. *Crows again.* Crows seemed to have flown into her life since she arrived at Anton's Walls and the Wardlaw Valley.

Crows and Sir Andrew Douglas. Eleanor smiled and wondered from where these vignettes came. She had never been prone to such bursts of imagination before she arrived at Anton's Walls, and now Sir Andrew accompanied her across half of Scotland.

Eleanor started the car again, hearing the mighty roar of the engine. She knew she had to follow Sir Andrew's route, although the twentieth-century road network did not exactly follow the mediaeval paths.

Eleanor smiled when a crow accompanied her as she headed in the direction the abbot had indicated all those hundreds of years ago. The crow flew beside the Crossley for fifteen minutes as if guiding her on the correct path.

"Who are you, crow?" Eleanor asked and parodied the words of old Martin's song as she drove.

"As I was driving all alane,

I saw yin corbie flying abane,"

Eleanor told herself the words made no sense and concentrated on driving the heavy car.

She stopped for petrol in a quiet village, and when she started again, the crow had returned, its slow wings somehow keeping pace with the car.

"What do you want, Crow?" Eleanor asked. "Are you with my handsome Sir Andrew?"

When Eleanor stopped for the packed lunch the hotel had generously provided, she heard hoofbeats where there was no horse to be seen and smelled the warm, somehow-familiar scent of a horse.

Are you with me, Andrew?

"Ce fut en mai

Au douz tens gai."

Eleanor smiled as the song entered her head, stretched on the car seat, and imagined the young knight sitting beside her, with his blue eyes smiling at her.

Go away, Sir Andrew. I have to concentrate on my driving. Eleanor shook her head. *I am following you, my long-dead friend, and I'll discover what happened to you.* She touched her ring, smiling.

Southern Scotland is well provided with roads running north to south, but travel from east to west is less encouraged. The topography of hill masses and broad rivers have always forced travellers onto specific routes, which the earls, lords and robber barons studded with watchful castles. Eleanor nearly forgot about Anton's Walls as she pursued her knight, looking for the guiding crow and touching the ring whenever she lost the trail.

Eleanor wondered why she accepted her descent into the supernatural as normal, but in the wake of the Great War, nothing seemed abnormal. After four years of poison gas, the death of millions, the fall of empires and the world shaken to its foundations, the world could no longer surprise her.

As she drove, negotiating the winding roads with a skill she had honed driving ambulances in France, Eleanor recalled her past. During her time as an army nurse in France and Belgium, she had witnessed enough daily horror to last a score of lifetimes. The ghost of a long-dead knight, as she believed her images of Sir Andrew to be, could not upset her.

What was one more dead man?

At times, the crow flew over farmland or moor where there was no road, and Eleanor had to scout around and study the Bartholomew map for the best route. Her heart was in her mouth when she searched for a sign, and twice she felt like abandoning her quest. However, the crow reappeared, or she heard the slow drumbeat of hooves and knew she was close to Sir Andrew's path and heading for Caercorbie.

I've heard of Caerlaverock, the Lark's Nest, but never Caercorbie, yet it seems to have been important. I wonder what happened? Why was that castle wiped from history?

Eleanor had to cross and recross the country, sometimes ignoring angry farmers as she bumped over farm tracks that guided her south and west. At other times she followed a metalled road, grateful for the relief the tarmac afforded the Crossley's beleaguered tyres.

You chose a most direct route, Sir Andrew, Eleanor thought as a pair of crows summoned her onto yet another rutted country road.

Two crows now? I must be getting close.

By the evening of that day, Eleanor had passed a dozen ruined castles, each one in a wilder position than the last as she probed deeper into the untamed hill country of the western Borderland. She thought most of the castles seemed newer than the fourteen century, although she wondered if Sir Andrew had visited their predecessors and, if so, what reception he got.

She filled the petrol tank twice more, much to the astonishment of the petrol pump attendants when they saw a lone woman driving a motor car.

"Does your husband know you're driving his car?" one young man asked, eyeing the Crossley.

"No," Eleanor answered honestly. "Does your mother know you ask cheeky questions?" She held his gaze until he looked away.

The further she drove, the less Eleanor saw of her guiding crows, and when the winter night crept in, the bird left her completely. She was in an unfamiliar part of the country, with darkness crowding down from the hills and bleak trees stretching naked branches to an uncaring sky.

The lights of an inn drew Eleanor like iron filings to a magnet. The building was whitewashed, with strangely old-fashioned lanterns bouncing their light before a fitful wind. Eleanor pulled up the Crossley in front and walked inside.

"Do you have a room for the night, please?"

The elderly lady at reception looked Eleanor up and down before she smiled. "You look tired, my dear," she said. "Have you been travelling long?"

"All day," Eleanor said. "I was glad to see the inn. I had contemplated spending the night in the car."

"We'll soon have you comfortable," the woman said. "Do you have any luggage?"

"Only one case."

"George will take care of it." The woman signalled to an equally elderly man who removed the bag from the boot of the Crossley and carried it into the inn. "You'll want supper?"

"Oh, yes, please," Eleanor said, suddenly realising she was hungry.

"In you come, my dear," the woman said. "I am Meg. Could you sign the register?"

Eleanor signed the leather-bond book, seeing the previous entry had been some weeks before. "I'm afraid I am unsure where I am," she said. "I got a little bit lost."

Meg smiled. "We are a bit out of the way," she said. "Only a few people use this road, which makes our guests all the more welcome. Mrs Machrie, I see?"

"Yes," Eleanor agreed.

"Is Mr Machrie not with you?"

"I'm a widow," Eleanor explained. "My husband died in the war."

Meg nodded understandingly. "Ah. I'm sorry, my dear. War is a terrible thing." She showed Eleanor her room, small and neat, smelling of beeswax and with a newly lit fire sparking in the grate. The brass of the double bed gleamed, and the pillows were white and soft.

"Supper will be ready in twenty minutes," Meg said. "I'll leave you to freshen up. The bathroom is at the end of the corridor."

The meal was simple, well-cooked, and satisfying, with George helping Meg and a rising wind hammering at the window.

"It's unusual for a traveller to come this way in winter," Meg observed. "Where are you headed?"

"A place called Caercorbie." Eleanor dropped her guard before these friendly people. "I'm not sure where it is, although I think it's in this area."

"Caercorbie?" Meg repeated the name as if it were a curse. She straightened up, stepping backwards. "Yes, I've heard of Caercorbie, although I haven't heard it mentioned for many years."

"I can't find it on the map," Eleanor said.

"No, you won't." Meg shook her head. "It has a different name now." She sat opposite Eleanor, with her broad face concerned. She removed her glasses, polished them on a snow-white napkin and replaced them on the bridge of her nose. "There are many stories connected to Caercorbie."

Eleanor felt excitement building inside her. "Do you know of a knight named Sir Andrew Douglas?"

Meg's brow furrowed in thought. "No," she said after a few moments. "I don't know that name."

Eleanor hid her disappointment. "It doesn't matter. Could you tell me what you know about Caercorbie?"

"Come over to the fire, my dear." Meg led the way, so they both sank into comfortable armed chairs, one on either side of the fire, as George cleared the table, listening without saying a word.

The heat was relaxing, and Meg seemed almost maternal as she stirred the fire with a poker. "What's your interest in Caercorbie, Mrs Machrie?"

"Somebody mentioned it yesterday," Eleanor replied cautiously. "I had never heard of the place."

"There's nothing to see," Meg said. "You'd just be wasting your time. There was a great evil in Caercorbie. It was so horrible that the weight of the evil pulled the castle under the ground." Although she smiled, Eleanor thought she looked worried, "or so the legend goes."

Eleanor returned the smile. "Have you heard of a man named de Soulis? Hugo de Soulis?"

Eleanor did not expect the look of horror that crossed Meg's face. "I am familiar with the name," Meg said, trying to control her emotions.

"I heard he was associated with Caercorbie." Eleanor played out her fishing line, wondering what she might hook.

"He was." Meg caught the hook and held it tight. "De Soulis was the cause of the evil." She nearly spat out the name as if de Soulis had affected her personally. "He was worse than the Kaiser!"

"What did he do?" Eleanor played the line, drawing facts and legends from Meg.

"Great evil," Meg said. "According to the story, de Soulis held Satanic practises in Caercorbie, holding black masses in the castle dungeons, with human sacrifice upside down crosses and kidnapped children."

"I've never heard of such a thing in Scotland," Eleanor said. "I thought that was limited to fiction books set in Transylvania." She tried to make light of the matter, hoping to draw more stories from Meg. Every legend added a little to her store of knowledge, and even the wildest myth had some truthful basis.

"It happened," Meg said. "There was more evil in Caercorbie than in any other castle in the country, and when you think of the black deeds in Edinburgh and other places, that amounts to a terrible lot of evil. De Soulis called up a demon that the local people called Robin Redcap, a terrible creature that lived on human blood."

Meg was silent for a while, then added coal to the fire. "Him and that woman of his!"

A woman? I didn't know a woman was involved.

"When did this happen?" Eleanor asked. Despite her experiences during the Great War, she found herself shaking.

"Towards the end of the War of Independence," Meg said. "King Robert gave de Soulis lands to hold against the English, but he proved to be a cruel man. His familiar, Robin Redcap, granted de Soulis immortality, saying he could not be harmed by steel or rope. In return, Robin Redcap demanded blood and more blood. As long as he had blood to drink, Robin's cap remained red, but if the blood supply ran out, his cap would alter colour, and his powers would fade. If his powers faded, he could no longer protect de Soulis."

"So human blood gave Redcap its powers, and de Soulis continued his depredations," Eleanor said.

"The great evil did not stop," Meg confirmed. "All across southern Scotland and northern England, people had a saying:

Don't go by Caercorbie, for de Soulis will be there.

Time after time, a local man would raise his spear or take his knife and attack the evil lord, but Robin Redcap's enchantment protected him. The steel could not penetrate the supernatural armour."

"What happened?" Eleanor asked.

Meg spoke as if she had known de Soulis personally. "According to the legend, the people asked the king for help, and he sent a knight, a man skilled in battle, a knight who had defeated the English in a dozen battles and skirmishes."

Eleanor wondered if history had misrepresented Sir Andrew. "Did this knight defeat de Soulis?" she asked.

Meg shook her head in sorrow. "No. De Soulis threw him into a dungeon and starved him to death."

Eleanor thought of the lonely grave under the cellar at Anton's Walls. "That's terrible," she said.

Did Sir Andrew die in such a terrible manner?

Meg nodded. "Eventually, the people rose. They captured the castle, took de Soulis to an ancient sacred place, and killed him."

"How did they kill him if he could not be harmed by steel or rope?"

Meg shook her head. "The legend does not say. But the story doesn't end there. Caercorbie had so much evil that it sunk beneath the ground." She leaned closer to Eleanor. "Now, nobody knows where it once stood, and it is better that way. There should never be a monument to evil."

"Here you are, Meg!" George stood behind them, shaking his head. "Are you filling this young lady's head with more of your nonsense?"

"Meg is educating me," Eleanor defended her teacher.

George shook his head. "More likely she's spouting ancient rubbish." He drew up a seat beside the fire. "Meg's forgotten more of the old Border lore than Walter Scott ever wrote down."

Meg glanced at me and laughed. "I was telling Mrs Machrie about Caercorbie."

George grinned. "Old Caercorbie, tower so grim,

God grant you sink for sin

For reason of the evil deeds,

De Soulis did therein." George quoted a rhyme Eleanor had never heard before. "Nursery rhymes and old wives' tales," he said. "You don't want to take any notice of them."

"I won't," Eleanor said, but when she left the following morning, she looked for the two crows and thought of young Sir Andrew dying a lonely death at the hands of the evil de Soulis.

CHAPTER 10

"ROBERT POWRIE'S doing the work of ten men," Thomas enthused as he returned from Anton's Walls to find Eleanor lying on her bed. "I've never known a man work so hard. I wish I had him in the regiment during the war; we'd have defeated the Huns a year earlier!"

Eleanor laughed. "I'm glad you are making a new friend," she said.

"There's nothing he can't turn his hand to," Thomas said. He lowered his voice. "He only drinks wine, too. Not beer or whisky or even tea. Only red wine, and he's mean with it too. He never shares."

"I'm surprised he can find any wine here," Eleanor said.

"He told me he gets it from Hawick," Thomas told her. "More importantly, he's a keen fisherman and knows all the local angler's neuks[1] and pools."

"That is highly important." Eleanor did not keep the sarcasm from his voice. "When you two are not chatting about fishing and drinking, how is my house coming along?"

"Quickly," Thomas told her, smiling. "Have I shown you my new fishing fly?"

Should I tell Thomas that Sir Andrew travelled here to destroy some great evil and ended up under our cellar? No, it is best not to damage his recovery.

∿

While Thomas worked on his fishing skills and making Anton's Walls habitable, Eleanor continued her research. With no library in Newbigging, she drove over the winter-bleak hills to the mill town of Hawick. The town was dull under a leaden sky, with the mills quiet and the librarian pleased to see a customer.

"Can I help you?" The librarian was middle-aged, prim, with kindly eyes.

"I am trying to identify a mason's mark," Eleanor said.

The librarian raised her eyebrows. "That's an unusual request," she said, happy to have something different to do. "Give me a minute." She produced a catalogue from a shelf under the counter and leafed through the pages. "Here we are, Scottish Mason's Marks from the Twelfth to the Nineteenth Century." She smiled. "It's not one of our most-used books. Wait here, please. It's in our storeroom."

The librarian returned within ten minutes, holding a heavy, leather-bound volume. "It's a bit dusty," she apologised.

"That doesn't matter," Eleanor said, "It's the contents that interest me, not the condition."

Eleanor could feel the librarian watching her as she opened the book to the eighteenth century and compared the marks with the copy she had made.

"Are you all right?" The librarian walked over.

"I can't find what I'm looking for," Eleanor admitted.

"Can I help?" The librarian glanced at Eleanor's drawing. "A double V with a line above? Oh, you're hundreds of years away," she said.

"Am I? The house was built in the eighteenth century," Eleanor said.

"I've seen that mark before, and it's not from the eighteenth century," the librarian told her severely. "I'm no expert, but that mark is well known."

"Where?" Eleanor asked.

"Sweetheart Abbey," the librarian said. "It's the mark of Master James of Nantes; he worked on restoring buildings all across Europe. He helped restore Sweetheart, Kelso and Jedburgh Abbeys after the English destroyed them in the War of Independence. Where did you see his mark?"

"A house called Anton's Walls near Newbigging," Eleanor explained.

The librarian frowned. "I don't know that name," she admitted and listened as Eleanor described the house and its situation.

"It sounds like somebody cannibalised the stones from another site," the librarian decided. "That was a common practice in the eighteenth century when people thought nothing of robbing castles and abbeys, even Hadrian's Wall, for building stone."

"We considered that," Eleanor admitted. "Master James of Nantes, you say. Do you know anything about him?"

"Only what's in that book," the librarian admitted. "He worked in Scotland at the beginning of the fourteenth century and then disappeared from history. As far as I am aware, nobody knew what happened to him.

Eleanor took a deep breath. "Do you know anything about Hugo de Soulis?"

The librarian's expression altered. "De Soulis of Caercorbie?"

"That's him," Eleanor said.

"The Wicked Lord Soulis," the librarian spoke as if she had known him personally rather than referring to a man who had been dead for six hundred years. "Don't go to Caercorbie, for de Soulis will be there. He spread great evil around the Borders."

There's that phrase again, great evil.

"De Soulis is a man best forgotten," the librarian said.

"Do you have a book about him?"

"Are you a library member?" the librarian asked, evidently eager to increase her membership.

It took a few moments to fill in the requisite form, and then the librarian ushered Eleanor to the history section. Like most Border libraries, the local history shelves were full, showing a regional pride unsurpassed in any other part of Scotland.

"Try that one." The librarian knew which books to select. "And that one."

Complete with the four books she was allowed, Eleanor thanked the librarian and returned to the Crossley, prepared to learn all she could about Hugo de Soulis. She chased away the two crows that stood on the Crossley's bonnet and speeded up to leave them behind in Hawick.

Both crows were waiting outside the Wardlaw Inn, preening their feathers, and watching her arrive through bright, intelligent eyes.

~

Sir Andrew Douglas stood at the side of the lonely grave. His squire had been a promising young lad, eager to please, but the fever had struck with devastating suddenness, and he died within three days.

Sir Andrew had found a local priest to say the holy words, dug the grave himself and laid his squire in with genuine regret. Now he watched as the priest, duty done, rode away on a broken-down donkey. Sir Andrew stroked his hawk, patted the hound and mounted Kenneth, his palfrey, pausing only to chase away the two black crows that landed on the newly turned earth. He pushed on, allowing the horse to take its time, for he knew the direction and the route would unravel as he travelled the miles.

The day following the burial, he emerged from the scattered trees fringing the Ettrick Forest and saw the remnants of a small village. The church lay in blackened ruins, the manor house was a memory, and smoke curled slowly into the chill air. The only sound was the wails of a distressed woman.

Sir Andrew reined up and raised his voice. "I am Sir Andrew Douglas of Maintree! What has brought grief to this place?"

A stocky, middle-aged man emerged from one of the few houses still standing. With a great scar disfiguring his face and a long knife at the side of his belt, it was evident he had fought in the late wars. "A plague has descended on us, Sir Knight."

Sir Andrew backed his horse away. "A plague?" With the memory of his squire's death still vivid, he crossed himself to invoke Christ's protection.

"A plague of evil, good knight." The man faced Sir Andrew squarely, with respect but without fear, as befitted a veteran soldier.

"What sort of evil?" Sir Andrew asked, touching the hilt of his sword.

"The sort that stalks by night," the man replied. "An evil

that spews from the bowels of the earth and spreads to the people all around."

Sir Andrew watched the crow circle the thatched roofs of the cottages before it settled on a weather-stripped birch. A second crow joined the first, with both birds watching the knight.

"You are talking in riddles, my friend. Tell me more and speak plainly," Sir Andrew said, dismounting. He tossed the reins to a staring youth. "You, churl, care for my horses. I want them fed, watered, and groomed."

The youth nodded and led the horses away while the scarred man ushered Sir Andrew inside the closest cottage to the birch tree. The brachet – the hound -accompanied them, sniffing at the ground.

"Come inside, Sir Knight. We have little to offer, but you are welcome."

Sir Andrew entered by right of his rank and position. The cottage was built of loose stones and mud, with a simple roof of heather thatch. Twenty years of war with the English had created a near desert along both sides of the border, so the population had learned it was useless to build anything elaborate. People threw up their homes in a couple of days, and the inhabitants were prepared to abandon them and run for the hills whenever an enemy raiding party appeared.

The interior was as basic as the outside, with a beaten earth floor, a simple hearth, and a scattering of three-legged stools. Used to the wealthier homes of Haddingtonshire, Sir Andrew hid his surprise and accepted what hospitality there was as his hound sniffed the ground, turned in a tight circle and settled in front of the fire.

"I am Sir Andrew Douglas of Maintree," Sir Andrew announced again.

"Sim Armstrong," the scarred man introduced himself.

"My wife is Isabel." He did not mention the two children who stared at the knight or the little girl who immediately crouched beside the brachet.

"You are welcome, Sir Andrew." Isabel was as bold-eyed as her husband as she spooned broth from a pot into three wooden bowls and handed one to her guest.

Sir Andrew tasted the broth. "Venison and kale, I am beholden to you," he said. "Does the local lord not object to you killing deer?" He eyed the bow propped against the wall and the long spear above the fireplace.

Sim gave a cynical smile. "I hunt deer," he said. "Our lord," he made the sign of the cross in the air, "hunts children and young women."

Sir Andrew looked up. He was unused to churls speaking against their lord, yet instinctively knew he would be unwise to challenge Sim Armstrong. This Borderland was different from Haddingtonshire. "Why?"

Sim touched the haft of his spear. "We are not sure, Sir Andrew, for nobody has met him and survived, save those with Devil's favour. We know he leads his host, his men-at-arms, to raid for children and youths. He drains the country dry for his crafts."

"Which crafts?" Sir Andrew asked.

Isabel made the sign of the cross before speaking. "Devil worship, Sir Andrew, and dealing with a demon he calls Robin Redcap."

Sir Andrew felt a cold chill run up his spine. "Does this lord have a name?"

Sim glanced at Isabel, who straightened up before she replied. "He calls himself Sir Hugo de Soulis," she said. "We have other names for him."

Sir Andrew finished his soup. "I can imagine you have, Isabel," he said, still unsettled at the brazen way these people spoke about their liege lord and social superior. "Where can I find Sir Hugo de Soulis?"

"At his castle of Caercorbie," Sim said. "Over the Windy-door Nick, the hill pass there," he nodded through the open door towards a range of ragged hills, "and across the Deepsyke Moss. Caercorbie guards the slap over the further hills."

"The Guardian of the Slap," Sir Andrew said, and the name hung like a curse in the air.

"Yes, Sir Andrew," Sim agreed. "A dark guardian."

"I'll rest here tonight," Sir Andrew decided, "and leave at first light."

"God keep you safe, Sir Andrew," Isabel said.

Eleanor was tired when she woke and realised she had been digging her nails into her hands again. She sighed at the semi-circles of blood on her palms, glanced over at the sleeping Thomas and lifted one of the books from her bedside table. A moment later, she scratched a match and lit the gas light at the head of the bed, for electricity had not yet reached the Wardlaw Inn.

Thomas woke half an hour later, yawned, scratched his head, and sat up. "What are you reading, sister-of-mine?"

"What do you know about crows, Thomas?" Eleanor asked.

"They're birds," Thomas told her. "They're black and big, and they eat carrion."

"Do you know anything else?" Eleanor asked.

"Is there any more to know?"

"Wherever I go in the Borders," Eleanor said, "I see crows. Ever since old Martin sang that song in the Dryfe Arms, I've seen crows and always in pairs."

"You're imagining things," Thomas said. "Crows are

common everywhere. Martin's song has probably only made you more aware of them."

"Maybe," Eleanor said. She forced a smile. "I hope you're right, Thomas."

"I am right, sister-of-mine," he told her. "What time is breakfast?"

"An hour yet," Eleanor said. "I've been researching crows. In old folklore, people associate them with deaths and battles."

"We've seen enough of both," Thomas told her sternly.

"Too much," Eleanor agreed. "The Irish Gaelic word for crow was *badh*, which was also the name they gave to a battle goddess. Cathubodua, battle crow." She smiled, "their great queen was the Morrighan, who sometimes appeared as a crow and had an insatiable lust for men." Eleanor stopped as she realised that war also had a lust for men. Both the Morrighan and battle used men and discarded them. *Is the Morrighan only a symbol of war? Or a male perspective of women who suck them dry?*

"Is that so?" Thomas pretended interest as he checked his trench watch, shook it when he realised he had forgotten to wind it and asked the time from Eleanor.

"Half past six. Crows can also be harbingers of death," Eleanor persisted.

"That's cheery." Thomas dismissed the subject. "Come on, Eleanor. Think of something happier."

Eleanor nodded. A few weeks ago, such a conversation would have pushed Thomas back into the darkness. Now, he listened politely and moved on. "You're right, Tom," she said, smiling. On an impulse, she bent over and kissed him.

"Hey! What was that for?" Thomas pushed her away. "You've never done that before."

"Neither I have," Eleanor said, kissing him again as the music sounded.

"Ce fut en mai

Au douz tens gai."

"Enough of that," Thomas said, pushing himself out of bed. "Good God, woman, you're acting like a Frenchman!"

Eleanor laughed, watched him wash and smiled with memories of another man.

~

Eleanor drew up the Crossley behind the police car outside the Wardlaw Inn after another day at Hawick Library. Newbigging was busier than she had ever seen it, with knots of people gathered outside shops and standing in the road. Two horse-drawn carts stood beside each other, and a crowd of women watched Eleanor leave her car.

"What are the police doing here?" Eleanor asked Sharon, who stood outside the inn with her arms folded.

"It's a bad thing." Sharon shook her head. "Wee Johnnie Bell has gone missing."

"Has he wandered off?" Eleanor did not know the boy.

Sharon shook her head. "I don't know, Mrs Machrie. Mrs Bell is beside herself with worry. The police are organising a search."

"I'll help," Eleanor volunteered immediately. "So will Tom when he gets back."

"You're guests here," Sharon said. "You don't know the area."

"We'll do what we can," Eleanor insisted. "Tom will be at Anton's Wall's, but he won't be long."

The police accepted Eleanor's offer without any objections. "We're checking the fields outside the village," the heavily moustached sergeant Learmonth told her. "Constable Scott will issue you with a staff, and you can join the search party on the south."

Eleanor nodded. "What's Wee Johnnie Bell like?"

"Seven years old, corduroy trousers, grey shirt and a tweed jacket," the sergeant said. "He has a habit of wandering in the moors to get bird's eggs, but not at this time of year." He took a deep breath. "His ma's upset, naturally. She lost her husband in the last days of the war, and Wee Johnnie is the only man left in the house."

Eleanor nodded. "Let's hope we find him."

Sergeant Learmonth organised the search parties, with the villagers working close to Newbigging and the hill farmers and shepherds scouring the wilder country further out. Eleanor walked through the fields in company with a line of villagers, shining a lantern and shouting Johnnie's name.

After a couple of hours, Robert Powrie and the men working on Anton's Walls returned to the village, bringing Thomas in their cart. They joined the search without hesitation, adding their rough voices and determination to the others. Eleanor watched Powrie, smiling when she realised that Thomas was correct as he was amazingly energetic, organising his workmen with near military efficiency.

When the light died, Archie Elliot provided lanterns to those who had none, and the search continued, with hoarse voices sounding hollow to tired ears but nobody willing to stop.

"It's six in the morning." Martin sat on a drystone dyke, lighting his pipe by the light of a scimitar moon. "We've scoured all the fields twice and found nothing."

"The wee lad's vanished," Constable Scott agreed, shining his lantern along the base of the wall.

Exhaustion was familiar to Eleanor after her experiences in the war. She brushed it aside and looked at Thomas. "We can't give up," she said.

"We won't," Thomas promised. He glanced at his sister. "Anton's Walls can wait."

Eleanor agreed. A missing child was more important than redeveloping a house. "Come on," she said, pushing herself upright. "We'll keep going."

Martin lifted a quizzical eyebrow, winked at Thomas, and puffed smoke from his pipe. "We have to do what the ladies want," he said, frowned and looked at Eleanor again. He opened his mouth as if about to ask a question, shook his head and trudged away, suddenly looking very old.

Daylight brought a fine drizzle from the hills, and an hour after dawn, reinforcements arrived when three lorry loads of the Kings Own Scottish Borderers rolled into Newbigging.

"Come on, lads!" a young lieutenant with old eyes ordered, and the men leapt from the lorries, all khaki and keenness. Eleanor stepped closer to Thomas, prepared to see him return to the war, but instead, he sought out the officer and spoke to him for a few moments.

"I knew him in France," Thomas said. "He joined in '18, just before the German March offensive. He should have been promoted by now."

As the original volunteers withdrew to snatch some sleep, the soldiers took over the search, and the entire village held its breath.

After three days, the searchers found nothing.

"The wee lad's vanished," one stout woman said. "As if somebody spirited him away."

"Somebody or something." Martin looked no different than he had at the beginning of the search, an elderly man with a leathery countenance and a constitution that would never give up.

"Something?" Thomas asked. His eyes were like hollow pits in a drawn face.

Martin glanced at Eleanor as if for confirmation. "Aye. Something. Your sister understands." He tapped the bowl of his pipe against a rock, searched for tobacco and realised he had none. "We're doing no good here. Let's go to the Dryfe."

"It's shut," Thomas said.

"It will open for me," Martin told him. "Everything opens for me."

CHAPTER 11

DESPITE THE EARLY HOUR, the Dryfe was already open, with policemen and soldiers making up part of the clientele. Martin found them a table, and they slumped down as exhaustion washed over them.

"I hope you don't want white wine or anything fancy," Martin reminded Eleanor. "This place is not used to serving ladies."

Eleanor forced a smile through her tiredness. "I am used to rougher places than this," she said.

"It's begun again." Martin slumped down with his elbows on his knees and his pint glass half-full in front of him. At that minute, Eleanor could not estimate his age; he could have been anything from fifty to a hundred and fifty.

"What has started again?" Thomas asked.

"The great evil." Martin looked at Thomas through narrowed eyes.

Eleanor thought of de Soulis and her knight. "What do you mean?" She had already guessed the answer.

"Missing boys," Martin said grimly. "He's back."

"De Soulis?"

Superstitious nonsense. De Soulis is a mouldering skeleton buried in some unknown grave.

Martin nodded. "You know the story, then."

"Some of it," Eleanor admitted cautiously. "But that was hundreds of years ago, and it was only a legend."

Martin shook his head. "It was more than a legend, Mrs Machrie, and time can't diminish evil."

Thomas looked from Martin to Eleanor and back. "What are you talking about? Let me into the secret."

Eleanor related the basics of the de Soulis legend.

"A great evil?" Thomas repeated Eleanor's words. "What did he do?"

Martin shook his head. "We're not sure," he said. "The legends say he abducted local children for some devilish practices and had a familiar called Robin Redcap."

"That's a strange name for a demon," Thomas said.

"Evil can hide itself behind a flippant title," Martin admitted.

Eleanor nodded. "From what I've read, there was nothing amusing about Robin Redcap." She looked up. "If there is a connection between the missing boy and de Soulis, maybe we should try and find his old castle."

Martin nodded. "Aye, maybe." He stared into the contents of his tankard. "And maybe we should leave well alone."

"Where is it?" Thomas asked.

Martin shrugged. "Nobody knows," he said. "The legend says that the local folk slaked it – burned it to the ground- and other stories say it sunk beneath the ground under the weight of its sin."

Thomas grunted. "If you told me these legends before the war, I'd have laughed, but I served with men who saw the

Angels of Mons." [1] He snapped shut his mouth without mentioning the knight he had seen in the trenches.

Eleanor nodded. "There must be a record somewhere, a piece of masonry, some foundations or something."

"I saw shattered buildings in France," Thomas spoke slowly. "Modern shell fire blasted them to rubble." He took a long pull at his pint. "Even after a concentrated bombardment, some fragments remained."

Eleanor watched Thomas's eyes flicker as he relived the memories. "I'll find some old maps," she said brightly. "Caercorbie might be marked."

Martin watched her carefully. "I've got some," he said. "I believe I have copies of all the old Border maps. You're welcome to study them."

"Thank you," Eleanor said. "It seems selfish playing with old legends while a mother is worried sick about her child."

Martin raised his white eyebrows. "A hundred people have scoured the fields and hills without success. Maybe you can help find him with a map."

Eleanor nodded. "Maybe," she said. *Why do I feel as if Martin is testing me?*

∽

Eleanor arrived at Fairhope the following day, wondering about her unpleasant dreams.

"You still look tired," Martin told her.

"I had nightmares about young Johnnie Bell last night," Eleanor said.

"Aye." Martin nodded. "That's understandable. I've dug up all my maps." He ushered her into his kitchen, where a square window overlooked the farmyard and blue-and-white plates gleamed on a Dutch Dresser. Maps sat in a neat pile on the plain deal table.

"I don't know if they're any good, but you seem to know what you're doing."

Eleanor wondered if Martin was merely humouring her or if he was genuinely trying to help as she spread out the maps. She had expected a modern Bartholomew and maybe an estate plan, but Martin had a dozen maps of various ages, and she lifted two.

"These are excellent," she said. "John Leslie's map of Scotland: *Scotiae Regni Antiqvissima* and John Speed's *Map of the Kingdome of Scotland*." She laid them aside. "These maps date back to the sixteenth and seventeenth centuries."

"I've nothing older," Martin said. "And they are only copies."

"I didn't think you'd have anything this old," Eleanor said. She had purchased a magnifying glass from Elliot's and studied Leslie's map, with Martin watching from a chair in the corner of the room.

"I've found Deepsyke Muir," Eleanor said after a few moments. "There's a road marked through it."

Martin stepped across and borrowed the magnifying glass. "That's the old Deepsyke Muir Slap," he said. "The road through the moor and over the hills to Liddesdale. The Dark Slap, as people used to call it."

"There's a castle marked here," Eleanor said, "I think." She pointed to the spot, still ashamed of her blunt and broken nails.

"Aye," Martin put a wealth of meaning into the single word. "I see it."

Eleanor looked again. "The writing is hard to decipher. I think that's Anton's Walls."

"Aye," Martin agreed. "I'd say it was on the same spot."

When Eleanor looked up, Martin was staring at her, with his eyes troubled.

"Anthony Armstrong didn't build Anton's Walls until the eighteenth century," Eleanor said. "Two hundred years after this map was made."

"Aye," Martin said for the third time. He said no more.

Eleanor spoke slowly. "I think Anton's Walls sits on an earlier site," she said. "On the site of a castle." She heard a bird flutter outside the window and guessed it was a crow.

"Aye," Martin emphasised that single word. Where another man could have spoken for five minutes, Martin's single word told Eleanor all she needed to know.

"Caercorbie Castle," Eleanor said softly.

"Caercorbie Castle," Martin agreed. "The home of damned de Soulis and Redcap."

Eleanor had never heard Martin swear before. "Oh, dear Lord," she breathed. She thought of the mediaeval mason's mark on the basement stones, the strategic positioning of the house and the dark legends and shook her head.

The cellar beneath Anton's Walls is the dungeons of Caercorbie. The maker's marks belong there.

"Did you know?" Eleanor asked.

"Aye," he said. "I thought it best you found out yourself." Martin stared at Eleanor. "Or never found out at all. Now, will you leave that cursed place?"

"Ce fut en mai
Au douz tens gai
Que la saisons est bele,
Main me levai."

Eleanor took a deep breath as the words ran through her mind. "We've nowhere else to go," she said.

"You're better nowhere than at Anton's Walls," Martin grated. "Run while you still can. De Soulis has returned, woman! Burn the place down and run while you have your soul, Eleanor Armstrong!"

"De Soulis has been dead for six hundred years," Eleanor said quietly. "The dead can't return, and anyway, we've spent all our money renovating that house. We came here to speed Thomas's recovery, and the quiet is already helping him."

"There's no peace in hell," Martin said. "You know that the redcaps emerged from hell to infest Border keeps."

A few weeks before, Eleanor would have scoffed at any mention of redcaps or other supernatural entities. Since her visit to Maintree, the persistent crows and the images of Sir Andrew Douglas, she was not so sure.

"I'll speak to Thomas," Eleanor promised.

"You do that," Martin advised.

Neither mentioned young John Bell, although the young boy's presence was in the room.

CHAPTER 12

"Do we really want to live in Anton's Walls?" Eleanor asked as they sat in the lounge bar of the Wardlaw Inn.

Thomas smiled. "The renovations are complete," he said. "We have a generator for electricity, water and sewage, and I've even had two of the rooms painted and papered."

"Only two?" Eleanor asked.

"We can do the rest ourselves," Thomas told her. "I'll do the skilled work, and you can be my labourer."

Eleanor fought mixed emotions. She partly dreaded living with such a grim history while simultaneously wanting the peace of the moor and her own home and possessions around her. She also wanted to solve the mystery of what happened to Sir Andrew Douglas.

"I am not sure about living where so much evil occurred," Eleanor said.

Thomas took hold of her hands. "We've both seen the obscenity of war," he reminded quietly. "We know what it's like. Can you think of any corner of Europe, or anywhere else for that matter, where violence and evil have not occurred?"

Eleanor considered for a moment. "No," she said.

"Exactly," Thomas agreed. "I doubt the Wardlaw Valley is any different. We can be happy there, sister-of-mine."

Eleanor smiled at Thomas's enthusiasm. "It's good to have you back," she said, squeezing his hands. "We'll send for our furniture, although the carrier will have the devil's own job negotiating that track."

"They're Borderers," Thomas said. "They're used to these roads." He smiled, so like his old self that Eleanor wanted to hug him. "Once we're settled, I'll improve the road through the moss."

"The Dark Slap." Eleanor forced a smile. "Doesn't the thought of de Soulis worry you?"

Thomas shook his head. "No," he said softly. "Whatever he did centuries ago, I've seen worse, and so have you."

Eleanor closed her eyes, remembering the long line of wounded and gassed men waiting patiently outside the hospital. She did not wish to rekindle old memories, but Thomas peered into his schooner of Youngers beer and began to talk. "I've been in trenches where human bodies made up part of the walls and trenches where men drowned in liquid mud. I've seen men burn alive and others with their faces blown off and still survive, desperate to die."

Thomas's eyes darkened as he relived his wartime memories. He recounted incident after incident, with his voice low and bitter.

"That's enough, Thomas," Eleanor tried to bring him back to the present. "It's gone now."

Thomas stopped, although his eyes flicked from side to side as if he could see the images he described. "Enough?" he repeated. "Aye, enough." His grin was crooked. "After four years of horror, sister-of-mine, I doubt there's anything de Soulis can do to scare me."

"How about me?" Eleanor asked. She did not remind him that she had seen her share of horrors as a nurse in France. "What if I am scared?"

Thomas focussed on her, with his eyes returning to normal. "I'll look after you," he said.

"I know you will," Eleanor said as the music seeped into her mind.

> "Ce fut en mai
> Au douz tens gai
> Que la saisons est bele,
> Main me levai."

Eleanor smiled, with her eyes straying to the window. She saw a pair of farmhands walking down the street, each dressed in his weekend best. The taller was rather handsome, Eleanor thought, running her gaze from the jaunty angle of his cap to his newly shined shoes. She laughed, covering her mouth when she realised that others in the room were looking at her.

"That's the spirit, Eleanor," Thomas said, grinning.

The two farmhands were gone now, Eleanor noticed, but their memory lingered in her mind, together with the music of that song.

"Living in Anton's Walls could be fun," Eleanor said, smiling.

After a few fair days, the track across Deepsyke Moor was nearly dry, with only residual puddles to remind where the floods had been. Even the ford across the Deep Syke was passable without difficulty. A weak early spring sun lit the moss, casting short shadows from Blackhouse Tower and altering the atmosphere from foreboding to merely desolate.

"There." Thomas halted the Crossley twenty yards from Anton's Walls and switched off the engine. "Our new home."

The two crows flapped slowly in front of them, landed and began pecking at the ground.

~

Sir Andrew pushed Kenneth across the hill pass of Windydoor Nick, nodding to the occasional shepherd, and descended to the road across Deepsyke Muir. He led his charger, with his hound trotting at his side and the hawk secure on the saddle. Sir Andrew listened to the lonely call of the whaups[1] and saw a pair of peewits dancing nearby.

This is a lonely place, a far cry from Maintree.

When he saw Caercorbie in the distance, a triangular pile of stone standing on an island in the moor, Sir Andrew halted Kenneth and surveyed the area.

That's a fitting nest for a viper: grim, stark, and foreboding. I wat I'll find evil within the walls.

Sir Andrew touched the hilt of his sword. *God and Saint Bride, grant me the strength of the good Sir James of Douglas.*

As Sir Andrew descended the pass and rode onto the slap, he noted the castle's builder had used the moor as a natural moat, with only the road offering safe passage to Caercorbie and the pass over the distant hills. Sir Andrew examined the castle, noting the strength of its position, the twin towers guarding the formidable gatehouse and the arrow slits, which were the only windows in the blank stone walls. A flag hung from the taller of the two towers, although the distance was too great for Sir Andrew to distinguish the device.

Whoever built Caercorbie had an eye for defence. No attacker can get close without being seen, the moor is too wet to allow artillery close enough to bombard the castle, and the surrounds are unsuitable for any besieging army to camp.

Pushing slowly forward, Sir Andrew walked his horse

along the track, aware that the garrison of Caercorbie was watching him. He saw movement on the battlements and the flash of sunlight on armour, but the castle gate remained stoutly closed. As he drew closer, he saw the device on the flag, with horizontal red lines against a white background, with a red bend sinister, a diagonal stripe from top right to bottom left.

That is the device of Sir Hugo de Soulis.

"Hold!" the challenge came from the battlemented gate-house. "Who are you, and whither are you bound?"

Sir Andrew lifted a hand in greeting. "I am Sir Andrew Douglas of Maintree, and I am bound to Caercorbie." He waited for an acknowledgement.

The sentry passed the message to his superiors and replied a few moments later.

"Sir Hugo de Soulis bids you welcome, Sir Andrew."

The portcullis grated up, the iron-studded door opened, and two men emerged.

Sir Andrew touched the hilt of his sword and rode through the gate of Caercorbie, wondering if he were entering the portals of hell. The gate closed behind him, and the portcullis clanged down.

~

Eleanor eyed Anton's Walls, noting the workmen had repointed the stonework, repaired the roof and chimney repaired, and repainted the external door and windows. "You've done a good job in a short time," she said.

Thomas laughed. "That was Robert Powrie. He and his boys worked like drunken Trojans." He drove the final twenty yards to the front door, where the workers had levelled the ground and laid gravel for parking.

Eleanor tried to push the dark stories from her mind when

she stepped out of the car. The day was bright, and she had the new house in a peaceful setting to ease the turmoil in Thomas's mind. Everything was as she had planned, and she had no reason to worry.

Eleanor flinched as a crow hopped across the doorway and flapped away on slow wings. Crows are common birds.

"Another crow." Eleanor laughed.

"Where?" Thomas asked, smiling.

"Did you not see the crow at the door?"

"Not even a shadow of a crow," Thomas said. "You're imagining things, Eleanor. Now, in you come, sister-of-mine!" Thomas inserted his key in the door and pushed it open.

The second crow fluttered out as Eleanor stepped into her house.

"You saw that crow, surely," Eleanor said.

"There was no crow," Thomas said, laughing. "You've got crows on the brain. Let me show you around," he invited, grinning with enthusiasm. He pointed out all the work, from plastering to electrical and plumbing.

"It's a house fit for a queen," Thomas enthused.

"You've been busy," Eleanor agreed.

"Thank Robert for that," Thomas told her.

Eleanor smiled. Robert Powrie had made a good impression on Thomas. "Good old Robert," she said.

❧

Eleanor's nursing experience had hardened her to sleeping in unusual places, yet strange dreams disturbed her first night in her bedroom at Anton's Walls. She awoke with the French tune running through her head and a recollection of erotic dreams that left her alternatively smiling and embarrassed.

She rose, wondering from where the images came, stepped

to the window, and looked outside. Her bedroom faced the moor to the north, and she saw a collection of lights. She watched for a few moments, realised she was shivering with cold and returned to the warm cocoon of her bed.

"I saw lights last night," Eleanor reported the following morning.

"A passing car, perhaps," Thomas replied.

"There's no road in the moor." Eleanor kept her voice flat.

"Poachers, then," Thomas said.

"What are they poaching?" Eleanor asked. "There's no deer here, and it's too wet for rabbits and too dry for fish."

Thomas sighed. "Where about in the moor were the lights?"

"Over to the north," Eleanor said, chewing on a mouthful of toast and marmalade.

"I'll walk over and have a look," Thomas said. "I want to explore, anyway."

"I'll come with you," Eleanor told him. "I don't want you getting lost out there."

Nor do I want you falling into one of your black moods, walking into a patch of bogland and drowning.

Thomas grinned at her. "Good idea, sister-of-mine. We've hardly seen each other since we began to renovate the house."

The morning was clear and crisp, with a covering of frost making the ground brittle underfoot and reflecting the sun with a million pinpricks of light. A whaup circled above, calling as its curved beak recalled stories of the demons that lived in the eaves of houses.

No crows, thank God. Eleanor remembered her dreams of the previous night and felt the blood rushing to her face.

"It's a beautiful day," Thomas said cheerfully, stamping his boots and taking deep breaths.

"You seem to be enjoying it," Eleanor replied sourly, shivering inside her coat, scarf, and hat. "Over this way." She thumped her staff on the ground to test its solidity and set off, watching Thomas from the corner of her eye.

What would he think if he knew what I dreamed? She smiled. *He'd probably approve. I doubt he was a monk over in France.*

The moor was uneven, with rises of high ground alternating with dips where thin ice concealed treacherous areas of bogland. They walked slowly, checking their route, watching their surroundings, and occasionally turning back to view Anton's Walls from different angles.

"It's hard to believe we live here," Eleanor said. "It's so different from Edinburgh with its smoky streets, trams and crowds of people."

Thomas rested on his staff. "I don't feel I quite belong," he said. "I feel like an intruder."

Eleanor nodded. "I think we are intruders," she agreed. "Stooriefeet, as the locals call us. They've been here for centuries; they endured the Border wars, English invasions and the reivers." She stopped to survey the moor, where the gaunt shape of Blackhouse Tower thrust up as a reminder of the grim reality of life on the old frontier. "Through all that, they carved out their farms, and now we come along and gaily move in."

Yet you do belong, Eleanor. Your blood is from here, and in some ways, you are more at home in the Wardlaw Valley than you ever were in the city.

Thomas laughed. "You're right, Eleanor. Their ancestors have done the work, and we're exploiting them." He strode up a heathery ridge, stopping at the top to allow Eleanor to catch up. "But our ancestors were here, too."

"They were," Eleanor agreed. "Our name proves that." She joined Thomas at the summit of the ridge. "The Armstrongs came from this area."

"In a way," Thomas said, "we are coming home."

Yes, a little voice inside Eleanor's head shouted. *I'm coming home.*

"Home?" Eleanor shuddered. "Home to a place of conflict, murder, slaughter, and feuds. I wonder if we'd have been better to remain in Edinburgh."

"I don't think so," Thomas said. "Chase away these silly superstitious stories, sister-of-mine, and enjoy the place. Walter Scott gave this place romance, and here we are in one of the country's most fascinating areas. Enjoy it."

"Over there." Eleanor pointed to another, more prominent ridge a few hundred yards away. "That's where I saw the lights last night."

Thomas grunted. "It's like an island amidst bogland."

The heather-and-grass ridge rose fifty feet above a large area of sinister-looking marsh, with small pools of reed-fringed water interspersed with bright green moss that signified soft ground beneath.

"Why would anybody want to go there?" Eleanor asked, yet she knew she was correct. "Come on, Thomas."

"It's like Passchendaele," Thomas said, referring to a particularly horrific battle fought in deep mud.

"No!" Eleanor nudged him. "You're in the Scottish Borders, not Belgium." She looked across the moor, imagining how she could reach the ridge. "Over here, I think."

"Be careful, Eleanor," Thomas said as Eleanor began to probe at the bog with her staff.

"It's all right," Eleanor reassured him. "There's solid ground here, under an inch of mud."

"How the hell did you know that?" Thomas asked.

Eleanor shrugged. "I just knew," she said.

Thomas followed, testing the ground as Eleanor stepped into the marsh. "Come back if it gets deep," he said.

"I will," Eleanor said cheerfully. She peered ahead, taking one step at a time as she made her slow way towards the ridge. A skein of geese passed overhead, their call evocative in this timeless landscape. "It's like an old path here," Eleanor said. "A causeway through the marsh." She could see people walking together, men and women talking in a language she did not know.

That's crazy. What's happening to me?

When they were halfway, Eleanor stopped and prodded in front of her to find solid ground. "I've lost the causeway," she said. "It ends here." She looked ahead, judging the distance she had yet to cover as she touched the knight's ring in her pocket.

"How deep is the mud?" Thomas asked.

Eleanor pushed down her staff without touching the bottom. "Deep," she said. "Too deep to walk."

"Try on either side," Thomas suggested. "There might be a bend in the path."

Eleanor prodded to her left and right without success. "Nothing doing," she said, feeling suddenly abandoned.

"Let me." Thomas squeezed past her. "Sometimes shellfire destroyed the duckboards in the trenches, and we had to jump over gas-filled craters," he said. "The duckboards started a few yards further on."

Using his staff, Thomas leaned forward and prodded into the mud, working in a regular pattern.

"I thought so," he said a few moments later. "Here's something." He tapped the ground a few times. "Definitely solid. Stand back, Eleanor!"

When Eleanor obeyed, Thomas jumped over the intervening mud to land with a splash. "Solid as a rock," he said, ignoring the liquid filth that splattered him from ankles to shoulders. "Can you jump? I'll catch you."

"I can jump," Eleanor said. Taking a deep breath, she

launched herself over the gap to land in Thomas's arms. She remained there a moment, enjoying the security.

"There we are, sister-of-mine," Thomas said, grinning. "Safe as houses if not as dry. Lead on, MacDuff. You're in charge here."

Eleanor had nearly forgotten her original reason for entering the moor as she traced the causeway through the mire. She felt like an explorer tracing the forgotten road, with a sensation of triumph as she arrived at the heather ridge.

Something terrible happened in this place.

Something terrible? It's only a featureless rise in the middle of a bog, so why create a causeway to get here?

CHAPTER 13

"WELL, HERE WE ARE," Thomas said as he stamped the loose mud from his boots. "We've reached a windy ridge in the middle of a bog. Now show me your lights, sister-of-mine."

"We won't see them in daylight," Eleanor said. "I only wished to find this ridge to see why anybody would have lights here."

"You're welcome to inspect the place." Thomas looked around. "It's broader than I imagined, a ridge of heather, grass and bugger-all else."

Eleanor hid her disappointment. She did not know what she had expected to find but something more than this bleakness.

Yet it's the right place.

"There's some view, though," Thomas said. "This ridge would make a splendid OP – Observation Post. You can see all around from here." He circled, naming the landmarks, and automatically searching for the best fields of fire. "Yes, Eleanor, this is a very strategic place you have found for us."

"There's more here than only a view," Eleanor told him. "There's something else here, Thomas. I can feel it."

"You can feel it?" Thomas gave her a sideways look. "You're a nurse, Eleanor, not a clairvoyant. What do you mean?"

Eleanor shrugged. "I could feel when men were going to die, Thomas. I used to sit beside the young boys, holding their hands and reassuring them. I was their mother, their sister, their sweetheart, or their wife. I could sense death and hear its wings rustling. It's the same here. I can feel something."

"I can feel the wind blowing on my face." Thomas tried to make light of Eleanor's words. "Seriously though, sister-of-mine, I knew men who foretold their own death and others who knew when the enemy would attack. I think some of us have a hidden sixth sense that we can trigger." He touched her arm. "Maybe you have that gift."

Eleanor leaned closer, grateful for his support. "Thank you, Tom. I don't know what's here. I only know I can feel something." She looked around. "This is an uncanny place, Tom."

"It's evil," Thomas said and smiled. "Why the devil did I say that?"

"Because it is," Eleanor said and shuddered, looking around. "What's happened here, Tom?" She closed her eyes and saw a knight facing the opposite direction, his face, surcoat, and shield hidden.

Thomas shrugged. A rising wind ruffled his hair and scoured his face. "We're right in the heart of the old border between Scotland and England," he reminded. "One of the most hotly contested frontiers in the world. Romans, Angles, Scots, Britons, Norsemen, and English, have all fought and died here. Only God knows what's happened in this place, and He's turned his eyes away from humanity."

"Has he? What makes you say that?" Eleanor asked quickly. When she opened her eyes, the knight had vanished.

Thomas tapped his staff on the ground. "You and I both saw the horrors of war, sister-of-mine. What loving God would permit such things?"

Eleanor frowned. "Humanity causes wars, not God. Do that again?"

"Do what again?" Thomas asked.

"Tap your stick on the ground," Eleanor said, thumping her staff down.

"Like this?" Thomas tapped his stick.

"Yes, listen. Your stick makes a different sound to mine." Eleanor banged her stick three times. "Listen!"

"There's a rock under here," Thomas said. "You only have grass and heather." He tapped again, and both heard a dull ring, like a cracked bell.

"Rock doesn't sound like that," Eleanor said. "Let me see." Crouching, she tore at the turf with her fingers. "You're right, though, there's rock under here."

Thomas watched for a moment. "What the hell are you doing, Eleanor?"

"I want to see what's under here," Eleanor said. "You could help rather than standing like a prize idiot."

"I prefer to watch," Thomas said, sighed and pulled his clasp knife from his pocket. "Here," he said, opened it and passed it to Eleanor. "Use this."

Within ten minutes, Eleanor had burrowed half an inch into the turf and uncovered a section of flat stone. "See?" she said and began to follow the outline. Thomas watched, smiling as she traced a roughly oblong stone lying under half an inch of turf.

"This thing is about fifteen feet long," Eleanor said. "And there are more. I know there are."

"It's only a stone," Thomas protested. "Scotland has millions of the damned things."

"Help me find them." Ignoring Thomas's complaints, Eleanor walked along the ridge, prodding her staff into the ground. "Here's another," she said a few moments later. "Come on, Tom!"

"Why are we doing this?" Thomas asked as he joined her.

"I have an idea," Eleanor told him. "I'll tell you more later." She glanced upward, where grey clouds gathered, pregnant with menace. "Hurry, Tom."

Eleanor was faster in tracing the outline of the next recumbent stone. "That's two," she said and saw her crows arrive on the ridge. They stood on one spot, watching her as if attempting to convey a message.

"What's the matter, sister-of-mine?" Thomas asked as Eleanor stared towards the birds.

"I don't know," Eleanor said. "I think the crows are trying to help."

"Which crows?" Thomas asked, looking around.

"These crows." Eleanor pointed in the crows' direction.

Thomas looked puzzled. "You're imagining things, Eleanor."

"You're going blind in your old age," Eleanor told him, shook her head, and walked towards the birds which fluttered away on her approach. She thrust her staff into the turf, heard it strike a rock and dug again. "Here's a third stone," she said.

"Well done, the imaginary crows," Thomas said, unsure whether to laugh or be concerned. "They can find stones in the stoniest country in the world."

"Not just any stones," Eleanor said. "These are in a pattern. Can't you see?"

"A pattern?"

"They are the same distance apart and in a circle," Eleanor explained. "We are unearthing a stone circle. They are lying flat, but it's a definite circle."

Thomas grunted, looked over the ground and nodded. "You could be right," he said as Eleanor strode to where her crows waited.

The clouds darkened overhead, occasionally releasing a few heavy raindrops as a portend of what was to come. Eleanor worked quickly, locating and marking the outlines of each slumbering stone with Thomas good-naturedly helping. It was mid-afternoon before she finished, with the winter daylight already dimming.

"That's enough, now," Thomas told her. "It'll be dark soon, and we have to negotiate that causeway." He grinned. "We still haven't found the source of your light."

"No," Eleanor wiped the sweat from her forehead, "we haven't, but we found this stone circle, which could be more important."

"More important for what?" Thomas asked. "Were you thinking of turning into a druid and prancing around the stones to worship the moon or whatever druids did?"

"No." Eleanor shook her head. "I don't know why they're important," she admitted, "I just know it means something."

Thomas glanced upwards. "Well, I know the rain will drench us unless we return home quickly. Come on, sister-of-mine."

The light had faded in the last few moments, but Eleanor found the beginning of the causeway without any difficulty. Thomas followed her, marvelling at her sense of direction as she strode along the hidden path.

"I wish we had you in Flanders," he said. "You could have led patrols through No man's land."

Eleanor laughed. "My feet know the way," she said. She did not mention the two crows that flew before her, for she had come to accept them as part of her life. If they had befriended Sir Andrew, they could only be helpful.

~

Anton's Walls' living room looked comfortable, with a large fire glowing in the grate and electric lighting fighting the gloom. Eleanor sat in her favourite armchair on the left side of the fireplace, dipping into the pile of books she had brought from Hawick Library.

"This Hugo de Soulis was a bad man," she said as Thomas tied a fishing fly opposite her.

"I already knew that," Thomas said, holding up his fly and squinting to see if his knot was tight. "What else have you found?"

"The main story is the same in all these books," Eleanor indicated the pile beside her chair, "but some have details that others leave out."

"That's the way with books," Thomas said solemnly. "Authors twist the legends to suit their experiences. Do any of them mention that stone circle you found today?"

"Yes," Eleanor said. "Or rather, they might do."

"That's rather ambiguous," Thomas said. "Explain, sister-dear, or forever hold thy peace."

Eleanor marked her place with a slender finger and looked up. "Most books say that Hugo de Soulis sold his soul to the devil and had a familiar called Redcap. They all say that the local people rose against him and killed him. Some say they dragged him to a place called the Thirteen Stane Rig, boiled him to soup and drank him."

"That would stop his badness," Thomas said.

"It would," Eleanor agreed. "Thomas, how many stones did we uncover today?"

Thomas laid his fly aside. "I didn't count them," he confessed.

"Thirteen," Eleanor said. "That must have been the Thirteen Stone Rig."

"That makes sense," Thomas agreed politely but without much interest and began work on another fly. "I might try some coarse fishing," he said. "I'll have to ask the local landowner for permission."

"That's Sir Hugh Cummings," Eleanor replied without thinking.

Thomas nodded. "I know. I'll ask him where I can legally fish."

"According to this book," Eleanor said, "when the locals disposed of de Soulis, they buried his bones, then flattened the thirteen stones and threw earth over them."

"Why?" Thomas sighed and put aside his fly.

"So there was nothing to mark de Soulis's grave, and nobody would ever know where he was buried," Eleanor said.

"We uncovered the stones," Thomas said. "After you found them with the help of your imaginary crows."

Eleanor shivered, lifted the poker, poked the fire, and added more coal. A down draught blew blue-grey smoke into the room, and she coughed and waited for it to clear. "I know. Maybe we should cover them up again."

"Don't be daft!" Thomas grinned at her. "If de Soulis ever existed, he's long dead now and no harm to anyone. It's an old wives' tale to scare bairns and nothing else."

Eleanor shivered as the wind roared in the chimney. "I hope you are right, Thomas."

"Does that book tell you anything else?" Thomas had given up all hope of tying another fly.

"This one does." Eleanor lifted a thin volume entitled Tales from the Old West March. "It is more like a children's book and misses out some details, but it introduces a new character."

"Oh?" Thomas pretended polite interest. "Who?"

"Lady de Soulis," Eleanor said. "An old lady named Meg mentioned her, but none of the academics. Maybe they don't want to think of a woman involved."

"Maybe," Thomas said. "Some men still place women on pedestals. The evil lord was married then. I should have guessed as much. Those old knights needed an heir to pass on the family line, and legitimacy counted for a lot."

"I suppose so," Eleanor said. "This book claims she was the power behind the throne, and she was as bad, if not worse, than de Soulis."

Thomas nodded. "I'll remember that if I ever find myself in the fourteenth century." He grinned, "I'd have to borrow H. G. Wells' time machine."

Eleanor smiled absently and returned to her book. She hardly noticed when a lump of coal in the grate exploded, but when she looked up, Thomas was face down on the floor, with his mind back in the trenches and the exploding coal the harbinger of a German bombardment.

CHAPTER 14

SIR ANDREW RODE SLOWLY under the portcullis and into Caercorbie, with the guards watching his passage and two crows cawing inside the castle courtyard. A tall, smooth-faced man advanced to meet him with a middle-sized squire in a red cap leaning against the wall at his back.

"Well met, Sir Andrew, and welcome to Caercorbie." The tall, smooth-faced man stepped forward. "I am Sir Hugo de Soulis."

"Your name is known, Sir Hugo," Sir Andrew said, looking about him. The courtyard looked normal, with the hustle and bustle expected of a compact castle, servants and men-at-arms hurrying about their business and an elderly minstrel in one corner, strumming the strings of a harp. The minstrel studied him for a moment, then returned to his harp.

De Soulis snapped his fingers. "Grooms! See to Sir Andrew's horses!"

Two men ran to Sir Andrew, one taking the reins of Kenneth as he dismounted and the other attending to his charger.

"Enter, Sir Andrew," de Soulis said. "I have your quarters prepared, and my falconer will care for your hawk."

Sir Andrew stretched his legs, with his hound barking at one of the resident dogs. "My thanks, Sir Hugo. You must have seen me coming along the road."

"My messengers informed me a knight was approaching," Sir Hugo said with a tight smile. "They could not tell me your name."

"I did not see any messengers," Sir Andrew admitted.

"They saw you." Sir Hugo ushered his guest up a short flight of stone steps and through a tall doorway into the castle's great hall. Sir Andrew noticed that everything was built of stone. Stone flags on the ground, stone ceiling, stone walls, and stone steps. Yet the tapestries on the wall softened what could have been an austere chamber while the minstrel strummed sweet music in a corner.

"Sir Andrew Douglas!" The lady was tall with dark hair above a pale face. She greeted Sir Andrew with a slow smile and eyes that wandered from his forehead to his feet and back. "Welcome to Caercorbie, Sir Andrew."

"Thank you," Sir Andrew replied as the red-capped squire stood behind him, grinning foolishly.

"I will ensure your stay here is memorable," the lady told him. "First a bath, I think? And then some food. Let me take you to your quarters." Her smile revealed even white teeth. "I have had them prepared for you."

Sir Andrew bowed politely, immediately impressed. "My Lady," he said.

"Lady Marjorie de Soulis," the lady told him. "It is not often we have such a handsome young knight visiting Caercorbie." She led the way, speaking over her shoulder. "You may have heard the strangest rumours about us. They are all untrue, Sir Knight."

Sir Andrew followed, unconsciously breathing in Lady Marjory's perfume.

"Are you staying long, Sir Andrew?" Lady Marjory asked as she stopped at a chamber on the second level.

"I am unsure," Sir Andrew replied. He noticed his brachet sniffing at Lady Marjory's hand.

"We'll endeavour to help you decide," Lady Marjory said, ushering him into the room. "I hope you stay for a long time." She stepped aside. "You should be comfortable here. If you require anything, anything at all, let me know."

The room was well furnished with a bed, chest, and tapestries on the wall, with a window facing the internal courtyard.

"I will, my Lady," Sir Andrew said. He bowed again as Lady Marjory touched his shoulder with her forefinger.

"I will see you at the high table, Sir Andrew."

"Thank you, my Lady." Being invited to eat at the high table was an honour afforded only to the most important guests. Sir Andrew was surprised at the hospitality Lady Marjory showed him.

Perhaps the rumours are false, and de Soulis is only a baron holding a troubled frontier fortress. So far, only a distant holy man and a churl have given me evil tidings about Caercorbie. My experience has been the opposite. Sir Andrew viewed his comfortable quarters, stepped to the window, and looked out into the courtyard. Everything seemed normal. *I will remain a few nights and then resume my journey to Outremer.*

～

"Ce fut en mai
Au douz tens gai
Que la saisons est bele,
Main me levai."

Eleanor woke with the words of the French song in her head and a smile on her face.

When did I start to have that sort of dream? She stretched in the bed, with erotic images returning to her head. She lay back, smiling as she recalled incidents from her dream and the man with whom she had shared them.

Tall, blond and with blue eyes, he had been unpractised but vigorous. She had taught him to slow down and showed him some tricks that delighted them both.

From where did I obtain that knowledge? Eleanor wondered. *I must have inherited it from somewhere because it's certainly not from experience.* She laughed out loud, covered her mouth for fear of waking Thomas and closed her eyes to savour the memories.

Who were you, imaginary man?

The images were startlingly clear as if they had actually happened. Eleanor could recall every detail of the events.

What's happening to me? I saw hundreds of men when I was a nurse. Why this sudden erotic interest?

Pushing herself out of bed, Eleanor stepped to the window.

The moor was quiet, with a bright sky above the brown heather and weak sunlight highlighting the distant Thirteen Stane Rig. Helen remembered the knight on the ridge and smiled again.

You were a handsome chap, she said to herself. *And I would not turn you down.* She could not restrain her laugh, clapped a hand over her mouth and wondered what was for breakfast.

~

The estate factor had a small office in Newbigging, with a sign over the door and a light burning inside. Ignoring the Bentley parked outside, Thomas entered the office and rang the little bell on the counter.

"Hello there!" he called, looking around. The front office was compact and clean, bare of any luxuries. A map of the estate covered one wall, with Newbigging in the centre and map pins marking several properties. Thomas grunted as he realised how far the Cummings' lands extended.

"Good morning." A serious-faced young man emerged from a door at the back of the building, straightening his tie. He perched on a tall stool and faced Thomas. "Can I help you?"

"I want to fish the local rivers," Thomas explained. "Do I need to purchase a chit – a permit from the estate?"

The clerk looked Thomas up and down and gave a supercilious smile. "Well, now," he said. "That would depend on where you wish to fish and what sort of fishing you wish to do."

"Coarse fishing," Thomas said cheerfully.

The clerk sighed, removed a form from the top drawer of his desk and handed it over. "Fill that in and bring it back with the appropriate fee."

"I'll fill it in now." Thomas took the form, extracted a fountain pen from his inside pocket, wrote down his details and handed it back.

"Captain Thomas Armstrong." The clerk read the name.

"What was that name?" The door to the back room opened, and a tall woman stepped out. "Captain Armstrong?"

"That's me," Thomas admitted.

"I am Lady Fiona Cummings," the woman said. "I believe you have recently moved into Anton's Walls."

"That's correct, your Ladyship," Thomas said. He judged

Lady Fiona to be five foot seven in height, with an erect posture and level grey eyes that coolly surveyed him.

"Give me that form, Hunnam." Lady Fiona took the document and scanned it. "Pen!" Hunnam handed over his pen, and Lady Fiona wrote something on the bottom. "Hand me a permit."

When Hunnam produced a small slip of paper from another drawer, Lady Fiona scribbled something on the back and passed it to Thomas. "That should cover every eventuality," she said. "If you have any difficulties, mention my name."

Thomas glanced at the permit. Lady Fiona had written, "Captain Thomas Armstrong has my full permission to fish in all the rivers, lochs and waters of the estate."

"Thank you, your Ladyship," Thomas said. "That is very kind of you. What fee do I pay?"

"Where did you serve, Captain Armstrong?"

"Gallipoli, Flanders and France," Thomas told her.

"Then you've paid your fee in full," Lady Fiona said. "Anybody who survived that deserves free fishing. Did you see much action?"

"Some, Your Ladyship," Thomas said.

"Where?" Lady Fiona asked.

"Gallipoli, Flanders and France," Thomas repeated as the memories returned.

~

"Gas, gas, gas!" The warning shout carried along the trench, past the dog-leg bends and into the dugouts. "Gas, gas, gas!" The warning bell clattered its insane message as men reached frantically for gas masks.

Thomas dragged on his mask and scrambled out of the dugout to check on his men. Most were hauling on masks, but one recruit lay on the duckboards, clawing at his throat and gasping for air.

"Here!" Knowing the mask muffled his voice, Thomas held the boy's head and pulled on his mask. "Don't struggle!"

The boy stared at him in panic. He could not have been more than seventeen.

"Take deep breaths," Thomas ordered, with all the authority of rank and three extra years of life. He held the boy until he calmed down. "That's the way. Off you go and do your duty."

The men knew the drill, manning their stations on the trench wall, holding their Lee-Enfields, with lookouts with periscopes peering into No-man's land for German raiders or a full-scale assault. Gas shells usually heralded an attack or a trench raid, although the enemy might only be harassing the British trenches.

Grabbing a periscope, Thomas adjusted the height and stared into the ravaged wasteland between the British and German lines. A bank of grey-green mist showed the extent of the gas, but Thomas could see no movement beyond the vicious belts of barbed wire.

He glanced along the trench, where his men waited nervously. Sergeant Kilner walked along, checking each man, growling words of encouragement or reproach.

Thomas frowned when figures appeared in the gas, moving ominously quickly as they cut at the wire.

Trench raid!

When Thomas signalled to the Lewis gunners and gave the order to open fire, the hellish mechanical chatter punctured the day. He heard the explosion a second after the sound of its passage.

Whizz-bangs! The Huns are busy today.

The Borderers were firing now, with the crackle of

musketry adding to the machine guns and artillery shells. A man near Thomas fell, staring at his left arm, now detached from his body, and lying on the muddy duckboards. The private gaped for a full ten seconds, stooped to lift the detached limb and tried to push it back in place.

No longer vague shapes, the enemy was pushing through the wire, falling as the Borderers' bullets hit them, some screaming, others dying without a sound. One scared German soldier worked a flame thrower until the Lewis gunner cut him in half, and he lay engulfed in his own fire. Gasmasks concealed men's faces, so they appeared like aliens, strange beings moving in a green mist, firing and dying.

We're in hell, Thomas thought. *We've died and gone to hell.*

A Vickers heavy machine gun joined in the fight, scything into the desperate German attackers. Thomas fired his revolver, emptied the chamber, reloaded, and fired again, unaware he was yelling orders to his men.

The knight slid through the gas, his armour gleaming with moisture and the emblem on his shield indistinct.

"What the hell is that?" Thomas asked, with thoughts of the Angels of Mons running through his head. "What devilry have the Huns devised now?"

❧

"Captain Armstrong?" Lady Fiona held his arms. "Are you all right?"

Thomas gasped as the memories faded. He had been staring into Lady Fiona's eyes, remembering the horrors that her words had recovered. *I had forgotten about the knight I saw in France.*

"Yes, thank you," he said. "It's the war." He forced a smile. "It brings back these memories from time to time."

"I understand." Lady Fiona released him, with sympathy shadowing her eyes. "I lost two brothers in France."

Thomas stepped back. "Thank you for the permit," he felt himself colouring with embarrassment as the clerk stared at him, "and for the understanding."

"If you want to talk about things," Lady Fiona said, smiling. "Drop by anytime. I'm at Wardlaw House."

"Thank you." Thomas knew he would never use the invitation. He shook away the images, wondering about the knight in his recollection.

Where the hell had he sprung from, and how did I forget such an apparition?

CHAPTER 15

ELEANOR STOOD IN HER BEDROOM, staring across the moor to the distant hills. The central height was Dundreich, opposite Wardlaw on the opposite side of the pass, the original Deepsyke Slap, before people transferred the name to the road over the moss. These two peaks dominated the range, neither much above two thousand feet yet appearing like sentries glooming over the moor.

Everything here has a name and a meaning, Eleanor told herself. *Wardlaw, the watcher's hill, where men stood to watch for approaching enemies.* She knew the old lords of the Wardlaw Valley would have built a beacon fire on the summit, ready to light if English raiders appeared. Now, it was merely a hill with a memory of long-gone animosity. *I wonder what Dundreich means?*

Eleanor had read through her library books and learned all she could about the local area and Hugo de Soulis, yet felt she knew little. The books contained the same information, with little differences except for the inclusion of Lady de Soulis.

Who was Lady de Soulis, and why was history so quiet about her? Was it only masculine bias that relegated her to less than a footnote? Or was she so terrible even the historians could not bear to discuss her life?

Eleanor fretted, sighed, and stepped downstairs to the basement. Thomas had replaced the slabs over the grave until they decided what to do with the body.

"Do you want to remain here, Sir Andrew?" Eleanor asked. "Or should we transport you home to your family?"

Eleanor did not expect a reply, so she threw on a coat and hat, grabbed a walking stick and left the house. The moor beckoned, and she walked aimlessly, surprising herself when she found her feet following the line of the causeway. The path was familiar now, and Eleanor leapt the gap without effort and stepped onto the Thirteen Stane Rig. The stones lay as she had left them, an ominous circle on top of the ridge, with the wind whispering through the rough grass and a lone whaup calling in the distance.

"What happened here?" Eleanor asked the wind. "Did the local people genuinely boil and drink de Soulis? And what happened to Lady de Soulis? Only one book mentions her, and then only briefly."

She expected the crows to appear as they circled above her and landed in the centre of the circle, watching her through their bright, intelligent eyes. Eleanor walked around the ridge, stepping on each stone in turn, attempting to understand her feelings for this place.

"What are you trying to tell me, crows?" she asked as the crows remained where they were. "I know you have some message." Eleanor shook her head. "Look at me, walking in a circle in the middle of a moor, talking to a couple of imaginary birds! Anton's Walls is affecting me. Or have the memories of the war damaged my mind as they have with Thomas?"

That last was a terrifying thought. Eleanor has seen many

soldiers with shell shock, some so severely affected they could not function, others with flashbacks like Thomas and a few who were outwardly normal yet whose moods could swing in seconds. Eleanor remembered one soldier who would slide out of bed to fight imaginary Germans coming through the wall and another who held long conversations with an officer who had died in 1915.

Have my hospital experiences affected me, so I see imaginary birds?

On an impulse, Eleanor altered the direction she walked, from clockwise to anti-clockwise, sunwise. On her seventh circuit, both crows began to peck at the ground.

"Now, what are you doing?" Eleanor asked. She remembered how the crows had pecked around each recumbent stone on her previous visit. "Do you want me to dig there? Is that it?"

The crows stepped politely aside when Eleanor knelt in the centre of the circle and clawed at the ground. After a few moments, she knew she needed a tool and hurried back to Anton's Walls, hoping the weather remained fair. Returning with a garden fork and trowel, Eleanor attacked the ground, with the crows circling above, sunwise, on slow-flapping wings.

"You could help," Eleanor shouted. "After all, this is your idea!"

The crows continued to circle, never landing as Eleanor worked away. She cut back the top layer of turf and heather and thrust the fork into the hard ground beneath. Panting with effort, she shovelled away the dirt and small stones, forming a small pile at her side.

"What am I digging for?" she asked the crows. "What's down here? Buried treasure?"

The crows did not reply but continued to circle on lazy wings, never leaving the vicinity of the ridge and never landing.

Shaking her head at her folly, Eleanor dug on, finding a layer of black ash and then a flash of something white.

"What's that?" She picked it up curiously. "A scrap of bone," she said and tossed it aside. The next forkful contained more bones, and Eleanor looked more closely. "That's human remains," she said and dug with more care. "This is a grave."

Slowly, she unearthed most of the major bones of a human corpse, some shattered and some intact. The skull was last and deepest as if somebody had thrown the corpse headfirst into a shallow grave.

"You must be Hugo de Soulis." Eleanor crouched beside the grave without feeling any revulsion or horror. "Good afternoon, Sir Hugo."

If this is de Soulis, then at least part of the legend is true. Sir Hugo has an association with the Thirteen Stane Rig.

Helen looked up as the crows continued to circle, dark shapes against the clouding sky.

∾

"Do you like hunting, Sir Andrew?" de Soulis asked.

"I do." Sir Andrew had been pleasantly surprised at the hospitality de Soulis had offered him. He had expected a surly tyrant and instead found an affable young man with a passingly fair unmarried sister.

More than passingly fair, he corrected himself. *Lady Marjory is a very handsome lady.*

"We have some fine hunting here, Sir Andrew," Lady Marjory told him, meeting his gaze boldly. "Deer, wild boar, game birds, and others that are even more interesting."

"More interesting?" Sir Andrew asked with genuine interest. "I usually hunt deer on Lammermuir or send my hawk after whatever she can find."

"Ah, Lammermuir," de Soulis said and glanced at his sister. "The rolling moorland around the Blackadder River."

"That's correct," Sir Andrew was surprised that de Soulis was familiar with the area. "Deer hunts can last a full day there."

"We'll show you a different kind of hunt," de Soulis promised. "One you will never forget." He looked at his sister, and they laughed together.

"You intrigue me, Sir Hugo," Sir Andrew said. "I can only think you mean wild boars or wolves. I have never hunted either."

De Soulis and his sister laughed again. "What we hunt can be more dangerous than a boar or a wolf," the sister said. "The most dangerous prey in the world."

Sir Andrew raised his eyebrows in pretended mockery. "You have dragons here?" He smiled at his attempted humour.

The sister laughed again. "Not even one dragon," she said. "We have the creatures who hunted dragons to extinction."

"I am even more intrigued," Sir Andrew said and wondered at de Soulis's laughter.

"We will show you anon," de Soulis said, with a broad smile on his smooth face. When he lifted a finger, his squire ran to his side. "Ensure Sir Andrew's hound is well cared for, Robin," de Soulis said. "He will have work soon."

❧

"Well, I had a good day," Thomas said as he strolled into the living room. "I met Lady Fiona Cummings, and you could not imagine a nicer lady."

Eleanor looked up from the pages of a library book. "I met somebody today as well," she said.

"I'm glad to hear that," Thomas said. "It's good to make

friends. Lady Fiona has given me permission to fish anywhere on her lands and even invited me to call on her."

"I met Hugo de Soulis," Eleanor said.

Thomas threw himself onto a chair and smiled. "Lady Fiona could not have been more pleasant," he said, then frowned. "What did you say?"

"I said I met Hugo de Soulis," Eleanor told him.

"Hugo de Soulis has been dead for centuries," Thomas said quietly, reaching for the whisky decanter. "How could you meet him?"

"I dug him up," Eleanor explained.

Thomas poured them both a dram of whisky, added water to Eleanor's glass and handed it over. "Why did you dig up another dead man?"

"The crows told me to," Eleanor said and closed her mouth. *Why did I say that? Either this place or my war experiences are affecting me.*

"The what?" Thomas stared at her. "Sister-of-mine, there are no crows. I think you're nearly as mad as I am." He sipped at his whisky, shaking his head, and smiling fondly. "Tell me more, you grave-robbing little rogue!"

Pleased to see his good humour return, Eleanor nodded. "I think I am worse than you," she said. "While you were sweet talking Lady Fiona, I was conversing with a pair of crows and digging up a six-hundred-year-old skeleton."

"Did Sir Hugo also talk to you?" Thomas asked lightly.

"No." Eleanor shook her head. "He just lay there, all white and bony."

Thomas sat down. "I don't understand," he said. "Why dig up a skeleton? Is that not against the law?"

Eleanor shrugged. "Is it? Is that not body snatching you're thinking of? I don't intend to sell the thing for medical research."

"What do you intend to do with it?" Thomas asked.

"Burying it back underground, I suppose," Eleanor said. She frowned. "I don't know why I dug the blasted thing up in the first place."

Thomas scratched his head. "Nor do I. You should take up fishing, Eleanor, rather than involve yourself with this nonsense."

Eleanor finished her whisky and looked for more. "I also read that some people think de Soulis was a Knight Templar."

Thomas grunted. "Is that so? I thought the Templars dedicated themselves to protecting the Holy Land."

"The Saracens kicked them out in 1291. They weren't only warriors, they were also economists and bankers," Eleanor said. "Money men need a stable world to generate a profit, so maybe de Soulis prayed to the devil to stop the English war."

Thomas grunted. "Is stability what money men want? Many companies profited by the Great War when the world was anything but stable."

"Men who profit from wars are as evil as the wars themselves," Eleanor said, hoping she did not send Thomas back to a dark place.

"Soldiers live for warfare," Thomas reminded. "It's their reason for existence."

"Soldiers and mediaeval knights," Eleanor mused as she visualised her handsome knight once more.

~

Sir Andrew lay in his quarters, pleased that Sir Hugo had found him a chamber to himself rather than having him share with the household knights and other visitors. He realised he was the only visitor and smiled.

Caercorbie's evil reputation must have put travellers off.

While Sir Andrew had expected cold stone, tapestries hung from the walls, and the bed was of furs, with a covering over the window to keep out the worst of the draughts. He stretched on the bed, wondering if the tales were all exaggerated. So far, Sir Hugo had proved the consummate host, attending to all his needs, and entertaining him with the itinerant harper.

"It's a strange thing," Sir Hugo had said, "that even in the worst years of the war, minstrels are sacrosanct. They travel between armies, singing their songs of love and endeavour to friends and foes alike." He raises his voice. "Sing for us, Minstrel! Sing a song of love from the warmth of Provence!"

The minstrel, an elderly man with grey hair that flopped across his eyes, lifted his small harp, and strummed the strings, sending sweet music through the hall. His voice took on a new timbre as he sang, becoming more youthful as if he adopted the character of the lovers in the song. Even his appearance altered, Sir Andrew noticed, as if the words melted away the years back to the minstrel's long-gone youth.

Sir Andrew's hound sat at his feet as he sat at the high table with Sir Hugo on his left and Lady Marjory two places down. Two household knights were at Sir Andrew's side, with lesser people seated at the two tables that stretched at right angles towards the arched doorway. Servants hurried around with plates and bowls while the aroma of cooked meat filled the air.

"You keep a splendid table, Sir Hugo," Sir Andrew said.

"All my sister's doing." Sir Hugo jerked a thumb at Lady Marjory, who looked across him to nod to Sir Andrew.

When the minstrel sang an old favourite about a man watching a young knight woo his lover in a garden, Lady Marjory lifted her gaze towards Sir Andrew once more and smiled.

The minstrel strummed calloused fingers across his harp strings.

"Ce fut en mai
Au douz tens gai
Que la saisons est bele,
Main me levai,
Joer m'alai
Lez une fontenele."

"Splendid!" Lady Marjory approved. "Now, another song." She threw a chicken leg to the minstrel. "Eat, my musical friend and give me a song of battle, of brave men fighting for their lives, endeavour and bravery against the Saracens!"

The minstrel caught the chicken, bit into the meat, chewed, swallowed, and obeyed, making the hall echo with the clash of steel on steel, of the raucous battle cries of "Diex aie! God be with us!" that the Normans roared at the Battle of Hastings.

The men in the hall echoed the cry, laughing as they recounted deeds they imagined they had done in the English wars. Knights and men-at-arms pounded the pommels of their knives on the table, boasting of their valour.

Sir Andrew hid his jealousy, wishing he had been old enough to fight at Bannockburn, Stirling Bridge, Glen Trool or any of the other score or so victorious encounters. He looked for ladies to impress and frowned when he realised there were none. Lady Marjory was the only woman below fifty in the hall.

That's unusual.

Sir Andrew caught the minstrel's gaze fixed on him and wondered why a lowborn man should dare to stare at a knight. He held the minstrel's eyes, expecting the man to look away, but without warning, the minstrel laid his harp aside and stood up. He looked even older as he lifted his head and began another song, with his voice harsh, as unpleasant as the words he intoned.

"As I was walking all alane,
I heard twa corbies making a mane;
The tane unto the t'other say,
"Where sall we gan and dine today?"

"Not that one!" Sir Hugo shouted, half rising from his seat. "I forbid you to sing that song, Minstrel!"

The minstrel closed his mouth and sat down, but his gaze remained fixed on Sir Andrew as if attempting to convey a message. That song in the language of the common people altered the atmosphere in the hall. Sir Hugo rose early, with the others following their lord's lead. Sir Andrew could do no less and, after attending to his horses and his hawk, retired to his chamber. It had been an interesting first day in Caercorbie and nothing like he expected. Without a squire to do the menial work, he checked his mail for flakes of rust, polished his sword and prayed before sliding into bed.

"Guide me, St Bride," [1]Sir Andrew prayed. "Help me be a good knight and combat evil wherever I may find it."

The tap at the door alerted Sir Andrew, and he groped for his sword, realised that no midnight assassin would warn him and stood up.

"Sir Andrew." Lady Marjory entered the chamber as silent as a spectre, with a long gown fastened at her throat with a red silken cord. Without another word, she took his hand and escorted him back to the bed.

"My lady?" Sir Andrew asked.

"There is no point in sleeping alone when you can sleep with me," Lady Marjory smiled at him. "You are a lusty knight and wifeless, so I shall be your woman and do anything that may please you."

Sir Andrew smiled, hiding his surprise. "You are very welcome, my Lady. I shall strive to be worthy of you."

Lady Marjory unfastened the silken cord at her throat, and her dress fell to the floor. As naked as a baby, she smiled at Sir Andrew. "All you have to do, Sir Knight, is accept your werd, your fate."

Andrew stared at her with his heart pounding. "You do me great honour, my Lady." He threw back the covers and watched as she slid gracefully into his bed.

"I yield to your mercy, gentle knight," Lady Marjory said with a wickedly mischievous smile. "And hope you will yield to mine."

As Lady Marjory's hand began to explore, Andrew smiled. "Right willingly," he gasped and allowed her to demonstrate.

Lady Marjory smiled and softly began to sing.

"Ce fut en mai
Au douz tens gai
Que la saisons est bele,
Main me levai,
Joer m'alai
Lez une fontenele."

CHAPTER 16

Martin stared. "You did what?"

"I dug up de Soulis," Eleanor admitted.

They sat in the Dryfe Arms with the last rain of a passing squall pattering against the window and the barman hovering to listen to their conversation. By now, the villagers were accustomed to seeing Eleanor and Thomas, and although they did not speak, nor did they stare. Only Wally Nixon glared at them with his red hat thrust to the back of his head.

"You dug him up?" Martin repeated. "Dear God, why?" He shook his head. "No, never mind why. It doesn't matter. Bury him again, now, this very minute. You can't allow such evil to see daylight or moonlight, God help us."

"It's all right," Eleanor said. "He's dead."

"That sort of creature can avoid death," Martin said cryptically and added. "I'd like to know why you think it was de Soulis. Where was he?"

"Buried in the Thirteen Stane Rig," Eleanor explained.

Martin shuddered, and his hand gripped his schooner glass. "How do you know about the Thirteen Stane Rig?" he asked quietly, looking directly at Eleanor. "The location has been lost for centuries."

"We found it," Eleanor said. "We followed a causeway through the moor, and the crows showed us where the stones were."

"The crows." Martin looked away. "Oh, dear God, preserve us from stupidity. I thought you understood my song." He lowered his voice to a hiss. "It was a warning to let well alone, Mrs Machrie! I hoped you would heed it."

"I can bury him again," Eleanor suggested.

"Now! Do it now," Martin said, "and pray to God we are not too late."

"We could pray to St Bride," Eleanor said and frowned. *From where did that name come?*

Martin started and rose immediately. "There is not a moment to waste. Mr Armstrong, take us in your car. We'll need spades and hurry for the love of God."

Eleanor shook her head. "It's only old bones, Mr Crozier. The dead don't bite. How many dead bodies have you seen, Thomas?" She regretted her words as soon as she spoke, for her brother's eyes darkened again.

"Thousands, Eleanor," he replied as he drifted back to the battlefields, with visions of acres of corpses returning. "Torn, mutilated, swollen, obscene."

Eleanor nudged him with a sharp elbow. "Thomas!"

Thomas nodded, and his eyes cleared. "I've seen thousands," he repeated Eleanor's words. "I can assure you that skeletons don't bite."

"This one does," Martin said. "You've no idea what you're dealing with here. Take us to Deepsyke Muir, Mr Armstrong, if you value your soul!"

Thomas shrugged. "Anything to oblige, Mr Crozier. Come on, sister-of-mine, let's undo what you've done!"

Martin was already waiting for them at the door.

With a collection of spades and forks in the boot, Thomas drove the Crossley to Anton's Walls, obeying Martin's constant urging for more speed.

"What's the urgency, Mr Crozier?" Eleanor asked as they rounded a curve, and Thomas swerved around a startled sheep.

"There is an evil in that place," Martin said. "Something that surfaces in certain conditions."

"What conditions?" Eleanor asked, holding onto the dashboard as Thomas threw the Crossley around a sharp bend and gunned up a short, steep slope.

"There are times when an evil descends on the world," Martin said, "or on parts of the world. In times of great famine or upheaval caused by war or invasion, a badness settles on some places and allows something far worse to escape."

"To escape from where?" Eleanor asked.

"I don't know," Martin admitted. "Hell, perhaps. Deepsyke Muir is such a place, on the borders of different ideas, where peoples and cultures clash. It attracts evil."

"We're talking about one man," Thomas reminded. "That's all. A man who died hundreds of years ago."

"No," Martin shook his head. "I'm talking about events that have occurred at least twice before when warfare has brought evil to the land."

Thomas turned off the metalled road onto the ancient track across the moor. Immediately they did, Eleanor noticed that the clouds began to gather and looked for her crows.

"When," she asked. "When did this evil descend on Deepsyke Moor?"

"This area had always been a borderland," Martin explained. "In the old days, the Roman Empire stopped a few miles away at Carlisle. South of Hadrian's Wall was the Empire, a civilisation fuelled by slavery and conquest. Northward of the wall, the nations and tribes lived in freedom, but the two cultures clashed in this borderland. I don't know what horrors happened in those days."

"No," Eleanor agreed as the Crossley banged into a rut that seemed to shake the bones from her body. "We can only guess." She scanned the moor for her crows, feeling slightly neglected when they failed to appear.

"We know that the Romans were scared of the druids," Martin said. "Druidism and Christianity were the two religions that offered a serious challenge to the Roman Empire. That is why the Romans fed Christians to the lions and targeted druidical sanctuaries. When the Romans destroyed the druid's headquarters on Anglesey in north Wales, some druids escaped by sea and landed in the lands of the Novantes, near here." He glanced sideways at Eleanor. "We think. That great black lump of a hill over there is called Dundreich, which we think means the Druid's Hill or fort. They became powerful in the area before St Ninian brought Christianity."

"I wondered at the name," Eleanor said. "It did not quite fit in."

"It's Celtic, like the first part of Caercorbie. Welsh if you like. *Caer* is Celtic, British for a castle, but *corbie* is Scots for a crow. The castle of the crows."

Eleanor dropped her guard. "Two crows follow me around."

Martin closed his eyes. "I warned you about them, Mrs Machrie."

Thomas spoke over his shoulder. "Eleanor is always talking about these blasted crows." He splashed through Deep Syke without slowing down, slewed sideways and pushed on towards Anton's Walls.

"Did you say the crows guided you towards the skeleton?" Martin asked.

"That's right." Eleanor heard the words of the French song inside her head.

Martin sighed. "If you see the crows, Mrs Machrie, say a prayer out loud. That might protect you."

"Are you being serious?" Eleanor asked. "That sounds like something out of Bram Stoker."

"It's nothing to laugh at, Mrs Machrie," Martin told her.

"I'll remember," Eleanor promised. "Please go on with your story."

Martin nodded. "When the Romans left, barbarian tribes attacked the lands they left vulnerable. Picts from the north, Gaels from Ireland, and the savage Germans from the continent. The people here, the original British tribes, formed themselves into small nations and fought back as best they could."

Eleanor nodded. She had a vague recollection of her schoolteachers mentioning the anarchy that followed the fall of the Roman Empire.

"The British kingdoms managed to repel the German, Irish and Picts, helped when Christianity reached the latter two peoples, and there were a few decades of prosperity in this part of the world." Martin stopped. "A short golden age before the next wave of horror began."

"What happened?" Eleanor asked.

"The initial German invasions had made great inroads into the British kingdoms," Martin explained. "But the British consolidated and fought back, holding them at bay. Unfortunately, the British then fought amongst themselves, and the German tribes, the Saxons, and Angles, saw their chance and began their aggression again."

"A way the Huns have," Thomas murmured.

"So it seems," Martin agreed without correcting Thomas's incorrect ethnic labelling.

"After the Saxon resurgence conquered most of the native

nations, only three British centres of power remained. Cornwall, Wales and what was known as the Men of the North or Penryn Rionyt, based in Galloway." Martin stopped for a moment. "This road, the Deepsyke Slap, led to the pass through the hills to Penryn Rionyt with Caercorbie, the Guardian of the Dark Slap."

"I see." Eleanor had grasped the castle's importance. "Our house is on the site of a border fortress. Thomas said the builder had an eye for defence."

"Nobody can pass Anton's Walls without the garrison seeing them," Thomas said. "The old castle would command the slap and the route between both hill passes."

Martin nodded. "Military appreciation has not changed much over the centuries. After the Anglo-Saxon resurgence, a great evil descended on this part of the world. King turned against king, and the Angles overran the country as far as the Forth and the kingdom of Strathclyde." He held onto the seat in front as the car bounced over a series of deep potholes.

"That was the first great evil," Eleanor said. "The coming of the Angles."

"Correct." Martin looked forward, to ascertain how far they were from Anton's Walls. "They brought a new culture and organised aggression."

"When was the second?"

"Edward Plantagenet of England opened the doors of the second great evil when he tried to conquer Scotland in 1296," Martin said. "Oh, there had been wars before, but he brought a vicious intensity that spread bloodshed and horror from the farthest north to the Solway. He was a demon in human form, and hell recognised him as one of its own."

Eleanor nodded. "I know Edward Plantagenet was an unpleasant person."

"He started a hatred that has never quite died," Martin

said, grunting as the Crossley lurched sideways. "We're nearly there, thank God. The war Plantagenet started unleashed terrible darkness across Scotland, particularly southern Scotland." He faced Eleanor again, "and now we are in another era of darkness."

Eleanor shook her head. "There's no war here."

"The Great War reached every corner of the world," Martin said. "Deepsyke Muir is more vulnerable to absorbing and emitting evil because of its situation and history."

Thomas eased the Crossley to a halt outside Anton's Walls and switched off the engine. "All right, Martin," Thomas said in his officer's voice. "This better not be a waste of time and effort."

Martin glowered at him. "You have no idea how important it could be," he said, scrambling out of the car.

Carrying their tools, they headed for the Thirteen Stane Rig, with Eleanor leading and Thomas bringing up the rear. They padded across the moor, skirting the treacherous areas of bogland and searching for the firmest patches of land.

"Here's the causeway." Now familiar with the route, Eleanor walked confidently, as if she had traversed Deepsyke Moor all her life. She moved quickly, ignoring the mud that splashed onto her skirt.

"There's a gap here." Eleanor pointed out the danger to Martin and leapt to the other side with barely a pause.

"Are you all right, Martin?" Thomas asked as Martin eyed the gap.

"I'm all right." Martin handed Thomas his tools, stepped back and jumped, landing on the edge of the causeway. He balanced for a moment and waited as Thomas tossed the tools to him.

"Eleanor's surging ahead," Thomas observed.

"She knows the way," Martin grunted with a twisted smile. "She's not as old as I am."

A whaup called over the moor, with the sun easing through low clouds to provide a sudden shaft of bright sunlight on the Thirteen Stone Rig.

"Dear Father in Heaven," Martin said as he clambered from the causeway onto the ridge. "There's a sight I hoped was gone forever." He gazed at the recumbent stones. "We'll have to cover them up or push them into the moss. Where's the skeleton, Mrs Machrie?"

"Here!" Eleanor said and strode to the centre of the circle. "Somewhere." She glanced around. "It was here."

"It's not here now," Martin said. "It's gone."

～

Sir Andrew watched as de Soulis's following of household knights and men-at-arms prepared for the hunt. A silent groom brought Kenneth, sleek and shining after his rest.

"We used to hunt in Outremer," Sir Hugo told him. "The climate was vastly different there, with sun and heat nearly all the year round."

"Outremer? The Saracens recaptured that years ago," Sir Andrew observed. "Did they allow you a pilgrimage to the Holy City?"

Sir Hugo glanced at him, smiling. "No. I was a soldier, a crusader."

"Acre fell in 1291," Sir Andrew said. "I didn't know Christianity still had a toehold in Outremer, the Holy Land."

Sir Hugo's smile widened across his youthful face. "I don't believe Christianity has," he said. Swinging onto his horse, he jabbed in his spurs and rode away from the castle. Sir Andrew followed, frowning.

If Sir Hugo had been a soldier in Acre, he had left thirty years ago, making him at least forty-six, yet he appeared scarcely older than twenty. Sir Andrew shook his head. *Perhaps I misunderstood.*

"Sir Hugo," Sir Andrew called, spurring to catch up. "How old are you?"

"Older than you imagine," de Soulis shouted as he spurred ahead.

Unsure what to think, Sir Andrew followed, with his horse's hooves kicking up clods of mud and a collection of riders from the castle riding alongside. Lady Marjory rode beside de Soulis and the silent squire with the red cap a few yards in the rear. The squire was not a good horseman, Sir Andrew noted, or perhaps the horse was scared, for the squire had to resort to the spurs and whip to keep his mount under control.

"Come on, Sir Andrew," de Soulis shouted over his shoulder. "We have things to show you!"

Lady Marjory made space for Sir Andrew at her side, and they led the cavalcade, crossing the moor with a dozen twists and turns.

"Over there is a stone circle." Sir Hugo nodded to a ridge, deep in the moor. "The ancients built it, and the churls call it the Thirteen Stane Rig and attribute all sorts of magical things to it." He laughed, throwing his head back as if he found everything a tremendous joke.

"What sort of things?" Sir Andrew asked.

"You'll have to ask them," de Soulis replied. "I never listen to the peasants." He pulled his horse to the north and then westward, riding easily toward the range of low hills. The moor gradually became more fertile, with a scattering of sheep grazing on patches of rough grass and the occasional shepherd's hut built of turf or unmortared stone. People worked in the long rigs of the fields, glimpsed in the distance.

Lady Marjory rode beside Sir Andrew, smiling. "Can you see anything unusual about our people?"

Sir Andrew had barely spared them a glance until Lady Marjory directed his attention in their direction.

"They're naked!" Sir Andrew said, staring.

"Only the women," Sir Hugo replied with a light laugh. "It's a little fancy of mine. Every few months, I demand that the women work naked in the fields, then I pick one or two of the most attractive as helpmates." He laughed again, with Lady Marjory joining in.[1]

"What do you think of that, Sir Andrew?" Lady Marjory asked. "I know you like the company of a willing woman." She smiled at him with her eyes dancing with mischief. "Sir Hugo must have his pleasures, and where better than from his own lands? The alternative would be to raid a neighbour, which would start a feud."

"Do the fathers and husbands not object?" Sir Andrew tried to conceal his disquiet.

"They might," Lady Marjory said, still smiling. She watched as de Soulis rode slowly around the fields, perusing his tenants with his squire a few yards behind. De Soulis reined up beside one female, leaned down from the saddle and spoke to her. When the woman recoiled, de Soulis laughed and gestured to his squire.

"Ah!" Lady Marjory said. "Hugo has selected a helpmate. I wonder if he wants more or if one woman will suffice for his needs."

Sir Andrew stirred uneasily in the saddle. He knew that de Soulis's actions were in contravention of the knightly oaths, but a gentleman could run his lands as he wished.

"He wants more." Lady Marjory watched Sir Andrew as de

Soulis halted his black horse and indicated a young, brown-haired woman. Sir Andrew estimated she was twelve years old.

The squire leaned from his saddle, wrapped his long arms around the girl and dragged her face-down over his horse. As she kicked and screamed, the squire gagged her, tied her ankles and wrists, and followed Sir Hugo.

"Do you wish a woman?" Lady Marjory enquired, turning an amused eye to Sir Andrew. "Or did you find me sufficiently satisfying?"

"More than satisfying, my lady," Sir Andrew replied, trying to avoid the terrified looks of the working women.

Lady Marjory smiled. "I am glad to hear it, Sir Andrew." She watched as her brother stopped at a small group of women and pointed to the smallest and youngest.

She's a little girl, Sir Andrew thought. *She can't be more than ten years old.*

When the girl screamed, a man ran from the neighbouring field and challenged Sir Hugo.

"That's my daughter, Sir Hugo!" the man complained. "She's only a child!"

"Now we'll see some sport," Lady Marjory said. "That oaf is the girl's father." She laughed. "The fool is trying to object."

Sir Andrew stirred unhappily in his saddle. "Perhaps he thinks his daughter is not yet ready for such an honour."

"It would appear so," Lady Marjory agreed, smiling.

De Soulis placed his horse between the father and the girl, fending the father off with his mailed feet and the flat of his sword. Grinning, Robin, the squire, lifted the girl one-handed, tied her expertly and placed her face down beside her bound companion.

"Take him!" de Soulis's voice carried easily across the fields, and three riders detached from the group and surrounded the protesting man. Sir Andrew expected the riders to kill him, but instead, they dismounted, knocked him uncon-scious with mailed fists and threw him over a spare horse.

"What will they do to him?" Sir Andrew asked.

"You'll see," Lady Marjory said, smiling. "I told you we would show you a better hunt than any you have experienced."

CHAPTER 17

"A SKELETON CAN'T JUST VANISH," Thomas said. "You must have buried it again or left it somewhere else."

"It was here." Eleanor pointed to the area of disturbed ground at the centre of the stone circle.

"It can't have walked away," Thomas said.

"Dear God," Martin knelt beside the empty grave. "He's lain here for six hundred years, and now he's out again."

Thomas smiled, shaking his head. "You talk as if de Soulis is walking around," he said. "It's a skeleton of a long-dead corpse. Good God, man, I've seen a thousand skeletons, and none could walk."

"It appears this one did," Eleanor said, realising that Thomas had returned to France.

Thomas huddled beside the trench wall, with the shells hammering down. The vicious whizz-bangs[1], the hellish coal boxes[2] and the hissing mortars all exploding in a terrible cacophony around him.

The dugout was gone, blasted open during the first few moments of the bombardment, and Bill Anderson, Lieutenant William Anderson, MC, his friend and companion, was gone with it. Number One section had vanished, obliterated by a single shell, and Private Willie Duff was shaking in fear with saliva drooling from his mouth as he cowered beside Wee John Slater. Nothing much remained of Slater, with his body torn away beneath the waist.

The shelling eased, inviting the Borderers to man the firing steps, and then intensified again, hammering the Borderers' position. One shell landed on the sandbag wall in front of Thomas, uncovering a dead man embedded in the mud. For an instant, Thomas stared into the sightless eyes of the semi-decomposed skull, with worms crawling through the apertures where the nose had been. He recoiled, and the knight reap-peared, riding his horse into the trench with the device on his shield less obscure. He stared at Thomas as if he had seen a ghost.

"What devilry is this?" the knight shouted, and although he spoke in a language Thomas did not know, he understood every word.

"Who are you?" Thomas asked.

The knight stared at Thomas, with the unicorn and sword on his shield glittering in the light of the shell bursts, and then he vanished, leaving Thomas dazed and confused.

"Here they come!" Sergeant Kilner roared as the British counter barrage began.

The knight had vanished before Thomas reached his place on the firing step, resting Private Slater's Lee-Enfield on top of that handy skull.

~

"Thomas!" Eleanor was shaking him, peering into his eyes. "Come back to me, Thomas."

Sunlight eased over the Thirteen Stone Rig, highlighting each recumbent stone. Thomas shook away the visions.

"Skeletons don't hurt," he repeated as the image of the knight faded with the anonymous skull. He grinned to prove he had not been scared.

"This one is missing," Martin sounded grim. "Sir Hugo de Soulis is back among us."

While Eleanor frowned, Thomas barked a laugh. "You make that sound as if he is walking free."

"God forbid," Martin said, shaking his head. "We must all prepare for dark days ahead." Taking hold of Eleanor's arm, he gazed into her eyes. "Leave Anton's Wa's, Mrs Machrie. It is not safe for you there."

"It's my home," Eleanor said. "Let the dead look after the dead."

"Get back to Edinburgh while there is still time," Martin said. "You've done enough damage here." He gasped and recoiled when both crows landed on the disturbed earth where the grave had been.

"Can you see these crows, Thomas?" Eleanor asked.

"Which crows?" Thomas frowned, looking all around.

"Can you see them, Mr Crozier?" Eleanor pointed to the birds.

"I can see them," Martin said. "Most people cannot."

"Why not?" Eleanor asked. "They are as plain as anything."

"You belong," Martin said softly. "You understand the spirit of the song, and that makes it very dangerous for you here. Go home, Mrs Machrie, before you cause more trouble."

"Who are so many people determined to get rid of me?" Eleanor asked. "You and Sir Hugh Cummings are both determined to send me away while Wally Nixon glares as if he hates me." She shook her head. "I may be Eleanor Machrie, but I am also Eleanor Armstrong, and I belong here." She looked around the bleak moor and the backdrop of long, grey-green hills. "My people have lived here for centuries, longer than de Soulis and his Norman forbears."

She stopped, wondering from where these ideas and words came. She had been born, raised, and educated in Edinburgh and had never visited the Borders until they bought Anton's Walls.

"Your people?" Martin asked softly, holding Eleanor's gaze.

"The Armstrongs," Eleanor reminded.

"I see," Martin said. "Well, we're doing no good here, so we'd better get back to Newbigging."

"Thomas will drive you," Eleanor said. "I'll stay at home."

Caercorbie was her home now. She belonged within these old grey walls, with the austere emptiness of the moor spreading around her. Deepsyke Moor was no longer a place of dread, but a sanctuary, a barrier against the encroachments of humanity. She watched the Crossley bump over the track and hugged herself, singing a song.

"Ce fut en mai
Au douz tens gai
Que la saisons est bele,
Main me levai,
Joer m'alai
Lez une fontenele."

From where did that song come? She asked herself. I must

have picked it up in France, but I don't remember. I even under-stand the lyrics. It's a love song.

"It happened in May,
when skies are gay
And green the plains and mountains,
At break of day
I rose to play
Beside a little fountain.

In the garden close
Where shone the rose
I heard a fiddle played; then
A handsome knight
that charmed my sight,
Was dancing with a maiden."

Eleanor smiled and sang, wishing she could hear a vielle playing to the words. *How do I know about vielles?* [3] *I must have learned more in France than I realised.*

There were no thoughts of skeletons as Eleanor sang her song, smiling as she thought of the young knight courting a pretty young shepherdess. She could see him plainly with his blond hair, blue eyes, and muscular body with two white scars.

Eleanor hugged herself, dancing with intricate steps around the room. In her mind, she was the shepherdess, a girl without a care in the world, enjoying the spring morning in France. Her knight was young, brave, and handsome, with his hair fashionably long and his sword sitting proudly at his side.

Oh, my handsome young knight, Eleanor thought. *Would you visit me at Caercorbie? Or are we too remote for such as yourself? Must I coax you to stay? That would be delightful for us both.*

The sun seemed stronger now, easing across the moorland, reflecting on the pools of water, so they seemed to sparkle enticingly. They were no longer menacing dark depths but pretty ponds where ducks dabbled, and fish swam close to the surface. The rutted track was a highway to her romantic castle, full of every pleasure a knight could wish for: good company, fine hunting, bold horses, and a woman ready for his love.

Eleanor could picture herself riding on her palfrey with her robes flowing around the horse's flanks and a circlet of spring flowers on her head.

"Both fair of face,
They turned with grace,
To tread their May-time measure;
The flowering place,
Their close embrace,
Their kisses brought them pleasure.

Cors orent gent
Et avenant
Et molt très bien dançoient ;
En acolant
Et en baisant
Molt biau se deduisoient."

Eleanor shook her head and turned away, still smiling. She saw the man out of the corner of her eye and stopped.

"Thomas?"

It had not been Thomas. She knew her brother and this man had felt differently and dressed differently. He had been in the same room.

"Is that you, Martin?" It had not been Martin but a taller, younger man.

"Hello?" Eleanor had seen too much horror in the military hospitals to be frightened by a strange man. Lifting the poker from beside the fire, she strode from the room.

"If you're trying to scare me, you've chosen the wrong woman," Eleanor shouted, gripping the poker as she opened doors and peered into rooms one by one. Every room was empty.

"Just as well for you," Eleanor shouted, laughing at herself. *All this mediaeval nonsense is affecting my nerves.* She replaced the poker and began to make up the fire, crumpling newspaper for the empty grate. Breaking sticks with her hands, she made a pyramid and added small pieces of coal.

I should have a maid to do this. I don't do manual labour in Caercorbie!

Eleanor smiled. From where did that thought come? She never had nor wanted a maidservant in her life, and she was in Anton's Walls, not Caercorbie. She shook her head, laughing at herself.

The man was back. Eleanor could sense him standing beside the door, watching her. She placed a couple of larger pieces of coal on top of the fire and leaned back to inspect her work. Grabbing the poker, she whirled around.

"Right, you! I've had about enough of this nonsense!"

The room was empty, with a shaft of sunlight easing through the window to gleam on the whisky decanter and accompanying glasses.

My imagination is playing tricks, Eleanor told herself. *I'll have a little drink, and then I'm going to light the fireand find a book to read. Fiction this time, and nothing mediaeval.*

Scratching a match, Eleanor applied it to the newspaper, waited to ensure the fire drew and stepped into the kitchen to wash her hands. The range was already smouldering, and she quarter-filled the kettle and placed it on top to boil while she selected a book.

Ignoring anything serious, Eleanor lifted out Jules Verne and Conan-Doyle before settling for Sapper's *Bulldog Drummond*, a light adventure story that an ex-Royal Engineer officer had written after the Great War.

That will do.

Eleanor sat beside the fire with a half-full glass of whisky in her hand and immersed herself in Captain Drummond's adventures against the evil Carl Petersen.

The song returned, sounding around the room as she read so that the rugged Drummond faded away and the handsome young knight was back. Eleanor sighed.

"I'm not afraid of you," she said. "Who are you?"

Eleanor could see him clearly now, a tall, very young man with a puzzled expression on his face as he looked at her from the shadow of the wall. He opened his mouth as if about to speak, and then he vanished, leaving only a memory.

"Goodbye, Sir Knight," Eleanor said and smiled. "Whoever you were, you were not Hugo de Soulis."

She knew that Sir Andrew Douglas was in the house, looking after her, and smiled with the most delicious sensations coursing through her body.

CHAPTER 18

"TAKE the women to my chamber in Caercorbie," de Soulis ordered, and the squire trotted away.

"Now, gentlemen, we have some sport."

De Soulis's followers laughed, grinning at each other in rising anticipation. Their dogs barked, with Sir Andrew's brachet as loud as the others.

"Take the churl with us," de Soulis commanded, and the riders pushed their prisoner ahead of them, encouraging him with prods of their swords and cuts with their whips.

The man stumbled, looking over his shoulder. When he shouted words of encouragement to his daughter, Lady Marjory laughed loudly, with the other riders following her example.

At the moor's edge, de Soulis shouted for the prisoner to come to him.

"You opposed my wishes," de Soulis said, with his followers listening in disciplined silence. "I could hang you for that, but I am a merciful man."

Lady Marjory smiled at Sir Andrew. "My brother's mercy is legendary," she murmured.

The man was around forty, Sir Andrew guessed, balding and stocky, with the face and bearing of a farmer.

"I will give you a chance to keep your life," de Soulis said. "Deepsyke Muir is ahead of you. I will release you and give you a start, and then we will hunt you down. If you reach that hill pass," he pointed to Windydoor Nick, three miles away, "you can live."

"My daughter," the farmer began, and de Soulis back-handed him across the face.

"I have given your daughter the honour of joining my household," de Soulis said. "You need not concern yourself with her again." He raised his voice. "Now, run!"

The farmer hesitated for a moment, then looked at the grinning, predatory faces of de Soulis's followers and stumbled into the moor.

"I promised you sport," de Soulis said to Sir Andrew. "I said we would hunt more dangerous prey than wild boar, and what is more dangerous than man?"

"Are you going to hunt that farmer?" Sir Andrew asked.

"We are," de Soulis confirmed. "I have given him a sporting chance."

"Allow him a count of three hundred," Lady Marjory said. "He is not fast on his feet and will make but poor sport if we catch him too quickly."

De Soulis laughed. "Three hundred it shall be." He counted the seconds, watching the farmer splash and stumble across the moor. When he reached two hundred and eighty, de Soulis lifted his hand, counted the final twenty and dropped his hand.

"Hunt!"

Immediately de Soulis spoke, his followers released the

hounds, kicked in their spurs, and raced forward onto the moor, shouting slogans.

"Come on, Sir Andrew!" Lady Marjory urged and pushed her horse forward. "Watch for the peat holes!"

Sir Andrew followed as de Soulis jumped a patch of soft ground to land with a thud.

"It's a fair contest, you see," Lady Marjory shouted as they raced side by side over the moor. "A man on foot is lighter; he can run over land that could not support a horse. That makes this a sporting occasion."

Sir Andrew guided his horse between two ominously green patches of ground and watched the fugitive run. He moved fast, glancing over his shoulder as de Soulis and the riders pursued him.

Hunting a man isn't a sport and breaks the knightly code.

Sir Andrew had seen several hangings as his father managed his lands and punished wrongdoers. He knew that thieves, murderers, and those who rebelled against lawful authority should be punished. Yet making game of a frightened man was outside the law.

The fugitive stumbled into an area of soft mud, yelled in fear and floundered, nearly falling. He slowed, hauled himself to a patch of dry ground and ran on.

"We've got him already!" one of the horsemen shouted in triumph and spurred forward. His horse stumbled into a hidden hole, and the rider slid forward, falling over the horse's neck as his companions laughed at his misfortune.

The fugitive leapt from one firm area to another, gasping with effort. The hills seemed as distant as ever, half hidden as ragged clouds drifted across the summits.

"He's giving us better sport than I thought!" Lady Marjory laughed. "Come on, boys, don't let him escape!"

The riders spread out, with another man falling but the rest outflanking the fugitive, laughing as they overtook him. One man-at-arms drew his sword as the hounds bounded ahead, barking wildly.

"Shall I order the dogs to kill?" the hound master asked.

"Not yet," de Soulis shouted.

The fugitive ran onto a long ridge, where a group of tall stones thrust to the careless sky.

"The Thirteen Stone Ridge!" Lady Marjory yelled, as excited as any of the men. "This is an old druidical sacred site," she explained to Sir Andrew, who nodded without interest.

The fugitive ran around the stones, desperate to escape the encircling horsemen, who avoided the bog. The hound master snarled at the dogs to get back, allowing the men to finish the hunt.

"Pen him in," Lady Marjory said as the horsemen pushed forward to the edge of the bog. Sir Andrew reined up outside the circle, watching without comment. De Soulis spurred his horse onto a hidden causeway and walked to the thirteen stones.

"Follow my lead!" de Soulis ordered, and one by one, the horsemen picked their way over the causeway. They formed up between the standing stones, facing their desperate quarry.

"Kill the churl!" Lady Marjory commanded, and the horsemen drew their swords. The fugitive waited for a moment and then jumped at his nearest attacker. The man reared back as the hunted man grabbed his sword and pushed him from the horse. Taken by surprise, the rider fell back, with only his stirrups holding him in place.

"I'll kill you, de Soulis!" the farmer shouted. Leaving the astonished man-at-arms to recover, he dashed across the rough grass toward de Soulis. As the other riders watched, too shocked to intervene, the hunted man yelled, leapt in the air, and thrust his sword at de Soulis.

"Get to hell, you fiend!"

When Sir Andrew tried to intervene, Lady Marjory grabbed his horse's bridle. "Leave them, Sir Andrew. This escapade is all part of the fun."

"Fun?" Sir Andrew's sword was half out of the scabbard.

"Watch," Lady Marjory said, smiling.

The fugitive put all his weight into the stroke and gasped as the sword crashed against de Soulis's stomach.

"Sir Hugo is not wearing armour, not even chain mail!" Sir Andrew said.

Lady Marjory laughed loudly. "That always astonishes the churls," she said.

The fugitive tried again, bringing his sword back and slashing at de Soulis's leg. Although the blade crashed above de Soulis's knee, it did not cut the skin.

"He'll try a third time," Lady Marjory said. "They always do."

"Always?" Sir Andrew asked as the fugitive stepped back and lunged at de Soulis's unprotected face.

"Always," Lady Marjory replied, laughing as the fugitive's sword made contact without inflicting any injury.

The fugitive swore, turned, and tried to run with de Soulis watching. When a household knight blocked the fugitive's retreat, de Soulis kicked his horse forward, drew his sword and sliced downwards. The quarry screamed as de Soulis's sword cut off his right hand.

"Kill him," de Soulis ordered, smiling, and the others followed, hacking at the man with their long swords.

～

"Somebody must have taken the skeleton away." Thomas tried to apply logic to the situation. "Dead men can't walk."

"That must be it," Eleanor agreed. She had decided not to mention the previous day's encounter with the handsome young knight. "Somebody's playing tricks on us. We know the locals don't like incomers, so they're trying to drive us away. Even Martin Crozier is keen to get rid of us."

"They're using all this superstitious nonsense to scare us back to Edinburgh," Thomas decided. "I'll bet Martin is at the heart of it with his supposed knowledge of everything local."

They sat in their living room with the fire bright between them and Eleanor's pile of library books at her side. She had temporarily discarded *Bulldog Drummond*, with a sprig of dead heather between the pages as a makeshift bookmark.

"Are we trying to convince ourselves?" Eleanor asked. "We both know that strange things have happened here, from the crows showing us where those old stones were to the grave in the basement and that wee boy disappearing."

"We're allowing old stories to alter our beliefs," Thomas said. "We've seen the reality of war and experienced horrors beyond anything that happened in the past. Crows are intelligent birds, that grave has been there for centuries, while little boys tend to wander off. These things are not supernatural." He sipped at a tumbler of whisky. "Mediaeval knights lived to fight; they were trained from childhood to kill people and welcomed war as their reason for existence. I'll bet there are hundreds, maybe thousands of graves scattered around Scotland, waiting for somebody to discover them."

Eleanor stared at the fire. "Aye. Maybe. I hope there are no more waiting around our house. One was disturbing. Two is damned unsettling."

"You've seen worse," Thomas said soberly.

"I have," Eleanor agreed, "and that worries me, Thomas. A couple more dead bodies should not disturb me, so why am I agitated? There's something different about these two."

"No," Thomas shook his head. "The only difference is that they are old and near our home. We'll contact the Douglas family and see if they want their knight back and forget old Martin's tales. He's probably a bit doolally[1] anyway."

Eleanor smiled. "You're probably right. I've got all these silly old tales in my head." She was silent for a moment, watching the glowing embers settle in the fire. "I am not sure about the crows, Tom. I see them, and you don't."

Thomas shrugged. "I was probably looking the wrong way," he said. "You often see things I don't."

Eleanor laughed and stood up. "You're probably right. Good night, Thomas." She halted at the door. "By the way, Tom, did you know that Hugh Cummings might be distantly related to de Soulis?"

Thomas shook his head. "No."

"The de Soulis family were important in mediaeval Scotland," Eleanor explained, with one hand resting on the door handle. "Our Hugo was a cousin of William de Soulis, Lord of Liddesdale, and Butler of Scotland, as you know. That was when Edward Longshanks, the English king, tried to conquer Scotland."

"The Hammer of the Scots," Thomas murmured.

"That's what he called himself," Eleanor said, "but as he failed, it's more true to say the Scots hammered him." She smiled. "Edward, Hammered by the Scots. He died still trying to conquer us. Anyway, William was a cousin of Alexander Comyn, Earl of Buchan, and the name Comyn evolved into Cumming, or Cummings."

Thomas lifted a hand in acknowledgement. "There's more old blood than ours, then," he said.

"The local families have long roots," Eleanor said. "Their blood has fertilised this land for centuries."

"That's a strange way of putting it," Thomas said.

"It's a strange place," Eleanor told him. "Despite your logic, Tom, the area seems to affect me." As she looked at her brother, she saw his face alter to the young knight, with the war-created lines disappearing and the hard press of Thomas's mouth softening.

"Affect you? I thought we had discounted all that rubbish," Thomas said.

"Oh, forgive me. I'm talking nonsense," Eleanor told him. *It was just a trick of the light.*

"We'll go to the Wardlaw Inn tomorrow and find them all laughing at us," Thomas said.

"You're probably right," Eleanor agreed, trying to shake the French music from her head as the young knight stood beside Thomas. *At least he can keep my bed warm tonight.*

～

Lady Marjory stood in the centre of the stone circle with her legs straddling the butchered corpse, smiling. "You can keep my bed warm tonight, Sir Andrew."

Sir Andrew started. After the farmer's slaughter, sleeping with Lady Marjory was not on his mind.

"I sense more death here," Lady Marjory said. "I can feel gentle blood soaking into this ground."

De Soulis cleaned his sword on the rough clothes of the dead farmer. "His blood was not gentle," he said. "He's only a churl, a peasant."

"I don't sense the blood of a churl," Lady Marjory replied. "It is the blood of a gentleman, a knight of the realm."

"Sir Andrew and I are the only gentlemen here," Sir Hugo said. "Unless you count the household knights." He snorted. "They are landless, little better than peasants."

"That is truth," Lady Marjory agreed. She glanced at Sir

Andrew. "This fair knight tried to aid you, Hugo. If I had not stopped him, he would have dispatched the churl."

De Soulis nodded toward Sir Andrew. "My thanks, Sir Andrew, but you will have noticed I have crafts to keep me safe."

"I noticed the farmer's sword could not hurt you," Sir Andrew replied cautiously.

"Neither steel nor rope can harm me," de Soulis said, grinning.

"You are not safe in this place," Lady Marjory told him. "Avoid the thirteen stones, Hugo."

Sir Andrew saw the two crows land beside the dead churl. One began to peck at the body.

"Topple the stones!" A sudden panic gripped de Soulis after Lady Marjory's words. "Knock them down so men will never find this spot again!"

"They are set deep in the ground," one of the riders said.

"Call up all the churls in the area," Sir Hugo ordered. "Force them to it! I want this place destroyed."

The household knights nodded. "We'll gather the churls, Sir Hugo."

Lady Marjory stepped closer to Sir Andrew and pressed her leg against his. "You are mine now, Andrew. Abide with me, and I will not let any harm befall you." She touched his arm.

Sir Andrew met her gaze and saw dark depths in her eyes. When she smiled, he was suddenly light-headed and dizzy. "You are a fair lady and passing wise, Lady Marjory." He felt her enter his mind, probing into the corners he would prefer to keep hidden. "Who are you, my Lady?"

"I am your fair lady, my Andrew, and that is all that matters."

Sir Andrew nodded, yet he sensed something wrong with

Lady Marjory. He met her gaze and saw something else behind her steady eyes, as if another presence lurked inside her, trying to contact him.

"You appear confused, Andrew," Lady Marjory said, tilting her head to one side as her mind probed into his thoughts.

"It is a small matter, Lady Marjory," Sir Andrew said. "I thought I saw a shadow in your eyes."

"The shadow of our future, Sir Andrew," Lady Marjory told him.

~

"Another!" Walter Nixon stood with his back to the bar and his arms on his hips, facing the room. "That's two bairns gone missing now!"

Thomas and Eleanor slipped into the inn and sidled to a table as far away from Wally as possible. "You sit there, sister-of-mine," Thomas said.

"Two bairns and no explanation!" Wally nearly shouted.

"Wally Nixon seems agitated," Thomas said as he ordered the drinks.

"Wally Nixon's always agitated about something." The barman fetched Thomas's order. "He's not a man to argue with."

"What's happened?" Thomas asked.

"A wee lassie has disappeared," the barman said. "That's the second bairn in six weeks."

Thomas felt a chill up his spine. "Is there a search party?"

"The factor is organising one right now," the barman said, sliding Thomas's drinks across to him. "That's why he's shouting across the bar."

"We'll help," Thomas volunteered when Wally finished speaking.

"You?" Wally faced him. "You're the cause of the problem. Everything was all right until you stooriefeet arrived." He glared at Thomas, secure in his superior height, weight and standing in the community. "We don't want you incomers in the area."

"Well, Mr Nixon." Thomas faced him with a faint smile. "We're here, we're staying, and we're offering to help."

"We don't need your help," Wally told him, "and we don't want your help. Get back to Edinburgh, where you belong." He hawked and spat on the floor. "Digging up bad old memories, unearthing skeletons and causing trouble."

"We're offering to help." Eleanor joined her brother. "If we don't join your search party, we'll look ourselves," she said. "Although I can't see much happening except a man with a big mouth making a lot of noise."

Thomas stepped in front of Eleanor as Wally made a move towards her.

"There's no need for any of this." Martin acted as peacemaker. "Mr Armstrong and Mrs Machrie did not kidnap the missing children."

Wally grunted. "How do you know, Martin? The bairns only went missing after they arrived."

"What would they want with children?" Martin asked.

"Toonies [2] are queer folk," Wally replied enigmatically. "I wouldn't like to think what they would do with them."

"We don't have any children hidden away," Thomas replied with surprising patience. He faced Wally with his left foot slightly forward, and his knees bent, waiting for the heavier man to attack.

"I want to search Anton's Walls." Wally leaned towards Thomas pugnaciously.

"You can want!" Eleanor replied.

"What's all this?" Sergeant Learmonth pushed into the

room with two uniformed constables behind him. "Who wants what?"

"Wally Nixon thinks Mr Armstrong has the two missing children hidden in his house, Sergeant Learmonth," Martin explained quickly.

"Have you?" Sergeant Learmonth asked.

"Of course not!" Eleanor replied first.

"What makes you think they have, Wally?" the sergeant asked.

"They're stooriefeet, and nothing happened until they arrived," Wally said. "And they've been digging up the druid's stones."

"Being stooriefeet doesn't necessarily mean they are kidnappers," the sergeant explained. "Not all incomers are bad."

"They dug up a lot of druid's stones," Wally said. "They found the Thirteen Stane Rig."

Sergeant Learmonth shuffled his feet. "Digging up stones is not a criminal offence," he said. "Enough now, Wally. Leave these good people alone and attend to your own business."

"Everyone's business is my business," Wally said. "I'm Mr Cummings' factor, remember."

The sergeant hardened his tone. "Leave the pub, Wally, or I'll take you in for creating a disturbance."

"I'm leaving," Wally said, glowering at Thomas. He stared at Eleanor; his eyes widened as if he had seen something. "Mrs Machrie." He nodded and stumbled from the pub.

"What was that all about?" Eleanor asked. She realised that Martin was watching her with his head tilted to one side.

"We're stooriefeet," Thomas said simply. "The locals don't want us here."

"We are locals," Eleanor said. "More local than many of

them. Our blood comes from here, but why did Mr Nixon decide to leave?"

"The police told him to," Thomas said.

"No." Eleanor shook her head. "It was nothing to do with the police. He was glowering at me when something made him leave."

Martin nodded. "You made him leave, Mrs Machrie," he said, watching Eleanor over the rim of his glass. "He saw something in you that scared him."

Before Eleanor could reply, Sergeant Learmonth began to organise a search party.

"Come on, lads, we've wasted enough time. Let's find this wee lassie."

CHAPTER 19

SIR ANDREW ROSE from his chamber before the first grey streaks of dawn and slipped out the door. Lady Marjory remained in his bed, white, naked, and sleeping soundly. Only the night watch was awake, grumbling on their posts on the tower as they leaned on their spears and stared into the star-lit dark.

Barefooted and with his dagger belted around his waist, Sir Andrew padded from his chamber, determined to explore the castle. De Soulis had been an excellent host, despite his unorthodox method of execution, but Sir Andrew was unhappy about his treatment of his people, especially the women.

As always in castles across Christendom, the servants slept in the great hall or wherever they could find space, with only the lord, his lady and privileged guests having the luxury of private apartments. Sir Andrew picked his way across sleeping bodies as he peered into chambers and rooms. As he expected, the household knights shared an apartment, the men-at-arms crammed into barracks, and the hounds were in their kennel.

There are few female servants, Sir Andrew confirmed, *and none are young. That is unusual. I will ask Lady Marjory why tomorrow.*

The moaning came from below. At first, Sir Andrew thought it was the wind, but when it continued, he realised there was not even a whisper of a breeze. He headed downwards with his feet slapping on the cold stone and his hand gripping the hilt of his dagger.

The stairs ended at a round-headed, iron-studded door that creaked when Sir Andrew pulled it open. He waited for a moment in case the noise had alerted the guard, then stepped on into darkness. The moaning intensified, with an occasional loud gasp and a single agonised scream.

Sir Andrew drew his dagger as he entered a small, stone-slabbed square with two heavy doors blocking access to three further chambers. Sir Andrew saw three iron bolts secured the first door, with two large keyholes. He drew the bolts, tried the door, and was not surprised to find it locked. Kneeling, he peered through the lower keyhole and gasped in horror.

Lying against the far wall, what remained of a man stared at him through sightless eyes. The man wore the clothes of a merchant or successful artisan; he had not the status of a knight but was far above the commonality. The man was emaciated by starvation and looked as if he had chewed on his arms in his hunger.

De Soulis has starved that unfortunate man to death. I wonder what faults he made to deserve such a terrible fate.

Withdrawing from that dungeon and keeping to the wall, Sir Andrew stepped slowly forward into darkness punctured by a flickering yellow light. Although Maintree Castle had a dungeon, it was seldom occupied, only for the occasional thief or English prisoner-of-war. He had never seen anybody tortured, yet when he rounded a stone pillar, he knew what was happening.

De Soulis and the squire stood underneath the younger of the two women de Soulis had grabbed the previous day. The child hung upside down from the ceiling, with her throat cut and the blood dripping into a stone trough. As de Soulis watched, the squire plunged his hat into the trough, removed it and sucked out the blood. As he did so, his red hair took on a brighter hue.

"St Bride, protect me!" Sir Andrew breathed. "What in the name of God is that?"

The squire straightened up, dipped a golden goblet in the blood and handed it to de Soulis, who drank greedily, with the blood running down his chin to drip to the stone slabs beneath.

"Well met, Robin," de Soulis said. "Well met indeed."

The squire dropped his cap into the trough again, then lifted his head. "I smell somebody," he snarled. When he turned around, Sir Andrew saw his appearance had changed. He was no longer a stocky, slightly shambling man of indeterminate age but a figure from a drunkard's nightmare.

Short in stature and thick of body, Robin looked much older, with his red hair straggling down to his shoulders, large, red eyes, distended nostrils, and a small mouth full of yellow fangs. His hands were long, with thin, talon-like fingers and long dirty nails, while he wore iron boots on his feet.

Sir Andrew involuntarily drew back, tightening the grip on his dagger.

"I smell somebody watching," Robin repeated and reached for an iron-bound pikestaff that leaned against the wall. He glared at de Soulis as if awaiting orders.

"Seek him," de Soulis commanded.

Robin grabbed the pikestaff and turned in Sir Andrew's direction, lifting his head and twitching his wide, flat nose.

Sir Andrew withdrew hastily. He glanced at the turnpike stairs leading to the great hall, realised he could not escape that way and dragged open the third and final door. Diving inside, he closed the door behind him and drew an iron bolt to keep it secure.

What sort of monster was that? A fiend. It was a fiend from the pit. By St Bride, it was a redcap!

Sir Andrew held his knife in his hand, wondering if he should have attacked the creature and de Soulis. He knew now that all the stories were true. De Soulis was working with a demon to terrorise the countryside. He had to stop this evil from spreading. That was his task as a knight sworn to protect the weak from the strong.

Footsteps sounded as de Soulis and Robin ran up the stairs. Sir Andrew took a deep breath, waited a few moments, and opened the door. A little light seeped in from the dungeon, allowing Sir Andrew to see he was in a sizeable, stone-flagged chamber lined with stone tables on which were jars and containers. He glanced in a few, realised they contained herbs and plants and lost interest. Returning to the dungeon, Sir Andrew glanced at the girl.

She hung upside down with the final few drops of her blood dripping into the deep metal trough. The look in her eyes spoke of unbelievable horror.

I am too late to save you, little one, but I will try to save others.

Climbing the stairs two at a time, Sir Andrew heard the noise above as de Soulis shouted orders.

"Get up! Sir Andrew Douglas is no longer welcome in Caercorbie! He has found the mason, James of Nantes and abused my hospitality. Find him and bring him to me!"

The dead man in the dungeon was James of Nantes, the mason who disappeared.

"Find him! I want him alive!" That was Lady Marjory's voice, with Sir Hugo shouting at the guards, urging them to greater effort. Men hurried around the castle with flaring torches, swearing at being awakened at this ungodly hour in the morning.

Sir Andrew hugged the shadows, cursing that he had left his sword in his quarters and determined to regain it before he left Caercorbie. Swords were more than mere weapons, they were nearly sacred objects and badges of honour and status. A knight without a horse and sword was less than a man. Bred only to fight and command, an unarmed knight was no use to anybody.

The door to his chamber had no lock, and Sir Andrew slid inside. His sword hung on the wall, encased in its scabbard. He dressed rapidly and awkwardly, wishing he had a squire to help, buckled on his sword and sighed with relief. Without his sword, he felt vulnerable; with it, he would face any enemy, man or demon.

Now I can face you, de Soulis, and that fiend from the pits of hell.

Sir Andrew ran to the courtyard, where a band of men-at-arms were preparing to ride outside to search for him.

I'll give you sport, by God, and you'll not live to gloat about it.

"There he is!" a pockmarked man-at-arms shouted as Sir Andrew made his way towards the stables. He jumped in front of Sir Andrew and slashed with his sword. Without thought, Sir Andrew drew his sword, beat down the man-at-arms' defence and thrust the point into his throat. The pockmarked man gurgled, reached for his wound, and collapsed, blood spouting onto the straw-strewn ground.

I've killed my first man. I am a warrior, a soldier.

There was no time for self-reflection. Sir Andrew stepped over the body and ran on, holding his sword. He ignored the shouting behind him and raced toward the stables, where a

single rush torch spread sputtering light. De Soulis had anticipated the move and sent four men to guard the door, but they
were still half sleeping and slow-moving.

"Stand aside!" Sir Andrew shouted, and two men, hearing
the voice of knightly authority, obediently stepped away. A
third stared at Sir Andrew, and only one lifted his poleaxe. Sir
Andrew parried the swing and thrust his sword into the man's
stomach as his father had advised.

*Two dead. Where are you, Sir Hugo? Face me like an
honourable knight rather than hiding behind your demon's
crafts.*

Two grooms looked startled when Sir Andrew burst in.
"Saddle my horse!" He decided to use the voice of authority
again.

"But Sir Hugo said," the younger of the grooms protested.

"Never mind that!" Sir Andrew ordered, pulling his saddle
from its rack, and throwing it at the groom. "Saddle my horse,
or it will be the worse for you!"

With Sir Andrew's bloody sword threatening him, the
groom hurried to obey. Within minutes, Sir Andrew had
sheathed his sword. He mounted Kenneth, kicked in his spurs,
and clattered across the courtyard.

"There he is!" a guard cried.

Sir Andrew knocked the guard to the ground, charged
through another two men-at-arms and trotted out of the gate.
Robin Redcap appeared in front of him in the guise of Sir
Hugo's squire.

Before Sir Andrew could draw his sword, Redcap had
jumped onto his horse's neck and thrust out his long claws.
Holding the reins with his left hand, Sir Andrew drew his
dagger and plunged it into the creature's stomach. Robin
Redcap smiled at him, showing a mouthful of pointed teeth,
plucked out the knife and threw it away.

"Jesus and St Bride, save me!" Sir Andrew said and swung his arm, unbalancing the redcap, so it fell off the horse, bounced and recovered. The creature followed the horse for a few yards but fell behind.

De Soulis appeared, standing in front of Sir Andrew with his hands on his hips, smiling. Sir Andrew swerved around him, swinging his sword. He felt the thrill as the long blade made contact with de Soulis's neck.

"You'll murder no more children!" Sir Andrew roared and realised de Soulis was unharmed, laughing at him.

"You will make good sport, Sir Andrew," de Soulis shouted as Sir Andrew spurred furiously. When a crossbow bolt buzzed past his shoulder, he sawed his reins to dodge any further bolts and headed into the moor.

The monks were correct. There is a great evil here.

CHAPTER 20

"Captain Armstrong!" Lady Fiona leaned out of the passenger window of her Bentley. "I hoped you would call in to see me!"

Thomas stopped at the side of the road and lifted his hat politely. "Good evening, Lady Fiona. I've been rather busy, I'm afraid."

"Terrible business about these children," Lady Fiona said. "Our factor accused you of being involved, I understand."

"He did," Thomas said, replacing his hat.

"I'll have a word with him," Lady Fiona promised. Something in her tone told Thomas that Wally Nixon would find the interview very uncomfortable.

"Thank you, your Ladyship, but I am sure he was acting for the best," Thomas said.

"I am sure he was not," Lady Fiona said grimly. "Are you very busy at present?"

"Not at present," Thomas said. "I was going for a walk."

"Good." Lady Fiona opened the car door. "Come with me

to Wardlaw House, and I'll tell you where you can find the best fishing."

Thomas hesitated, but the mention of fishing lured him in, as Lady Fiona intended. "Thank you, your Ladyship," he said, sliding into the Bentley.

"Take me home, Raymond," Lady Fiona ordered and sat back in her seat.

Wardlaw House was smaller than Thomas had expected, a neo-classical building two stories high with Doric columns at the door and a welcoming atmosphere.

Lady Fiona ushered Thomas through the outer hall and an arched doorway into an inner hall where classical statues vied for prominence with family portraits.

"Welcome to Wardlaw House," Lady Fiona said, smiling. "You might feel at home with our military ancestors."

Thomas realised that many of the males portrayed wore military uniforms, with scarlet predominating, although the older pictures showed unsmiling men in half armour.

"We are a military family, Captain Armstrong," Lady Fiona said. "Generation after generation of Cummings have fought for Crown and country," she smiled as if releasing a great secret, "and some have fought for their own ends."

Thomas nodded. "I have heard that the Cummings breed a martial kind of man."

"We have been called worse," Lady Fiona said. "Much worse!" Her laugh was open and free. "Come on, Captain Armstrong, and I will give you a tour of my house."

"Thank you," Thomas said, allowing Lady Fiona to show him around. Ignoring the servant's quarters, she introduced him to the public rooms and the oak-panelled library.

"Mostly history, the classics and military books," Lady Fiona said. "You may wish to return later and see if there is anything to your taste."

"Thank you." Thomas wondered why Lady Fiona was so hospitable to a stranger. "My sister would love your library."

"The fair Eleanor," Lady Fiona said. "Is she a book person?"

"Very much so," Thomas told her, smiling.

"She is welcome to visit," Lady Fiona said casually and stopped at a wall display of swords and flintlock muskets. "I grew up with military men," she explained. "My great uncle captured that sword from the Sikhs," she pointed to an elaborately decorated tulwar, "and my grandfather brought that one home from Crimea." She knew each weapon's history and spoke with the authority of an expert.

"That was my father's sword." Lady Fiona touched a curved sabre. "He died in the Boer War. I still have his revolver in my bedside drawer." She faced Thomas with a twisted smile. "I keep it there all the time. Would you like to see it?"

Thomas hid his surprise. "I don't think your husband would approve," he said, smiling. "If he found me in your bedroom, he might take offence."

"My husband?" Lady Fiona sounded surprised.

"Sir Hugh Cummings," Thomas said.

Lady Fiona laughed. "Oh, Captain Armstrong!" She touched his chest. "I am afraid I have given you quite the wrong idea. Hugh is my brother! My husband died at the Somme!"

"Oh!" Thomas felt himself flushing. "I am so sorry, Lady Fiona. I had no idea."

"Of course, the similarity of names." Lady Fiona smiled. "I married my second cousin, Lieutenant Iain Cummings of the Royal Scots."

Thomas struggled for words. "The Royals are a fine regiment, Lady Fiona," he said. "I served alongside them in Flanders." His eyes darkened as he returned.

~

Endless acres of mud and the harsh gleam of star shells reflecting on tangled barbed wire. A dead body hanging over the rusted strands, slowly decomposing. The smell of death in a hundred hideous forms and the furtive sounds of men preparing for a trench raid.

Thomas lowered his periscope, having scanned the area in front of the Borderers' trench. "Take nothing that rattles or reflects the light," he reminded. "Wear cap comforters[1] and the minimum of equipment. Bludgeons and maces, smoke-darken your bayonets and rub mud onto your cheekbones and foreheads."

The men obeyed, some grinning with repressed excitement, others trembling in apprehension. The veterans hid their fear, knowing what lay ahead. One or two exchanged dark humour.

"I'll take the lead," Thomas said. An officer had to lead. If an officer did not lead from the front, he would not last long in a Scottish infantry regiment. "Sergeant Maxwell, you command the rearguard."

"Aye, sir." Maxwell was a ten-year veteran, a man from Nithsdale whose ancestors had carved a bloody path through history. He nodded as if crossing No Man's Land was as easy as drilling a platoon on the barrack square. Thomas grunted. Maybe it was for Sergeant Maxwell.

"We'll crawl up the sap to the OP and strike across to the German trenches at point Z; that's the shell-shattered tree to our left centre."

The men nodded, already aware of their objectives.

"We want prisoners, so no killing unless we have to," Thomas reminded and saw men tapping their cudgels into the palms of their hands. After three years of war, the veterans were experts, those few who had survived. They knew the bloody reality of trench warfare with its quick, murderous raids to capture prisoners and gather information.

"Right, lads, follow me." Thomas ducked into the sap and crawled forward, ankle-deep in liquid mud, with his men following. He saw the knight again, with his chain mail reflecting the star shells and his face confused, shook the image from his head and continued.

～

"Captain Armstrong?" Lady Fiona held his shoulders. "Are you back?"

"I am," Thomas said. "I'm sorry, Lady Fiona. I was in the trenches again."

"I know, Captain," Lady Fiona said. "I understand. Iain was like that as well. He would just drift away with the same expression in his eyes."

"Thank you, Lady Fiona," Thomas said.

"It's good to have a real soldier back in the house," Lady Fiona said, allowing her hands to linger on Thomas's arms. "I feel that I have some of Iain back. He would understand how I feel; old soldiers do, don't they?"

"War can create a bond," Thomas agreed. "Battle and shared danger can bind men together."

Mrs Cummings pushed open a door. "Come in here, Captain." She sounded desperate. "Please come in here."

Thomas knew the door opened into her bedroom. "Lady Fiona, I don't think we should."

"Yes, we should, Captain Armstrong," Lady Fiona said. "We need each other." Propelling Thomas inside, she closed the door and turned the key in the lock.

～

"My brother had no interest in Anton's Walls until you arrived, Tom." Lady Fiona lay beside Thomas in the bed, leaning her head on her right hand and smiling down at him. "I don't know why he's acting as he is."

Thomas ran a hand down her smooth flank. "I think it's because we're incomers," he said. "Nobody likes strangers coming into their part of the world, altering the dynamics, buying up the property and believing they know better than people who have lived there for generations." He grinned. "You can't blame him for that."

"Do that again." Lady Fiona shifted slightly, pressing her hips forward.

Thomas obeyed, smiling with happy concentration.

"I don't know if Hugh is concerned about incomers," Lady Fiona said. "He's never shown any insecurities that way. I think he's scared of you."

"Of me?" Thomas asked. "I'm no threat to him."

Lady Fiona shifted closer. "Yes, you are," she said. "He was the man of the house, in charge of everything, the man who gave the orders, and then you came along. A decorated soldier who had fought in a dozen battles. My brother is very conscious that he avoided war service, so he struts, poses, and acts tough."

"Do you think I threaten his position?" Thomas asked.

"Perhaps," Lady Fiona said. "A little lower, please, and harder. That's my boy." She closed her eyes. "Now, I don't want to talk about Hugh anymore."

Thomas agreed. Hugh Cummings was the last thing on his mind at that moment.

~

"Sister-of-mine!" Thomas shouted as he pushed open Anton's Wall's front door. "Are you in?"

"I'm in," Eleanor replied from the kitchen. "What's all the noise for, Tom?" She glanced at the clock. "It's only two in the afternoon. You're early."

"I've brought somebody to see you," Thomas replied. "This fellow is Robert Powrie."

Eleanor stood up from her chair at the kitchen table, patting her hair into place. "You might have given me some warning, Tom. I look a mess!"

"You look just fine, Mrs Machrie," Robert Powrie told her. He stood inside the door, smiling.

Eleanor had always seen Powrie in his working clothes, but dressed in a suit and tie, with a shine on his shoes, he appeared a different man.

"Please forgive my brother," Eleanor said. "He can be very impulsive at times. When he's not being overly cautious."

"We've worked together for weeks, Mrs Machrie," Powrie said. "I can forgive his faults." Powrie's smile made him look quite handsome, Eleanor thought.

"Come into the living room," Eleanor invited, showing the way. "Do you want tea or something stronger?"

"Tea would be most welcome." Powrie had a deep voice, but less of an accent than Eleanor remembered.

"I wanted you two to meet each other." When Thomas glanced at her, Eleanor realised how important it was for him that she should like Robert Powrie.

"Thomas has mentioned you more than once." Eleanor was determined to help her brother.

Powrie smiled. "That was kind of him. He's spoken of you a hundred times."

"I'll put the kettle on," Thomas said. "And leave you to get acquainted."

Eleanor realised she was grinning foolishly. "Thomas told me you worked very hard on this house."

"It is good to see it occupied again," Powrie told her.

"You knew my great uncle," Eleanor struggled for conversation, "Jock Armstrong."

"I did," Powrie agreed. "Old Jock was a bit of a character, a local worthy if you don't mind me saying."

"I never met the man," Eleanor admitted as the French tune slipped into her mind.

"Ce fut en mai

Au douz tens gai."

When Powrie laughed, he looked even more handsome, Eleanor thought and joined in the laughter.

"You two seem to be getting along," Thomas approved as he appeared with the teapot and cups on a tray.

"Eleanor has you well trained," Powrie said, still laughing.

"It's taken me some time," Eleanor said seriously. Powrie was quite a charmer, she realised, with his broad smile and muscular body. She allowed her gaze to drift over him as her mind strayed into places she usually only visited during lonely nights. She found herself smiling, felt Powrie's eyes on her and coloured.

"I won't take up more of your time," Powrie said.

"You're welcome to stay as long as you like," Eleanor replied.

"I'd better not." Powrie stood. "Tam insisted that I meet his sister."

"I'm glad he did," Eleanor said as the French song increased in volume inside her mind.

"Ce fut en mai

Au douz tens gai."

She watched as Powrie left Anton's Walls, with his horse and cart negotiating the slap without difficulty.

"He's a friendly chap," Eleanor said.

"You seemed quite taken by him," Thomas agreed. "You were chatting for hours."

"Nonsense!" Eleanor said. "It was only a few minutes." She looked at the clock for proof and started to see the time. Nearly five o'clock. Robert Powrie had been in the house for three hours.

CHAPTER 21

SERGEANT LEARMONTH STOPPED at the door of Anton's Walls. "Thank you for your patience, Captain Armstrong, and you, Mrs Machrie. I am sorry to have disturbed you."

"You are doing your duty, Sergeant," Thomas said. "With two children missing, you have to explore every possibility." He held out his hand. "As somebody accused us of kidnapping them, you had to investigate."

Learmonth shook Thomas's hand. "I am glad you understand, Captain Armstrong."

"You can tell that fool, Walter Nixon, that we are not hiding any children," Eleanor said shortly.

Sergeant Learmonth gave a faint smile. "I will," he said, replacing his diced cap. "I wish you both a good day."

Thomas watched the sergeant ride his bicycle down the rutted track and shook his head. Missing children always worried him. He remembered the refugees in Belgium at the beginning of the war and, later, during the German March offensive of 1918. Mothers had abandoned their houses, possessions and even their husbands, but never their children.

~

Smoke drifted from burning buildings, blue-grey against the pale blue sky. Overhead, a Sopwith Camel scout plane, identifiable by its straight top wings and dihedral-angled lower planes, searched for Germans, covering the British withdrawal.

Thomas had marshalled his men, checking how many he had left.

"Where's MacDonald?"

"Dead, sir," Sergeant Maxwell reported, with blood smeared over his face and a fresh tear across the breast of his tunic. The three gold stripes on his sleeve told of bitter experience at the front. "A Hun sniper got him outside Albert."[1]

"Forty-three men left," Thomas said. "We'll make a stand at that farmhouse," he pointed to a ruin that crowned a low ridge. "The longer we delay the Hun, the better chance we give the rest of the army."

"Yes, sir," Maxwell said. "The men are about done in, sir."

"I know," Thomas agreed. "So are the Huns." An officer had to think about the enemy as well as his men. He should have the ability to understand the Huns' weaknesses as well as their strengths.

Both men ducked as a nearby artillery battery opened up, sending salvoes of shells screaming toward the advancing Germans. The Camel dived, with its twin machine guns hammering at the enemy.

"Get to that farmhouse, boys!" Thomas shouted above the noise. "We'll stand there!"

He did not hear the explosion that lifted him from the ground and threw him against the stump of a tree. He only remembered lying there, dazed, while a man stared at him.

"Who are you?" Thomas asked as the knight lowered his

shield. Thomas saw the device, a rampant unicorn above a sword. "Where the devil did you come from?"

The knight opened his mouth, trying to communicate in a language Thomas did not understand. As the two warriors stared at each other over the gulf of six centuries, a woman hurried past, carrying two children.

"What are you telling me?" Thomas asked.

The knight pointed with a mailed finger, his eyes urgent.

"What is it?" Thomas asked, pushing himself upright. He heard harp music among the battle din. "Who are you?"

"Tom!" Eleanor said sharply. "Come back!"

Eleanor's voice cracked the image open, and Thomas returned to Anton's Walls.

"I'm back," Thomas said, smiling, as the harp music faded away.

"You don't go away as often as you used to," Eleanor said, "and you've never come back smiling before." She ushered him inside the house and onto a chair in the living room.

"I met a knight," Thomas told her and related his experience. "I think he was trying to tell me something. He's there every time I return to the front, slightly clearer each time."

"Did you meet him in France?" Eleanor asked. "Or only since you came to Anton's Walls?"

Thomas considered the question for a moment. "I'm not sure," he replied. "I have forgotten much of what happened during the war." He stared at the dying embers of the fire. "These memories are so vivid I think they are real. I saw that knight as clearly as I saw Sergeant Maxwell." He sighed. "I did see the knight in France, Eleanor, but I discarded the image. We were all a little mad there."

"That's not surprising," Eleanor told him. "This may sound stupid, but he sounds like Sir Andrew Douglas. Did you see the device on his shield?"

Thomas nodded. "I did," he said. "It was a unicorn above a sword."

"Like this?" Eleanor slipped the ring from her finger and passed it to Thomas.

"Yes," Thomas said. "That's the device I saw."

"That's good," Eleanor said. "I'd like to think my Sir Andrew helped you at the front."

Thomas closed his eyes. "I am not sure that's correct," he said. "I think he was trying to tell me something."

"What?" Eleanor asked.

"He was pointing to a refugee carrying children," Thomas remembered. "He was warning me about children."

"Missing children?" Eleanor asked.

"Children in danger," Thomas said, and they looked at each other.

$\sim$

"This way, Sir Knight." The minstrel leaned on the trunk of a tree, strumming his harp.

"You?" Sir Andrew reined up his palfrey. He glanced over his shoulder in the direction of the castle. "What are you doing here?"

"The same as you, Sir Andrew, escaping from Caercorbie." The minstrel ran his fingers across the taut strings of his harp. "When you arrived, I wondered if you were on the side of good or evil."

"I wondered the same about you," Sir Andrew admitted.

The minstrel smiled. "A minstrel can enter where even angels fear to tread. Sometimes good has to adopt a disguise to recognise where true evil lies." He gave a low whistle, and Sim Armstrong appeared with a short spear in his hand. "You will remember this man?"

"Sim Armstrong!" Sir Andrew dismounted. "You were correct when you said Sir Hugo de Soulis is an unpleasant man."

Sim leaned on his spear. "Aye." He waited for the knight to continue.

"He is in league with a creature the likes of which I have never seen before," Sir Andrew said.

"Robin Redcap," the minstrel said. "A demon from the nethermost pits of hell."

Sir Andrew remembered the glimpse he had. "You speak truth," he said. "A doleful fiend. What do you know about it?"

The minstrel grunted. "Not enough, Sir Andrew, yet too much. The redcaps are demons that infest many castles in the marches, live off human blood and befriend the lord of the castle. When they have eaten, their caps glow red; otherwise, they are white or without colour."

"Can they be killed?" Sir Andrew asked.

The minstrel screwed up his face. "I do not know," he said. "I have heard that the name of the Lord repels their powers."

Sir Andrew nodded grimly. "I thrust my dagger to the hilt in the creature's belly, and it merely laughed at me. When I said the Lord's name, it fell off my horse."

"It will rise again, for even the Lord's name is insufficient to destroy such evil," the minstrel said. He led Sir Andrew through a tangle of woodland to a clearing, where a score of people appeared. "Welcome to our world," he said with a smile. "We hid here when Edward Plantagenet's soldiers murdered and ravaged along the Border, and now we hide from another great evil."

Sir Andrew nodded when more people arrived, men, women, and children. Some glowered at the newcomer; others accepted his presence without expression. A few stared straight ahead as if repeating some terrible event inside their head.

"De Soulis is equally protected," the minstrel said. "I heard that neither rope nor steel can hurt him."

Sir Andrew nodded. "I saw a man cut him three times, and de Soulis was unhurt. I did the same, without effect, even though a priest blessed my sword," he touched the weapon at his side.

"A single blessing is not sufficient," the minstrel agreed. "Do you intend to remain with us, Sir Andrew, or escape to a better place?"

"I swore a holy oath to defend the good against evil," Sir Andrew said. "I intend to fight the Saracens and redeem the Holy Land for Christianity, but I cannot leave this evil behind me."

The minstrel nodded. "Evil stalks everywhere," he said cryptically.

"We have just cause to wage mighty war against Sir Hug de Soulis."

"We are fighting an unholy trinity," the minstrel said. "Sir Hugo de Soulis, his familiar, Robin Redcap, and Lady Marjory."

Sir Andrew touched the hilt of his sword. "We shall see how they fare against the steel of a true knight."

"You are young, Sir Andrew, and have never met evil face-to-face. Yet you already know your sword will be insufficient," the minstrel said. "You will need more than a single blessing."

"You know a great deal about my needs, Minstrel!" Sir Andrew had been raised to command and was unused to a raggedly dressed minstrel giving advice.

"I have been fighting evil for a long time," the minstrel replied mildly. He smiled. "I have long prayed for a good knight to help."

Sir Andrew swallowed his pride. "What must I do, Sir Minstrel?"

"Strengthen your sword, Sir Andrew," the minstrel replied. "The steel is powerful against physical enemies, but what you will face is of the spirit, and you must have spiritual strength in addition to sharp steel."

"How can I do that?" Sir Andrew asked.

"Come with me, and I will show you," the minstrel told him.

Sir Andrew nodded. He realised that his early training had not prepared him for facing supernatural evil. "What should I call you, Minstrel?"

The minstrel's smile took decades off his age. "Minstrel will suffice, Sir Andrew."

"Sir Minstrel it shall be," Sir Andrew acknowledged.

~

Eleanor smiled as the familiar music drifted into her bedroom. She stretched on the bed, wondering what had happened to the time and where her strange, but no longer unwelcome, dreams originated. The music was soft and evocative, a reminder of days long ago.

"Ce fut en mai
Au douz tens gai
Que la saisons est bele,
Main me levai,
Joer m'alai
Lez une fontenele."

She looked up to see the young knight standing by the side of the bed, smiling down upon her. Light gleamed from the blond hair that flowed past his ears and reflected from his blue eyes.

"Good evening, Sir Andrew," Eleanor said. "I wondered when you would appear." She sat up in bed. "We've met before, haven't we? And you know my brother, I believe."

The knight extended a hand, stretching out to her, with his expression a mixture of yearning and shock.

"But you're dead," Eleanor reminded. "You've been dead and buried for six hundred years."

Sir Andrew's smile did not falter, and Eleanor realised he could not hear her. The knight existed in his own realm and time.

"You lived in Caercorbie, didn't you?" Eleanor asked. "Did you have a lover here? A sweetheart? Is it your music I can hear?" She sang the opening few words of the song.

"Ce fut en mai

Au douz tens gai,"

The knight remained beside Eleanor's bed with his eyes sparkling and his welcoming smile fixed.

"What do you want, Sir Andrew?" Eleanor asked. "How can I help you?"

Sir Andrew leaned forward, and then his expression altered from longing to disbelief and then dislike.

"Sir Andrew? Tell me how I can help!"

The image faded, leaving nothing but a memory and the whisper of a song.

"Ce fut en mai

Au douz tens gai

Que la saisons est bele,

Main me levai,

Joer m'alai

Lez une fontenele."

Eleanor shivered. *I know somebody is sending me a*

message, but I don't understand what. What are you trying to say?

The sudden laughter surprised Eleanor, rebounding from the walls and surrounding her. She looked around to see the source of the amusement and stopped, knowing it was herself. She was laughing without cause and in a voice she did not recognise.

Oh, dear Lord in heaven. Am I going mad? Has the war damaged me as it has Thomas?

Eleanor pulled up the covers as the French song ran through her mind, repeating itself endlessly.

"Leave me!" Eleanor pleaded. "Leave me in peace!"

CHAPTER 22

"I'LL SHOW you the best fishing in the Borders, Thomas," Robert Powrie said, smiling. "We'll find the trout in the Wardlaw River."

"Lady Fiona has given me permission to fish anywhere on her lands," Thomas said.

Powrie laughed. "I've been fishing the Wardlaw without the Cummings' permission for as long as I can remember," he said. "And, believe me, that's a long time. Meet me at the war memorial at ten tonight."

"Night-time fishing?" Thomas asked.

"Night-time fishing," Powrie confirmed. "Have you ever burned the water?"[1]

"Is that not illegal?" Thomas asked.

"Only if the gamekeepers catch you," Powrie said, with his smile broadening. "That's part of the fun, so make sure nobody sees you."

Thomas nodded. He did not like to poach on Lady Fiona's lands, but Robert had been more than helpful with Anton's Walls and had completed the work in an amazingly short time.

"I don't like to poach," he said, "But once can't do much damage. Or, if you prefer, I can try and get you a permit."

Powrie laughed again. "I'll show you real fishing," he said. "One trip with me, and you'll never forget it."

Thomas nodded, trying to balance his conscience with loyalty for a man who had befriended him. "I'll be there," he said. There was something persuasive about Robert Powrie. Perhaps it was his smile or general friendliness, but people were always eager to follow his wishes.

I'm no exception, Thomas told himself. *I'm meeting him tonight, acting against my better judgement rather than hurt his feelings.*

Powrie was waiting at the war memorial, dressed in battered khaki and with a soft cap comforter over his head.

"Glad you could come, Tam," he said with his ready smile. "This way." He set off with a long, loping stride that covered the ground quickly. Thomas matched him step for step as they walked through two fields, vaulting the drystane dykes with ease as they headed toward Wardlaw House.

"We're beyond the legal beats," Powrie told Thomas as they reached a low boundary wall. Powrie scaled the stonework with the speed of long practice and waited for Thomas to join him. "Only the Cummings family or their predecessors have ever fished here."

The river Wardlaw was broad between plantations of mature trees, with a boathouse on the opposite bank and two salmon cobles drawn up on a shingle shore.

"There's a neuk here that only the laird uses." Powrie grinned through the dark. "The trout gather here, close to the bank." He lowered his voice to a harsh whisper. "The old laird used it for wenching too. He and I shared some fine sport here."

"The old laird?" Thomas was having second thoughts about trespassing on Lady Fiona's water. "Who was he?"

"Hugh's father, Charles Cummings," Powrie said. "He was a rogue of the first water." He smiled. "I told you I was older than I look."

"Not that old, surely," Thomas said and smiled when Powrie shook his head and gave his infectious laugh.

"Remember, we're on Cummings' private beat," Powrie said. "If Himself happens to come along, run."

"Run?" Thomas repeated.

"Like Auld Hornie was prodding his flaming trident into your arse," Powrie said. He produced a lantern, shielded the wick from the persistent wind and struck a match. Within a minute, a soft glow illuminated the river, reflecting off the rippling water and showing the lower branches of the surrounding trees.

"I am not cut out to be a poacher," Thomas said. He had supported the rule of law all his life, and here he was, breaking the law and poaching fish that belonged to a woman who had shown him nothing but kindness. *More than kindness,* he told himself, as he thought of his visit to Wardlaw House.

"I think I'll leave you to it," Powrie said just as a shout broke the stillness of the night.

"What?" Thomas asked, but Powrie had vanished, and rough voices broke the silence of the night.

"What the hell are you doing?"

A rush of boots followed the shout, and three stalwart men burst through the thickets. Thomas froze in a sudden glare of lanterns.

∼

The star shell burst above him, terrifyingly brilliant in its harsh light. Thomas froze, half crouched in the hellish waste of No Man's Land. He knew that movement would attract a torrent of machine-gun fire from the German trenches. Behind him, the men of the raiding party followed their officer, praying no German lookout spotted them in their vulnerability.

The star shell remained in place for seconds that seemed like hours, picking out every detail of the ruined landscape. Thomas saw the skeletal remains of the man hanging on the German barbed wire and the half-decomposed body of a German soldier sitting in a shell hole, grinning at the world.

The light slowly faded as the sun sunk to earth and darkness returned. Thomas let out his breath in a long gasp.

"Right, lads, on we go."

∼

"Right, lads!" a harsh voice sounded. "We've found ourselves a poacher! Let's see who he is!"

The lights shone into Thomas's face as the three men crowded around him. Walter Nixon, the factor and two hard-eyed gamekeepers.

"It's that bloody stooriefoot!" Walter Nixon grated, with his red hat pulled low over his forehead. "Come on, you incomer bastard! Sir Hugh will want a word with you!"

Thomas wondered if he should resist. He imagined the sheer pleasure of planting a fist in Wally Nixon's face but knew the factor was in the right. Instead of fighting, he smiled and raised his arms.

"You caught me fair and square," he said. "Take me to Sir Hugh." He did not resist when one of the gamekeepers put a massive hand on the small of his back and pushed.

∼

The holy man was unlike any priest Sir Andrew had seen. Rather than live in a grand stone-built abbey or cathedral, surrounded by the glory of the Lord, he inhabited a small, mud-and-wood built hut in the middle of the forest.

"Is this the knight?" The holy man wore a single robe of dirty white, with his head shaved ear-to-ear in a pattern Sir Andrew had never seen before.

"This is he," the minstrel said. "He is Sir Andrew Douglas of Maintree, bound for the crusades."

The priest emerged from his hut and eyed Sir Andrew up and down. "He is very young."

"I am old enough." Sir Andrew did not enjoy people discussing him as if he were a horse or a new servant.

"He has fire, though," the priest continued as if Sir Andrew had not spoken. Leaning forward, he felt Sir Andrew's biceps. "And strength. He will need both if he is to fight Sir Hugo de Soulis and Redcap."

"And Lady Marjory," the minstrel said.

"Aye, and Lady Marjory, a great clerk of necromancy and the worst of the three, for she hides her evil behind a sweet smile." The priest prodded Sir Andrew again. "Did she seduce you, boy?"

"I am no boy!" Sir Andrew protested.

"Did she use your body?" the priest insisted. "Yes, she did." He answered his question. "That is the way she has. Her seduction will weaken your resolve against her, as she intends."

"It will not!" Sir Andrew replied hotly.

"Perhaps," the priest held out his hand. "Give me your sword."

When Sir Andrew drew his sword and handed it over, the priest ran two fingers over the blade. "You have had it blessed, I feel."

"Yes," Sir Andrew agreed. He did not know what to call this strange holy man. "What are you, father? Franciscan?"

"What?" The priest threw Sir Andrew a look of contempt. "I am not of the Romish Church. I am of the true religion before the Roman Catholics came here."

Sir Andrew flinched. "Heresy!"

"Damn your heresy, Sir Knight! We were Christian before Rome ever poked its long nose into Scotland."

"You are of the Columban Church?" [2]Sir Andrew said.

The priest grunted and handed back Sir Andrew's sword. "Hold this," he said and slouched into his hut. He returned a moment later with a battered leather bottle and the most beautiful Bible that Sir Andrew had ever seen.

"Blessed water," the priest explained and uncorked the bottle. Taking back the sword, he opened the Bible, placed the weapon on top, and smeared blessed water on the blade.

"That will destroy any evil," the priest said, turned the sword around and repeated the procedure. He muttered words in a language that Sir Andrew did not understand but was neither Norman-French, Latin, Scots, nor English. [3]"You can't use this blade to fight against good." The priest ran his hands over the steel. "Understand?"

"I understand," Sir Andrew said.

"If you use it for the cause of evil, the power will rebound," the holy man said. "Be careful in the causes you choose."

"I have vowed to fight for good," Sir Andrew boasted.

"All knights make that vow," the holy man reminded. "Very few keep it, as their behaviour in war proves. Now drink some of this." He handed over the leather bottle.

"Drink it?" Sir Andrew repeated.

"You'd better be blessed inside as out," the priest said and watched as Sir Andrew obeyed. When the knight handed back the bottle, the priest emptied it into the palm of his hand and sprinkled water over him, muttering in that same strange language.

"Stand still," the holy man ordered testily. "I haven't finished yet."

Sir Andrew obeyed as the priest made the sign of the cross over him and intoned a blessing.

"Now you have a fighting chance, Andrew Douglas," the priest said. "Your path won't be easy, but you have the sword and armour of the Lord supporting you. You must supply the fortitude, bravery, and skill." His eyes filled with sudden compassion. "It will be dangerous, Andrew."

"That is truth, Sir Priest." Sir Andrew noticed the priest had altered his form of address. "It is my knightly duty to fight evil wherever I find it."

"God bless you," the priest said, making the sign of the cross again. "He reverted to Latin and then Scots. "May He supply you with all your needs for the tribulations that lie ahead."

Sir Andrew stiffened as a vision came to him. He was in a dark landscape of mud and pregnant grey clouds, with a strange green mist seething over the land. Evil-looking creatures with the bodies of men but the faces of pigs, with huge eyes and a long tube for a mouth, carried short, misshapen spears.

Where am I? Who are these creatures?

Sounds such as Sir Andrew had never heard filled the air. A loud, terrible clatter mixed with the screams of dying and injured men as a terrible steel carriage rolled forward of its own accord, emitting fire. Men, hundreds, thousands of men, and the strange, pig-faced creatures faced each other with fear and hatred.

One man faced him, staring as if in disbelief.

Sir Andrew gripped his sword, asking where he was. The man continued to stare, shouting in some strange language.

"Sir Andrew!" The minstrel held his shoulder. "Sir Andrew! Are you all right?"

Sir Andrew nodded. "I have just seen what hell is like," he said. "A terrible place full of monsters, where fire and mist kill people."

The priest nodded. "That must be what will occur unless you defeat de Soulis and his ilk."

Sir Andrew nodded, shaking after his encounter with hell. "I was mounted and riding forward. I did not know anybody, save for one man who faced me."

"Who was that man?" the minstrel asked.

"I do not know his name," Sir Andrew said. "I only know we were linked."

The minstrel held Sir Andrew's gaze. "You are shielded now, Sir Andrew, and your sword is blessed. What are your intentions?"

They began to walk back to the clearing, following the intricate windings of the path only the locals knew.

"I intend to find this demon, this Robin Redcap, and place a hard sword betwixt its head and its shoulders." Sir Andrew patted the hilt of his sword.

"And the others? Sir Hugo de Soulis and the woman?"

Sir Andrew considered for a few moments. "After I have dealt with the demon, I shall pursue Sir Hugo. I cannot kill the woman, for a true knight does not make war on women."

"Edward Plantagenet massacred women in Berwick and placed his female prisoners in cages, exposed to the mockery of the world," the minstrel reminded.

"Edward Plantagenet was not a true knight," Sir Andrew said. "He abused the knightly code with every action he took." He shook his head. "I shall not wage war on a woman."

"Lady Marjory is not a woman," the minstrel replied. "She is a vixen, a creature that manipulates people, and is guilty of every conceivable sin."

Sir Andrew closed his eyes, remembering his nights with Lady Marjory. He had not been a virgin when he arrived at Caercorbie, but his previous women had been passing fancies, while Lady Marjory was a more profound attraction. Sir Andrew smiled, recalling the sheen of her white skin, the feel of her under him and her soft laughter in his ear. "She is a woman," he repeated. "A knight does not make war on women."

"Come with me, Sir Andrew," the minstrel said. "Let me show you the reality of that thing you call a woman."

CHAPTER 23

⤫

Sɪʀ Hᴜɢʜ Cᴜᴍᴍɪɴɢs frowned when he saw Wally and his gamekeepers escorting Thomas into the house. He met them in the hall beneath the watchful portraits of previous Cummings. "What the devil is all this about?"

"We found this man poaching, Sir Hugh," Wally said. "He was burning the water on your private beat."

"The blasted stooriefoot," Cummings said. "Well, Armstrong? What have you got to say for yourself?"

"Nothing," Thomas said. "Guilty as charged."

"It's the police court for you in the morning, my man," Cummings said. "Night poaching and using an illegal method. We don't take that lightly here, let me tell you. Especially when city people come to steal our fish."

Thomas refused to defend himself, although he wondered how the factor found him so quickly and how Robert Powrie vanished so readily.

"I'll demand a heavy fine for you, Armstrong, and a custodial sentence if I can get it," Cummings sounded pleased with himself.

All the men looked around when Lady Fiona descended the stairs from the bedrooms above. She wore a quilted housecoat over her nightdress and soft slippers on her feet. "What's all the noise?" she asked sharply.

"Nixon and Anderson caught this man poaching, Fiona," Cummings said. "Bold as brass on my private beat."

"Good evening, Captain Armstrong." Lady Fiona emphasised Thomas's military rank. "It's all right, Hugh, I gave him permission to fish on our waters."

Cumming's face reddened with anger. "You gave him permission to poach on my private beat?"

"I gave Captain Armstrong permission to fish anywhere he liked in our land," Lady Fiona replied easily. "You men can leave us now."

"What?" Cummings spluttered.

"Leave us!" Lady Fiona repeated. She waited until she was alone with Thomas before slamming the door shut. She faced Thomas, her eyes burning with anger. "What the hell do you think you are playing at, Captain Armstrong?"

Thomas stepped back, as much in admiration as surprise. "Thank you for defending me, your Ladyship." He saw the genuine anger in her eyes.

"Defend you!" Lady Fiona repeated. "Good God, man, you deserve... "She controlled herself. "Why, Thomas?"

"It's a long story," Thomas said, not wishing to implicate Robert Powrie.

Lady Fiona narrowed her eyes. "Who told you about the private beat? Nobody outside the family ever fishes there."

"I cannot say." Thomas felt like a schoolboy standing before the headmaster.

"Powrie," Lady Fiona decided. "It was Robert Powrie, wasn't it?"

Thomas nodded miserably. Despite holding the king's

commission, he felt like a ten-year-old boy before Lady Fiona's relentless anger.

"Aye, I thought so. Roaring Rab Powrie causes more trouble than any half dozen men in the valley." Lady Fiona said. "He is a friend of my brother and a worse companion I could not imagine." She frowned. "I would not be surprised if he gave Hugh a tip you were coming."

"That would explain how Sir Hugh caught me so quickly." Thomas accepted Lady Fiona's assessment of his friend. "I've been a complete fool," he said, "and I've betrayed your trust, Lady Fiona. I hope you can forgive me."

"Yes, you have been a fool," Lady Fiona agreed. "And you have betrayed my trust, but Rab Powrie is a very persuasive man. He could beguile a loan from a taxman and sell salt water to a sailor." She shook her head, smiling. "You're not the first to fall for his charming smile, and you won't be the last."

"I was an infantry officer, for God's sake," Thomas castigated himself. "I should know better than to allow somebody to fool me."

Lady Fiona smiled. "Don't be silly, Thomas. Roaring Rab has been fooling people for a very long time. He has twisted Hugh around his little finger and enjoys nothing better than leading visitors and newcomers astray."

"I feel such an idiot," Thomas said.

"You'll know next time," Lady Fiona reassured him. She stepped back, smiling and shaking her head as her anger dissipated. "It's too early to be up, and I'm too wide awake to return to bed. How about a nightcap, Thomas?"

"That would be most welcome, your Ladyship, but I fear I have already intruded too much on your hospitality."

Lady Fiona shook her head. "You are not a married man, are you, Captain?"

"No, your Ladyship," Thomas said. "I left school and went to Sandhurst, and then the war started."

"How old are you?" Lady Fiona asked curiously.

"Twenty-five, your Ladyship."

Lady Fiona shook her head. "Younger than I thought, Captain."

"I cannot help my age, Lady Fiona."

"Nor can I," Lady Fiona said. "I am nearly twenty-nine. Come with me. Thomas, this old woman has things to teach you."

～

Sir Andrew lay face down on the ground with his arms spread in the shape of a cross. "Sweet Jesus, and Saint Bride, grant me the strength to defeat this great evil." He hugged the heather within the circle of thirteen ancient stones.

The wind whispered around him, lifting his blond hair, and ruffling his clothes. He lay still, praying out loud.

"I will be fighting evil, Lord. An evil that is impervious to steel. Grant me the fortitude to succeed and the strength to overcome the wiles and crafts of the fiend known as Robin Redcap."

Sir Andrew stood and lifted his sword, so the blade glinted in the moonlight, and the shadow of the quillons [1] made a cross pointing towards the distant bulk of Caercorbie.

"By St Bride, Sir Hugo de Soulis, I am coming to clean up your nest of evil."

He stood, staring towards Caercorbie while a distant owl hooted across the moor and then sheathed his sword and strode onto the causeway.

～

Wally Nixon stopped at the door of Blackhouse Tower and pressed two cartridges into the breach of his shotgun. "This place has been empty for as long as I can remember," he shouted. "Nobody's lived here since Adam picked apples in the Garden of Eden, so how is the door open?"

The crowd behind him roared, shaking their fists.

"And how did Peter Maharg see a light when he passed last night?"

The crowd shouted again, waiting for Wally to lead them. They were scared after losing two children; they wanted a scapegoat, a reason, and an end to their constant worry.

Wally continued, bolstering his courage as much as encouraging the crowd. "We know who the culprit is, don't we? Come on, boys!" Wally looked for moral and physical support before he acted, needing mass approval to cover him if he was mistaken. Raising his size twelve boot, he rammed it against the sagging door, sending it hammering backwards. "Follow me!"

Wally stepped inside the tower, holding his shotgun ready in case anybody lurked inside.

The tower was a hollow shell, with a vaulted ground floor that the builders had designed as a storeroom or stable and a turnpike, a circular staircase, spiralling to the upper floors. The ground floor was empty of everything except dirt, cobwebs, and a family of rats, which scurried to the furthest corner on hearing the invading humans.

"Nothing here!" Alison Bell reported, holding a broom handle like a staff. She was John Bell's aunt and had nearly given up on finding her nephew alive.

"They could be upstairs," Wally suggested, looking at the crumbling stone stairs.

"Lead on, MacDuff." Alison Bell gripped her staff determinedly.

"It's probably a waste of time," Wally replied.

Alison sighed and pushed him aside. "I'll go," she said.

"Yes," Wally replied, looking at the worn stairs. "You are lighter than I am."

Alison kept to the inside of the staircase, hugging the wall as she climbed to the next storey.

"Up here!" she shouted a moment later. "I've found them!"

"What?" Wally climbed the steps two at a time, with the others crowding behind him.

The children lay on the heavy if part-rotted, wooden floor. Wee John Bell was dead, with a pale, wan appearance and Angie Brown lay with her wrists and ankles tied, huge-eyed and petrified.

"It's all right, darling," Alison Bell said, roughly comforting. "We're here to make sure you come to no harm."

"Wee Tam's dead," Wally said, surprisingly sympathetic.

"There's been bad work here," Alison said, lifting the terrified Angie. "Terrible, awful work."

"There's been that all right," Wally agreed. "Look at Wee Tam. Somebody's cut his throat and bled him like a pig." He used deliberately harsh language to hide his tears.

"Who would do that?" Alison whispered, removing Angie's gag, and untying her. "Who did this to you, darling? Tell me, sweetheart. You're safe now."

Angie was crying, clinging to Alison. "A man," she said. "A big man and a woman."

"Who?" Wally grabbed the child. "Who was it? Tell me!"

"No, that will never do." Alison pushed Wally aside. "You're only frightening the girl. Let me." She softened her voice. "You're safe now, darling. Tell me who did this to you."

The girl was shaking, staring at Wally. "A big man and a woman," she repeated. "A monster."

"Do you know who they were?" Alison asked. "Have you seen them before?"

"I don't know," the girl said, burrowing closer into Alison's coat. "I can't say who they were."

"Strangers," Wally growled. "It's these bloody stooriefeet, I tell you!"

"Aye!" a wiry, long-faced man in the crowd shouted. "These bloody stooriefeet!" others growled, desperate to find a way of assuaging their anger and fear.

"Is that what the lassie said?" Somebody further back in the crowd asked, and within seconds the message passed from person to person.

"The stooriefeet! Little Angie Brown said the stooriefeet grabbed her. They murdered Wee Tam and were going to kill her."

"They're in Anton's Wa's!" Wally shouted as the crowd surged down the stairs. Wally pointed across the moor to the house. "That's where they are!"

"Let's get them!" a woman shouted.

"Burn them out!" Wally shouted, lifting his shotgun in the air.

"Burn out the stooriefeet!" The crowd's anger rose as they encouraged each other to violence. They surged out of Blackhouse Tower and towards Anton's Walls, shouting, waving their fists, and whipping up their courage with loud words.

Wally Nixon marched in front, "Burn them out!"

"Burn them out!" people took up Wally's chant, with Angie Brown nearly forgotten as hysteria took control. One man tried a shortcut and floundered in the Deep Syke, sinking thigh-deep in liquid mud. Only his wife tried to help as the others continued to march forward.

Eighty-strong, they headed for Anton's Walls, determined to seek revenge for the death of Wee John Bell. A thoughtful few had brought lanterns, which they lit as the light faded; the bold pushed to the front as the more timorous drifted to the back.

"Burn the stooriefeet!"

～

"Something's happening out there." Thomas heard the noise and moved to the window. "I can see a lot of lights on the slap."

"Let me see." Eleanor stepped beside him. "A crowd of people is heading this way."

"I wonder why?" Thomas asked. He shrugged. "We'll find out soon enough."

Eleanor opened the window, and they heard the shouting. "They're very loud."

Thomas sighed. "I'll go and see what the fuss is all about." He shook his head. "It's probably something stupid; it usually is when a mob gathers."

"I'll come with you," Eleanor decided.

"Better not, sister-of-mine," Thomas told her. "It could get ugly. Mobs have a way of acting without brains. A bit like politicians, if not quite as dangerous."

"That's why I'm coming with you," Eleanor told him. "Come on, Tom."

When they opened the front door, the mob was closer, dozens strong, as it marched along the track.

"There they are!" Alison shrieked. "Standing bold as brass!" She raised her voice to a piercing scream. "There are the murderers!"

"They're coming to see us." Thomas pushed Eleanor behind him. "Maybe a housewarming party." He grinned at his wry joke.

"Aye, maybe," Eleanor said. "They don't sound very welcoming."

Thomas stepped forward to the garden gate and raised his hands. "What's the commotion?"

"We've found the bairns!" Wally replied from the front of the crowd. He stopped twenty yards from Anton's Walls, with his followers shuffling to a halt behind him.

"Well done!" Eleanor shouted. "Are they all right?" She glanced at Thomas, who stepped through the gate and faced them. "Be careful, Tom."

"You too, sister-of-mine," Thomas said. "This lot is not friendly." He lifted his chin and raised his voice. "What do you want, Mr Nixon?"

"You!" Wally replied. "We've come for you!" He brandished his shotgun.

"Why?" Thomas did not move as some of the mob shouted threats.

"We're going to burn you alive!" a woman yelled as a thin youth threw a clod of earth that landed three feet wide.

"You murdered Johnny Bell!" Wally pushed forward to stand in front of the crowd. He faced Thomas, holding his shotgun in both hands.

"We did not!" Thomas denied. "What makes you think that?"

The mob were screaming now, edging closer as they encouraged each other with wild threats.

"Angie Brown told us!" Wally edged forward and eased back the hammer of his shotgun.

"I'm glad she's safe." Thomas ignored the implied threat and stepped closer to the crowd. "Where did you find her?"

Another missile spiralled through the air to bounce on the ground a few yards from Thomas's feet.

"Blackhouse Tower," Wally shouted. "Where you left her!"

"Why?" Thomas knew there was no point in arguing with a mob but thought Wally might have some influence over them. "Why would we do that?" He heard Eleanor step beside him and hissed. "Get back, Eleanor! This lot could do anything!"

"We're going to burn you out!" Wally shouted. "We're going to show you what we do to stooriefeet who murder our bairns."

Thomas began to reply when Eleanor put a firm hand on his arm and stepped forward.

The music eased through her mind, making her smile.

"Ce fut en mai
Au douz tens gai
Que la saisons est bele,
Main me levai."

"Walter Nixon," she said, with her voice clear. "You are leading a mob to attack us and our house." She moved forward, ignoring a hail of badly thrown missiles. "Are you going to shoot me, Wally?"

Wally raised his shotgun, pointing it at her. "Get back!" He tucked the stock against his cheek and closed one eye.

"Are you going to shoot me?" Eleanor repeated. "Here I am." She stood still and spread her arms to the side. "You can't miss from this range."

"Eleanor!" Thomas hurried to her side.

"Get back, Tom! I know what I'm doing!" Eleanor hissed urgently. She held Wally's gaze as the crowd stilled.

"You know who I am, Wally," Eleanor smiled, "and I know who and what you are."

"What?" The shotgun's muzzle wavered as Wally tried to break Eleanor's gaze. He failed, and she continued to stare into his eyes.

"We know each other, don't we?" Eleanor said as the music

entered her head, growing louder, dominating her thoughts, and controlling her words.

"Yes." Wally lowered his shotgun. His eyes widened.

"Go home, Wally," Eleanor ordered. "Go home and take these misguided people with you." She moved forward one slow step at a time until she was nearly nose-to-nose with the factor. She heard the rustle of wings as the crows passed her to perch on the garden gate, watching the crowd.

"I'll have that, my lad." Thomas stepped forward and took Wally's shotgun. He eased down the hammers, broke the weapon and extracted the cartridges. "We don't want you hurting anybody, do we?"

"Go home, Wally," Eleanor repeated and lifted her voice. "You've come to the wrong place, people. There's nothing here for you. Go home now and look after the child."

A farm cart rumbled behind the crowd. "Make way! Police!" Sergeant Learmonth jumped out and pushed forward with Martin at his side. "What's all this? What's all the commotion? Get home, or I'll arrest the whole lot of you."

The crowd began to disintegrate, some still glaring at Thomas and Eleanor, others shamefaced and embarrassed. One by one, and then in groups, the people turned away until only Martin and Learmonth were outside Anton's Walls.

Thomas put an arm around Eleanor's shoulders. "You were magnificent," he said as she sagged against him.

"Was I?" Eleanor asked, shaking with reaction. "I must have acted by instinct. I can't remember anything about it." There were no crows on the garden gate.

Martin hurried to Eleanor's side. "I've never seen anybody master Wally like that, Mrs Machrie. What did you say to him?"

"I can't remember," Eleanor said. "I honestly don't know what came over me."

Madness again, as with that ghostly knight, the erotic dreams, non-existent crows, and the crazed laughter. Am I going mad? I can't remember anything from the last few moments.

"Whatever it was," Thomas told her, "it worked. Look!"

Sergeant Learmonth ushered the final stragglers down the track, glancing at Eleanor from time to time.

"Come away in, Martin," Thomas invited. "I'm sure you have things to tell us."

CHAPTER 24

"Come with me," the minstrel said. "I'll show you Mossend."

"I don't know that name," Sir Andrew admitted.

"Once I show you the village," the minstrel told him, "you'll never forget it."

Caercorbie cast its gloomy shadow across the ground as the minstrel circled to the north, halted to check for any patrols, and guided Sir Andrew onto an ancient causeway across the moor.

"The old people made this causeway," the minstrel explained. "It leads to the Thirteen Stane Rig."

"The druids?" Sir Andrew asked.

"Long before the druids," the minstrel said, taking long, confident strides. "Walk where I walk and don't stray, or you'll sink in the bog. The Deep Syke is at its deepest here."

The path passed the rig and pushed on, arrow straight, to the opposite side of the moor, where a straggle of silver birch trees marked the beginning of more fertile land.

Sir Andrew smelt smoke before they reached the village and grunted at a stench he did not recognise. "What's that?"

"It's a combination of roasting and rotting human flesh," the minstrel told him as they arrived at the outskirts of what had once been a village. Not a single house remained standing, with waist-high rubble walls and patches of nettles revealing the destruction of a once-thriving community. Decomposing bodies lay scattered among the ruins, with a fur of insects feasting on the flesh.

"Do you notice anything amiss, Sir Andrew?" the minstrel asked as the knight gagged at the stench.

"Some raiding party has destroyed this place," Sir Andrew stated.

"Look again, Sir Knight. What do you notice about the dead?"

Sir Andrew frowned, still uncomfortable with a minstrel giving him orders. Minstrels were privileged people, able to pass between warring armies without molestation, but they were inferior in rank to a knight. "They are all elderly," he said at last.

"They are," the minstrel agreed. "There is nobody here under thirty years of age and few under forty."

"The men could all be at the war," Sir Andrew said.

"We are in a time of truce," the minstrel reminded. "And the women? There are no young women and no children."

"Not one," Sir Andrew agreed. "Why is that?"

"Your Lady Marjory and de Soulis have taken them," the minstrel replied. "There is a great evil in Caercorbie, Sir Andrew, greater than you yet understand, and Lady Marjory is the fountainhead."

Sir Andrew took a deep breath and touched the hilt of his sword. "By Saint Bride," he said, "she fooled me."

"She fools everybody," the minstrel told him. "She uses her charm and crafts to inveigle men into her confidence, uses them for her lusts and discards them. Did you look at her household knights and men-at-arms?"

Sir Andrew considered the question. "I did not," he admitted. "They were all the same, with similar appearances, looks and actions. Not one stood out from the mass." He shook his head. "I didn't speak to any of them."

"Nor they to you, Sir Andrew," the minstrel said. "They are hollow men. Lady Marjory has drained them of their souls."

"I don't understand," Sir Andrew admitted. "Is she a witch?"

"She was only a woman, but a demon has possessed her," the minstrel said. "The moment she used her crafts, you were doomed to succumb to her charms."

Sir Andrew crossed himself, praying. "I escaped," he reminded. "Has she condemned me to hell?"

The minstrel touched Sir Andrew's sword. "Did a holy priest not bless your sword when you took the oaths of knighthood?"

"He did," Sir Andrew said.

"And did a priest not make you drink blessed water?"

"He did," Sir Andrew agreed.

"That blessing saved your soul," the minstrel informed him. "Now look around you, Sir Andrew, and remember. When you face Lady Marjory, you see only the body of a woman, but the evil is inside, controlling everything she does."

Sir Andrew nodded.

Buzzing flies rose from the dead bodies while a family of rats emerged from the chest cavity of a half-consumed man, with things crawling from a putrefying eye socket.

"Remember this place, Sir Andrew, when next you meet Lady Fiona. She is a shell, with the demon inside her." The minstrel lowered his voice. "I do not know if anything of the original woman remains within the body, but, Sir Knight, if you kill her with a blessed blade, you will save her soul as you take her life." He placed a hand on Sir Andrew's arm. "You will be doing only good, Sir Knight."

"I understand," Sir Andrew said, touching the hilt of his sword. "By St Bride, I understand."

∾

Martin glanced around the comfortable, if austere, living room before accepting Eleanor's invitation to sit down.

"You'll have heard what happened," Martin said. "Wally Nixon found the missing children in Blackhouse Tower. John Bell is dead, and Angie Brown is still alive."

"We gathered that," Thomas said, pouring three glasses of whisky.

Martin tasted the whisky. "That's the real Mackay," he said, smacking his lips. "The surviving child, Angie Brown, said two people abducted her, a big man and a woman, and she mentioned a monster." He glanced at Thomas. "You're a big man, and Mrs Machrie is a woman, and as incomers, you are naturally the prime suspects."

"Naturally," Eleanor said. "Always blame the stooriefeet."

"Maybe they have cause." Martin fixed her with his level gaze.

"We didn't abduct any children," Eleanor denied hotly.

"Perhaps not," Martin said, sipping at his whisky. "But you may have inadvertently helped it happen. Newbigging was a quiet village when Jock Armstrong lived here," he made a gesture that included all of Anton's Walls, "but since you arrived, the old ghosts have awoken."

"What do you mean?" Thomas asked.

"I mean, you have disturbed them," Martin said. "An evil that has lain dormant for six hundred years has stirred again.

You uncovered the thirteen standing stones, found Sir Andrew Douglas's skeleton, and dug up de Soulis." He finished his whisky. "Any of these incidents could have disturbed the past, especially when combined with the rift the Great War caused. It would have been better to leave well alone, Mrs Machrie, as Jock Armstrong did."

Thomas poured more whisky into their glasses. "Maybe things are better out in the open, so we can deal with them once and for all. We've just fought the war to end all wars; let's end this evil as well."

Eleanor nodded vigorously. "Let's bring good out of badness."

Martin shook his head. "Only God can defeat evil. The rest of us can only dissipate it or send it back to hell, where it will reform and return in a different form."

"Let's do that, then," Eleanor said as Thomas poked life into the fire and added half a dozen lumps of coal. "Let's send it back to hell."

Martin looked at the infant flames that licked around the coal. "The evil is here," he said. "It is among us now, residing in somebody, or some people, who we speak to daily. We don't know who they are, and they may not even know the evil is within them."

"Where is it?" Thomas asked. "I have a Webley revolver upstairs, and I'm a good shot. I'd defy anybody to return with half a dozen bullets in him."

"You're a brave man, Captain Armstrong," Martin said. "But you haven't met a power like this before."

"Try me," Thomas challenged. "I fought Johnny Turk and the Huns for four years. I am not afraid of a walking skeleton or whatever it is."

"I am sure you're not, Captain," Martin said gently. "Unfortunately, the evil will not return as a skeleton."

Eleanor finished her whisky. "How will it return, Martin? How can we recognise it? Will it be a crow?!

"Did you see young John Bell?" Martin replied to Eleanor's question with a question.

"No," Eleanor said after a glance at Thomas.

"If you had, you'd notice how white he looked," Martin said. "Something drained him of blood."

"Drained him?" Eleanor repeated. "Redcap?"

"Redcap," Martin said flatly. "Redcaps have been among us for centuries, haunting the Border towers, waiting their chance to return. As I have said, the Great War opened the portal and allowed evil to thrive."

"Are you saying there is a redcap among us now?" Eleanor sought confirmation.

"Yes," Martin said. "I don't know who or where. It will have been living with us as a normal person, but once it saw the opportunity, it would thrive."

"Dear God." Thomas leaned back in his chair.

"Dear God indeed," Martin agreed. "This particular brand of evil comes as a threesome, a man, a woman and a demon, the redcap. Human blood gives the redcap powers, which he passes on to the man and woman. They are the fountainheads of evil."

"A threesome like de Soulis, Robin Redcap and Lady de Soulis," Eleanor said.

"You've got it," Martin said.

"De Soulis and his woman are long gone," Eleanor said. "Does that mean that three others have taken their place?"

"Yes," Martin nodded.

"Who might they be?" Eleanor asked.

"I do not know," Martin replied. "I'd guess somebody with power and influence so the redcap can use the evil most effectively."

"How can we tell?" Thomas asked.

"Look for a woman with a voracious sexual appetite," Martin said. "I do apologise for the language, Mrs Machrie."

"It's quite all right," Eleanor said. "Women probably know more about sex than men do." She glanced apologetically at Thomas, who looked at her in some surprise.

"A woman with an appetite for sex," Thomas murmured, thinking of his recent escapades with Lady Fiona.

"What else?" Eleanor asked, feeling the colour drain from her face.

"A powerful man," Martin replied.

Sir Hugh Cummings and Lady Fiona, Thomas thought. *Cummings is the most powerful man in the Wardlaw Valley.*

"Must they be together?" Eleanor asked as her heartbeat increased.

"No," Martin replied. "They might not even know each other, but both must have a connection with the redcap."

"How does it work?" Thomas asked, wondering how to approach Sir Hugh and what to do with Lady Fiona.

"Human blood gives the redcap power," Martin said. "He transfers some power to the man and introduces a demon into the woman, and they perform the evil deeds. Normally the redcap will ensure the man is safe from human weapons, steel, and rope."

"Including a revolver bullet?" Thomas asked grimly. "It's made of lead, not steel."

"I'd imagine so," Martin said. "Demons are clever creatures."

Thomas grunted, a professional soldier considering what other weapons he could choose.

"How about the female?" Eleanor asked.

Martin held Eleanor's gaze. "I am not sure about the woman, Mrs Machrie, but I believe she is the fountainhead, the vessel in which the demon's spirit lives."

Eleanor nodded. "Can we remove the demon from her, or do we have to kill them both?"

Martin looked away. "I don't believe that is possible. The demon will have intertwined itself in her. It will be part of her. We know the Gaels had a word for this demon."

"What word?" Eleanor asked, wondering who "we" might be.

"They confused the demon with a goddess or a great queen and called it Morrighan, a war-mongering female with an insatiable lust for men. The Arthurian tales had Morgan le Fay, derived from the same demonic creature." Martin sat back, cradling his whisky.

They sat in silence for a while. "How do we come into this?" Thomas asked.

"I am unsure," Martin replied. "I suspect it's because you're living in Anton's Walls, and you interfered by finding the graves and standing stones." He shrugged. "And you, Captain Armstrong, are a warrior, as de Soulis was."

"As was Sir Andrew Douglas," Eleanor said. "My handsome knight."

Martin's eyes were troubled as he viewed Eleanor. "Sir Andrew as well," he said and swallowed more of Thomas's whisky. "You, madam, are the lynchpin. You see the crows, understand the songs, and feel the atmosphere."

"I do," Eleanor agreed. *I feel it too well.*

"I say again that I think you're in danger here, Mrs Machrie," Martin said. "I've tried to warn you off on numerous occasions."

"You have," Eleanor agreed. "And you, Mr Crozier." She spoke levelly, holding his gaze. "What is your position here? Don't tell me you are only a local historian because I would not believe that for a second."

Martin smiled. "I am here to maintain balance," he said.

"Evil cannot be allowed to flourish. I try to ensure nobody allows it in, either deliberately or accidentally." He sighed, nursing his glass. "Unfortunately, Mrs Machrie, my warnings did not work, and you allowed it in. Now we must strive to put the genie back in its bottle and insert a cork."

"How?" Thomas asked. "You know more about this sort of thing than I do. I will fight it if you tell me how."

Martin stood up. "Thank you for the offer, Captain Armstrong. Once I devise a strategy, I'll let you know. In the meantime, I'll head back to Fairhope. My cart is outside." He smiled. "Good evening, Captain, and you, Mrs Machrie."

~

"God forbid I should fail you," Sir Andrew said to the assembled people in the forest clearing. After three weeks, he knew most people by name and habit, from Sim Armstrong to Ill Will, a straggle-haired youth from the hill country. Sir Andrew had been raised as a knight, a member of the elite warrior class who viewed others as inferior beings to be treated kindly but with contempt. Now he saw they were men and women, human beings who shared much the same dreams, fears, and tribulations as himself.

"Tomorrow, I ride to Caercorbie to face Sir Hugo de Soulis and his creature."

The people listened silently, and one woman brushed back her dark hair and smiled at him. Isabel Elliot stepped forward from the mass.

"You shall not go alone, Sir Andrew. Sim and I will join you." Isabel waited for the muted shouts of approval from the crowd.

"De Soulis and his creature have powers beyond steel," Sir Andrew said. "My sword and armour have been blessed."

Sim nodded. "Blessed armour or not, one man, however brave, cannot fight a trio of evil and a castle full of household knights and men-at-arms. We will help." He lifted his chin. "This is our land; we were here before de Soulis and before the Saxon invaders. We shall defend it against this evil." He smiled. "Most of us are experienced fighters, Sir Andrew. We defend this frontier against English incursion." He touched the haft of his spear.

Sir Andrew had learned something of the Borderers' tenacity. "I shall be proud to have you at my side," he said.

"I would like the minstrel to be with us," Isabel Elliot said.

"Dismay you not," Sir Andrew replied formally. "The minstrel will help."

"We should all pray tonight," Isabel said, "for we are embarking against forces darker even than Edward Longshanks and his legions."

Although some of the gathered host showed their disdain, for years of unremitting warfare had disillusioned them, the majority knelt on the damp grass and prayed for divine help. Sir Andrew joined them, leading by example.

Sir Andrew slept in his hut that night, knowing the morning would bring dangers. Before he slept, he prayed again, lying face down on the ground facing east, with his arms spread in the shape of a cross.

"Holy Father, grant me the strength to perform the acts necessary to cleanse this place of evil," he prayed. "I know I am unworthy of your trust, but I will endeavour to follow the path you have prepared for me."

When he stood up, he saw a woman sitting inside the doorway.

"Good lady." Sir Andrew recognised the dark-haired woman who had smiled at him in the forest clearing. "You'd be better with your husband."

"I have no husband, Sir Andrew," the woman said. "And you'll need more than spiritual help." She extended her hand. "Let me relax you for tomorrow."

"Who are you?" Sir Andrew asked.

"Does that matter?" the woman replied. "I am a woman, and I may not fight, and you are a lusty knight." She smiled, showing surprisingly white teeth. "A lusty knight needs a woman, and I want to help defeat this great evil."

"I would fain know your name," Sir Andrew said.

"Ellen," the woman told him. "Ellen of Netherhope."

Sir Andrew smiled. "You are a passing fair lady, Ellen of Netherhope, and right welcome in my bed." He pulled the cover aside and watched as Ellen removed her clothes.

～

"Well, sister-of-mine," Thomas said. "Now we know what we're dealing with, we must create a plan of assault."

"Yes, Thomas," Eleanor agreed, with her mind elsewhere.

"If this demonic possession is true," Thomas said, "it's obvious who the enemy is."

"Yes," Eleanor agreed again.

"It's Sir Hugh Cummings and Lady Fiona," Thomas continued. "You found out that they are of the same blood, and Sir Hugh is undoubtedly the most powerful man in the area."

"He is," Eleanor said.

"While Lady Fiona has a voracious sexual appetite," Thomas said.

"Has she?" Eleanor asked.

"She has," Thomas said. "She has seduced me on more than one occasion."

"You dog!" Eleanor gasped in surprise. "I have been trying to pair you with Sharon, the waitress, all this time."

"Sharon?" Thomas smiled. "She's a decent girl but spoken for."

"Oh," Eleanor said. "I didn't know."

"I checked as soon as we arrived. We have Cummings and Lady Fiona." Thomas returned to his subject. "We can also guess who the redcap is."

"Who?"

"Wally Nixon," Thomas told her. "As the factor, he knows the Cummingses well, and we have had multiple examples of what a nasty little toad he is."

Eleanor nodded. "Maybe," she said, suddenly desperate to be alone. "Sorry, Thomas, I can't talk about this now. I must go to bed."

As Eleanor mounted the stairs, one thought repeated itself in her head. *The Morrighan is within me. I have these erotic dreams every night; I wake up with blood on my hands, and her symbol of two crows guide me. The demon is within me.*

CHAPTER 25

ELEANOR WOKE WITH A START, staring at the ceiling. The covers had tangled around her legs after another restless night. She gasped for breath, wondering at the increasing intensity of her dreams.

Who was that man with whom I spent the night? It was not Sir Andrew; please God, it was not Sir Hugo! Dear God, the Morrighan is within me, and I am damned!

Kicking off the covers, Eleanor stood up, wondered anew at the blood on her hands and stepped to the window. A Huntsman's moon ghosted over the moor, highlighting the Thirteen Stane Rig, and emphasising the stark beauty of the scene. She looked down at herself, realised she was naked and shrugged, humming the song that sprang into her mind.

"Ce fut en mai
Au douz tens gai
Que la saisons est bele,
Main me levai."

I must have been too hot during the night. No matter, we are all naked under our clothes.

Leaving the bedroom, Eleanor walked downstairs and threw open the front door, allowing the night air to cool her. She took a deep breath, watching the moonlight play across the moor and listening to the lonely call of an owl.

"You'll frighten the horses dressed like that," Thomas joined her. "What are you up to, sister-of-mine?"

Eleanor glanced over her shoulder. "Watching the moon," she said. "Did I wake you?"

"No, Eleanor." Thomas removed his dressing gown and slipped it over her shoulders. "You'll catch your death walking about stark."

"No, I won't," Eleanor said, leaning into him. "You'll keep me warm. I was thinking we need a herb garden."

"You *need* to put some clothes on," Thomas told her severely.

Eleanor laughed. "I'm not cold."

"Get back to bed," Thomas said. "It's three in the morning."

"I know," Eleanor said, humming the song. "I've always loved the night."

"Since when?" Thomas asked. "When you were wee, you were afraid of the dark."

"Never!" Eleanor laughed, with the harsh sound echoing from the stone walls. Slipping off Thomas's dressing gown, she handed it back and returned to bed, emphasising the swing of her hips.

～

They left shortly after midnight with a thin wind whistling through the trees and stark branches reaching skyward as if in supplication to a watchful God. Sir Andrew led, with his twice-blessed sword bouncing beside his saddle and his face set like flint.

"Godspeed, Sir Andrew," Ellen of Netherhope lifted her hand in farewell. "May God grant you strength."

Sir Andrew looked down at her. "Live well, my lady."

"I am no lady," Ellen replied, "yet I am your woman whenever you want me."

"You are as much a lady as any I have ever met," Sir Andrew told her, held her hand briefly and released her.

Ellen watched Sir Andrew ride away, then joined the throng that followed the fighting men. All the men were armed, some carrying the ubiquitous Scottish spear and others more basic farming implements, sickles, flails, and sturdy staffs. For all their weapons' rustic simplicity, no observer could doubt the menace with which the host marched. Many of the men had taken part in the battles and skirmishes of the war with England and were used to bloodshed. They were not simple farmers marching in ignorance but frontiersmen of the most volatile borderland in Christendom.

Somebody started to sing, the words ancient, recalling bloody fights from centuries ago, and then only the steady tramp of feet disturbed the silence. They left the woodland behind and threaded onto the Windydoor Nick pass, climbing up the narrow path with a dizzying fall on their left and a burn churning white and sinister hundreds of feet below.

The men tramped in front, aware of the danger they faced yet determined to overcome the enemy. Equally grim-faced, the women lifted the hems of their skirts and picked up any weapons they saw, mostly fallen branches and fist-sized stones.

Sir Andrew dismounted to lead his horse, resting it for the ordeal ahead. He halted at the pass's summit, allowing the others to catch up. The darkness of Deepsyke Muir spread before them, punctuated only by the single lantern King Robert demanded the holder of Caercorbie showed to guide travellers across the slap.

"There is our target," Sir Andrew said softly. "It will be a hard nut to crack without siege engines."

"Hard indeed," Sim Armstrong said, resting on his spear. When he smiled, the scars on his face writhed like adders disturbed by a careless foot. "Do you have a plan?"

"I have," Sir Andrew told him. "We have a man inside the castle, ready to open a privy postern at dawn."

Sim nodded slowly. "The Good Sir James of Douglas used similar stratagems when he recaptured castles from the English." He raised an eyebrow. "Are you related to Sir James of Douglas?"

"Distantly," Sir Andrew said proudly.

Sim touched the scar on his left cheek. "I got this when we took Castle Perilous from the enemy."[1]

Sir Andrew hid his envy. "I was too young to take part," he admitted and swallowed his knightly pride. "I would fain ask your advice as a veteran soldier, Sim."

"Strike when the guard changes," Sim said, "and all is confusion inside Caercorbie, with men running to and fro and sergeants shouting orders." He grinned without any humour.

Sir Andrew nodded. "Nobody will notice one more man moving at such a time," he said.

"Everybody will be too eager to get to their post; they won't be concerned about a stranger," Sim tapped the butt of his spear on the ground. "I heard that steel cannot kill Sir Hugo."

"It cannot," Sir Andrew replied. "I have seen a man thrust a sword into him without causing an injury."

Sim nodded. "I have heard the like before. Pray that the priest's blessing strengthened your sword, Sir Andrew."

"I hope so," Sir Andrew replied. "By the blood of Christ and the love of St Bride, I hope so." He looked into the dark again. "Now, move forward, Sim, to get into position before dawn."

"We'll not let you down, Sir Andrew," Sim told him.

Still leading Kenneth, Sir Andrew marched ahead with his sword bouncing beside the saddle and the stars brilliant above. "I would have looked for a darker night," he said. "Clouds conceal the good as well as the evil."

"We will use whatever God provides," Sim said philosophically.

An owl rose as they stepped onto the road through the slap, soaring on ghost-quiet wings that alarmed the more impressionable men. Ignoring their unease, Sir Andrew removed the mail from his horse and slipped it on, with Sim helping to fasten the buckles.

"I had a squire once," Sir Andrew said. "And a hound and a hawk." He gave a nervous grin. "After this night, I may regain my hawk and hound."

Sim did not reply, for his world did not include such extravagances. "That's the last buckle, Sir Andrew."

"Thank you, Sim. Now I am ready to face de Soulis," Sir Andrew said. They had discussed their plan of attack, but Sir Andrew knew that churls were not dependable. "Do you remember what to do?"

"I do," Sim said and repeated his part.

Sir Andrew listened. "That's correct. Conceal yourself in the moss and wait for my signal," he ordered. "If you don't hear anything by half an hour after daybreak, then I am dead or captured, and you must return to the forest."

Sim nodded. "I understand," he said.

"God be with us all," Sir Andrew said and crossed himself. "Take care of my mount." Dismounting, he handed the palfrey to Sim and made his way towards Caercorbie.

~

The music came again, soft and melodious, and this time, Eleanor expected Sir Andrew to appear.

"Ce fut en mai

Au ouz tens gai."

"I missed you, Sir Knight," Eleanor said when the figure materialised beside her bed. "You want me, don't you? You think I am the lover you once knew."

Who am I? Am I Eleanor Armstrong of Edinburgh and Anton's Walls or a creature from the dark past?

Sir Andrew stood in the same position as before, with his right hand extended and a look of longing on his face.

"Do you want to share my bed?" Eleanor asked. "It's a long time since a man shared my bed." She smiled. "It's a longer time since a woman shared yours!"

She reached forward, but her hand slid through the memory that was Sir Andrew.

"You have the desire but not the means, Sir Knight," Eleanor said sadly. "And I have the means and the desire. We are out of time, Sir Andrew. Some things are never meant to happen."

On an impulse, she pulled back the covers. "I don't know how to help," she said and cringed as the music altered. One moment the soft Old French words of the love song eased into the room, and the next came the harsh Border accents of the *Twa Corbies*.

The words rattled around the room.

"In behind yon auld fail dyke,

I wot there lies a new-slain knight;

And naebody kens that he lies there

But his hawk, his hound, and lady fair."

Eleanor slid out of bed. "I am not that lady fair," she nearly shouted. "I am Eleanor Armstrong, and I am trying to help you, Sir Andrew!!"

In reply, Sir Andrew pointed a finger at her and slowly faded away, leaving Eleanor with an impression of terrible sadness and a faint hint of a green haze in the room.

What's happening to me?

"What's wrong, sister-of-mine?" Thomas hammered on the door. "Eleanor? Are you all right?"

"I'm all right," Eleanor replied, opening the door. "It was a dream, I think." When she glanced at the window, both crows stood on the ledge outside, looking in through intelligent, hard eyes.

No, she told herself. *It was not a dream.*

"What's happening to me, Thomas?" Eleanor asked urgently. "I feel as if somebody is inside me, tearing at my mind to get out." She stopped. "Or to take over."

"It was the war." Thomas held her arms. "It affected us all, sister-of-mine. It got me through shell shock, and now it's got you."

"Oh, God," Eleanor said, holding out her arms. "I hope we can rid ourselves of this nightmare soon, Thomas."

"We will," Thomas said, holding her tight. He closed his eyes, and the bombardment started again, the relentless hammer of German artillery pulverising the British trenches.

~

The men spoke loudly to conceal their boredom, telling bawdy jokes and discussing women and drink, as soldiers have done for thousands of years. Sir Andrew crept along the shadow of the wall, hearing the sentry's conversation without paying attention to the words.

Caercorbie had a single postern gate, hidden in an angle of the wall, with a barred iron yett[2] on the outside and a studded wooden door inside. Sir Andrew crouched a sword's length from the iron yett, checked the time by the moon and waited.

He heard a rustling above as two crows flew lazily past without stopping. A sentry coughed and dropped his spear to be roughly reprimanded by a sharp-tongued sergeant, and somewhere in the moor, an owl hooted.

The night grew darker as dawn approached. The stars faded, and a slight rain pattered down. Sir Andrew did not move except to touch the wheel pommel of his sword. He heard the soft stringing of a harp and stepped forward as the minstrel pushed open the iron yett.

"Sir Andrew?"

"I'm here," Sir Andrew said, crawling through the small gap. Both the yett and the wooden door were open, and he eased inside the castle. "Well, met, Sir Minstrel."

"Hurry." The minstrel glanced over his shoulder. "Evil stalks tonight."

Sir Andrew looked around. "Stay safe, Minstrel. You've done your bit."

When the minstrel made the sign of the cross and withdrew, Sir Andrew crossed rapidly to the gatehouse. He knew the castle's layout, how many men guarded the portcullis and the sentry's beats, so he avoided them easily. As he remembered, the steps to the gatehouse were unguarded, with a single spluttering torch providing poor light and casting shifting shadows across the courtyard.

Taking the stairs two at a time, Sir Andrew ran to the gatehouse door and pushed it open. The four-man guard stared as he burst in, so he killed one before the others realised what was happening. The second was in the act of drawing his dagger as Sir Andrew plunged his sword into his belly, and the third threw a dart that nearly connected. Sir Andrew killed him with a swift thrust to the throat, then finished the fourth, a thin-faced youth who cowered on the floor begging for mercy.

I have killed another four men.

A simple pulley and chain mechanism worked the portcullis, and Andrew threw his weight behind it. He knew the noise of the chain would alert the others in the castle, so he worked quickly, hauling the portcullis halfway up.

That's far enough to allow access. Look down on me, St Bride. Put your cloak of protection over this knight.

Dragging the dead bodies across the floor to jam the mechanism open, Sir Andrew dashed down the stairs to the gate.

"There he is!" a man-at-arms roared from the courtyard. "It's Sir Andrew Douglas!"

A group of men-at-arms gathered at the foot of the stairs, pointing at Sir Andrew as he ran toward them. Knowing he had no choice, Sir Andrew pointed his sword in front of him like a lance and crashed into them. While some flinched aside from the sharp steel, others tried to meet him with maces, daggers, or swords. Sir Andrew brushed them aside and gasped as a sword crashed against his chest, with the chain mail deflecting the blade but the force forcing the mail into his flesh. He smashed the pommel of his sword against the man's teeth and pushed on.

"That's Sir Andrew!" The shout came from the Knight's Tower as two household knights appeared, one in full mail and both carrying swords. Sir Andrew eyed them for a second, knowing they represented a more formidable challenge than the men-at-arms.

They can wait. Open the gate.

The gate sat before him, with a double wooden bar holding it secure and long bolts thrust into the stone slabs beneath. Without hesitation, Sir Andrew put his shoulder beneath the uppermost of the wooden bars and heaved. The bar slid from its slots and clattered on the ground.

He heard the household knights clattering across the courtyard and knew he would have to fight them. A spear thudded into the gate at Sir Andrew's side, shaking the wood. He turned as the spearman withdrew his weapon, poised, and lunged again. Sir Andrew used his sword like an axe to chop the head from the weapon, leaving the spearman stupefied with only a long pole in his hands.

The door shuddered as people on the far side rammed something solid against it. Sir Andrew lifted the second bar and fell back as a press of bodies thrust the door open and charged into the castle.

Sim Armstrong was first in, short spear in his hand and his scarred face determined. "Well met, Sir Andrew!" He looked around the castle as his men immediately engaged the garrison. "Where will I find de Soulis?"

"Over there," Sir Andrew indicated the Lord's Tower. "Come with me!"

The household knights had rallied the men-at-arms and led them against the invaders, roaring a battle cry.

"Let them fight!" Sim had taken charge. "If we kill the head of the dragon, the body will wither!"

Sir Andrew nodded, although he was desperate to try conclusions with knights of equal social class and training. The good Sir James of Douglas had not won renown by engaging men-at-arms.

"Sir Andrew!" Sim urged.

"Follow me!" Sir Andrew led the way to the Lord's Tower, gasping at the pain from his bruised ribs. A crossbow bolt hissed past him to thump into the body of one of his followers. Other bolts followed, most missing their targets. As the archers reloaded, the Borderers crashed into them with spears, staffs, flails, and captured swords.

The fight was swift and brutal, leaving the bowmen crumpled in pools of blood. A household knight ran towards them with a shield protecting his body and his sword raised. Sir Andrew stood on guard as his father had taught him, searching for weaknesses before he acted.

The knight ran with his head back, barely looking at his enemy. Sir Andrew waited until he closed, sidestepped, and thrust into the man's side, putting all his weight behind the blow. The knight screamed, dropped his shield and sword, and crumpled to the ground.

"Sir Andrew!" Sim shouted. "Leave them for others!"

I have bested a knight in fair fight. Now I can hold up my head in the company of my peers.

Sim pushed open the tower door and plunged inside with Sir Andrew at his heels, blood dripping from his sword and ready to kill.

CHAPTER 26

THEY SAT around the table in Martin's kitchen with a large fire spreading heat and mugs of sweet tea in their hands.

"I have worked out a plan of operation," Thomas said.

"I thought you had," Martin replied, slurping his tea.

"As I see it," Thomas continued, "the opposition consists of three people. Sir Hugh Cummings, Lady Fiona Cummings, and the redcap, who I believe is the factor, Walter Nixon."

"You may be correct," Martin agreed.

"What do you think, Mr Crozier?" Eleanor asked. "I hoped you might have some insight into these creatures."

"No more than you do." Martin shook his head.

"Can you not see into people's souls?" Eleanor asked.

"Not until they reveal themselves," Martin said. "Why do you ask?"

Because I think a demon has possessed me. "It might help identify Redcap," Eleanor said.

"I agree with Thomas's suggestion of Sir Hugh and Lady Fiona Cummings," Martin said. "They are the most powerful people in the area and distantly related by blood to de Soulis. I am unsure about Wally Nixon."

"How can we find out?" Eleanor asked.

"Visit his house," Thomas replied immediately.

"Do you expect him to have a sign on display?" Eleanor allowed her stress to speak for her. "Maybe a notice above the door stating: I am a redcap?"

"I don't know what to expect," Thomas replied. "But in war, one gathers intelligence about the enemy before one acts."

"Yes, Captain Armstrong," Eleanor said. "What do you intend?"

"A trench raid," Thomas said. "I'll visit his house tonight and see what's there."

"Take care, Tom."

Thomas grinned at her. "I always do," he said.

What would you think if you knew your sister was a demon?

❧

Sir Andrew had no sooner entered the Lord's Tower when he heard the screaming from below.

"Sim!" Sir Andrew shouted and ran to the turnpike stair. With his sword in his hand, he headed downward. The smell of raw blood increased with every step, and when he arrived at the lowest chamber, he saw de Soulis and Redcap bending over the metal trough. A body hung above, obscenely white as blood dripped from a gashed throat.

"When I drink this blood," Redcap grated, "I will have the strength of ten men."

"You foul fiends," Sir Andrew snarled. "I'll drain your strength with my sword."

Redcap looked up, dripping blood from his cap and his

mouth. "No steel can injure me," he boasted, showing his pointed teeth.

Without replying, Sir Andrew thrust at de Soulis, who sidestepped to avoid the blow.

"Don't you remember?" de Soulis laughed. "I cannot be hurt by steel or rope."

"My steel is blessed," Sir Andrew shouted and slashed sideways. His blade jarred against de Soulis's arm and rebounded without inflicting any injury. He grunted, hiding his disappointment.

The holy man's blessing did not work!

De Soulis laughed. "You cannot hurt me," he said. "I will leave my friend Robin to deal with you," he smiled as he slid from the chamber. "I am sure he will find a way."

Redcap stepped between Sir Andrew and the door, with his cap crimson with blood and his talons extended. "No mortal sword can kill me," he hissed. "And everybody I kill descends to hell for eternity."

Sir Andrew remembered that place of mud, fire, and metal monsters. "I've been there," he said, "and I returned."

St Bride, heed my prayers and guide my sword. Give me your blessing to remove this evil creature from our world and send it to hell.

Redcap crouched, his red eyes glaring balefully at Sir Andrew and his claws ready to slash. "You won't return a second time," he said and leapt forward.

Sir Andrew waited until the creature was in mid-flight and thrust forward with his sword. He expected a quick kill if the holy man's blessing worked, but Redcap twisted in the air, slashing with hooked claws. Sir Andrew was a fraction late in drawing back, and three hooked claws raked down his face, gouging deep and drawing blood.

"You missed, Sir Andrew," Redcap gloated, landed, and bounced sideways, spitting blood into the knight's eyes.

Sir Andrew said nothing as he slashed his sword sideways, depending on the long blade to prevent Redcap from avoiding the blow. This time Redcap lay on the ground, sprang up and grabbed Sir Andrew around the throat, pressing his talons deep into the flesh.

"In the name of God and Saint Bride!" Sir Andrew shouted, remembering how the Lord's name had unsettled the creature in their previous encounter.

Redcap gave a long screech and fell to roll across the slabs. Sir Andrew followed, stabbing with his sword as the creature twisted and turned.

"Steel can't hurt me!" It grated triumphantly.

"Blessed steel can," Sir Andrew said. "In the name of the Lord and Saint Bride!" He thrust for the creature's stomach, smiling grimly when the blade sunk deep. The creature shrieked, writhing as the blessed steel ripped through its flesh. "Die, you repulsive monster!" Sir Andrew twisted his sword, tearing into Redcap's vitals. He pulled the blade out and plunged it back in, ignoring the blood that spattered over him. "Get back to hell where you belong!"

Redcap screamed as Sir Andrew tore his sword sideways, removed it and thrust it in a third time before finally slicing off the creature's head. Redcap glared at him and opened its red eyes until the knight was looking into a fiery pit.

"Sweet Jesus, send this fiend to hell," Sir Andrew prayed, and Redcap vanished, leaving only a smear of blood on the slabs.

Sir Andrew gasped with a mixture of horror and exhaustion. He crouched on the slabs, listening to the breath rasping in his lungs and feeling the wounds on his face sting. Lifting a rag from the ground, he cleaned the blood from his sword.

"Sim!"

There was no reply. Two crows appeared, pecked at the pool on the ground, cawed and flew up the stairs.

"Sir Andrew!" Sim burst into the dungeon with blood dripping from his spear and a fresh wound on his chest. "Redcap?"

"Back in hell," Sir Andrew told him.

"Two men-at-arms delayed me." Sim glanced around the dungeon, shaking his head at the horror. "Where is de Soulis?"

"He ran when I fought Redcap," Sir Andrew replied. "I'll have to find him."

Sliding his sword back into its sheath, Sir Andrew left the dungeon and dashed upstairs to find the castle in an uproar.

❧

Eleanor parked the Crossley beneath a copse of trees on the outskirts of Newbigging, a hundred yards from Wally's tied house. "Are you sure about this, Tom?"

Thomas pulled the cap comforter over his head, smeared mud across his cheekbones and winked. "It's all right, sister-of-mine," he said. "I've done this sort of thing before."

"We're not at war," Eleanor said. "And breaking into somebody's house is against the law."

Thomas grinned as the familiar sensation of mixed excitement and fear churned inside him. "I don't think Sergeant Learmonth is as dangerous as the Prussian Guards," he told her.

"Are you certain Wally is not inside?" Eleanor asked.

"Quite certain," Thomas told her. "Martin spread a rumour that I am poaching again, and Wally's taken two of the gamies to ambush me."

"Be careful, Thomas. I'll be here when you come out."

Eleanor sat in the driving seat, watching as her brother turned into a soldier once more.

Thomas slipped out of the passenger seat, stepped into the shadows at the side of the road and moved silently towards Wally's house. It was larger than most in the village, a solid, three-bedroomed, stone-built villa that sat within a third of an acre of garden ground. Thomas moved to the back of the house, climbed the eight-foot-tall garden wall and lay still, searching for signs of occupancy.

He knew that Wally was unmarried but did not know if he had any guests or relatives staying with him.

When he saw no movement in the houses, Thomas crossed the garden, trying each window in succession. The ground floor windows were locked, but a handy drainpipe allowed access to the floor above. Thomas inched along a narrow ledge to find the bathroom window ajar. It was the work of a moment to force up the sash and enter the house.

Thomas paused in case the noise of his entry had roused anybody. When he realised the house was silent, he moved on, entering each room in turn. Wally kept his house pristine, without a speck of dust and each piece of furniture perfectly aligned with the next. Thomas found nothing to indicate Wally was a redcap. He returned the way he had come, carefully returning the bathroom window to its previous position before descending the drainpipe and hurrying to the Crossley.

"Any luck?" Eleanor asked.

"It was a washout," Thomas replied. "The place was as clean as a sterilised whistle. I didn't see anything a monk would not have."

Eleanor sighed. "We're back at square one, then."

"Nearly." Thomas forced a grin. "At least that's one man we can score off the list."

"Wally was our only suspect," Eleanor reminded.

"Blast the man!" Thomas said. "Why couldn't he be Redcap and make it easy for us?"

Eleanor started the engine. "Life is never as tidy as one wishes," she said. "Sometimes people one thinks are evil are not, and sometimes people one thinks are good harbour evil."

"That was very profound," Thomas said. "Take us home, sister-of-mine."

Eleanor eased them through Newbigging's main street, with the Wardlaw Inn looking forlorn in the dark and the Dryfe as battered as a third-rate boxer.

"Stop!" Thomas commanded suddenly, and Eleanor obediently braked.

"What's the matter?"

"There's Robert Powrie," Thomas said. "I haven't seen him since he abandoned me for Nixon and the gamies."

"What are you going to do?"

"Confront him," Thomas said, opening the car door.

"Tom! We've got enough trouble without you looking for more!"

"Aye, right." Thomas slammed the door as his anger mounted. He stormed across the road. "Robert! Robert Powrie!"

Robert turned at once with an ingratiating smile. "Thomas! I hoped to meet you!"

"I bet you did," Robert said. "That was a dirty trick you played on me the other day."

Robert's smile did not fade. "It was no trick, Tom. I told you we were poaching."

"You ran away and left me to shoulder all the blame." Thomas tried to control his anger.

"I warned you," Robert repeated.

Thomas's punch landed on Robert's cheekbone, sending the heavier man staggering backwards. He prepared for

Robert's counter as Eleanor ran from the Crossley and grabbed his arm.

"That's enough, Tom. Enough!" Eleanor stepped between her brother and Robert. "Get in the car. Now!"

Thomas waited until Robert backed away, mouthing threats before he followed Eleanor's advice.

"Silly boy," Eleanor said. "Do you feel better now?"

Thomas nursed his bruised and bloody knuckles. "Yes," he said.

Eleanor smiled as the music eased into her head. "Let me kiss it better." She lifted Thomas's hand and kissed the injury, licking away the blood.

CHAPTER 27

When Sir Andrew emerged from the Lord's Tower, he found Sim Armstrong's host fighting the castle garrison, with warriors gasping and swearing as they exchanged blows. Dead men lay alongside writhing wounded on the ground as Sim's men gradually overcame the garrison.

"Where's de Soulis!" Sir Andrew asked. "Has anybody seen de Soulis?"

"No!" Ill Will replied as he hefted a wood axe. He paused, panting for breath.

"He ran out the postern!" The minstrel appeared from the stables.

"He can't get away," Sir Andrew said. "He will merely start his evil elsewhere."

The minstrel nodded, wordless.

Sim finished off a cursing household knight with a thrust of his spear. "This fight is about done, Sir Andrew." He ran out the main gate, with Sir Andrew at his side and the others following.

"De Soulis has escaped!" The words ran through Caercorbie, passing from person to person.

"Catch him!" Men and women left the castle in a noisy stream, charging onto the moor and spreading out to search.

The moor looked empty, expanding in an ugly, undulating smear to the distant hills.

"That way," the minstrel said. "They always run that way." He nodded towards the northeast.

Before Sir Andrew could ask who always ran in that direction, Sim was striding over the moor, splashing through the mud, and avoiding the deep peat holes and sinister pools.

"He murdered my daughter!" a distraught woman shouted, with tears weeping from her eyes. "She's in the dungeon, stark naked and upside down."

Sir Andrew could only imagine the horror of making such a discovery. He heard the crowd's anger, mingled with grief at the losses they had endured. Sim's host set up a united wail, a combination of grief and bitter anger that made the short hairs at the back of Sir Andrew's neck bristle.

"I saw her," a gaunt-faced woman said shrilly. "I saw others there. Young women, girls, our girls, naked as babies and drained of their blood."

Sir Andrew closed his eyes, hating this truth that spread around the common people. He felt their anger rise, forcing away reason.

"They bled them into a trough and drank the blood!" the first woman shrieked. "They are monsters, demons from hell!"

"They are," Sir Andrew confirmed. "Redcap was a fiend. I needed a twice-blessed sword to kill him."

"Fiends!" The cry resounded from man to woman and back as the crowd lifted their makeshift weapons and shook them in the air. "Catch the fiends!"

"Kill them all," the gaunt-faced woman demanded. "Kill de Soulis and that hell bitch he calls his sister!"

Those people not already on the moor surged forward, chanting, "Fiends! Fiends!" as they hunted for de Soulis and Lady Fiona. The minstrel watched, nodding as Sim tried to organise the mob.

They needed little organisation. Decades of vicious warfare against English invaders had augmented intuitive martial skills, and Sim's ragged host formed a double line that swept into the moor. The younger and more agile men acted as scouts, probing into every hidden corner, thrusting eager spears into deep pools, and poking into the occasional copse and bush. Behind the outliers came the older men in a solid wave that would not stop until it achieved its objective. The woman made up the rear, encouraging their men and pushing on any laggards.

"De Soulis will be at the Thirteen Stane Rig," the minstrel said. "It was a sanctuary site long ago and attracts fugitives like dung attracts flies."

"The Thirteen Stane Rig." The crowd roared and headed in that direction. Local people, they knew the secrets of the moor and stopped at the quagmire around the ridge. A thin line of men circled the now recumbent circle, ensuring that de Soulis could not escape.

"There is a causeway," the minstrel said.

"We know the way." Sim led them, with Sir Andrew striding at his side. "De Soulis had us topple the stones, but we know the ridge."

The people followed, no longer a howling mob but grimly silent as they splashed over the causeway.

"There he is!" a youth yelled and fired a short hunting bow.

De Soulis stood inside the circle with a sneer on his face and his sword in his hand. He did not flinch as the arrow burrowed into the ground at his feet.

"The first churl to approach me will die," de Soulis snarled. "And the second!" He brandished his sword, brave at the end. "Who dares to face me?"

"I dare!" one young man shouted and advanced with his spear held, ready to thrust.

De Soulis waited until the spearman committed himself, then twisted aside, hacked off the steel spear point, advanced two paces and thrust his sword into the man's chest. When the spearman fell, de Soulis finished him with a simple jab at his throat.

"One less!" de Soulis shouted, recovering his sword. "Who is next?"

His bravery deserves a better cause, Sir Andrew thought.

"Come, Sir Andrew," de Soulis invited. "Let me die by a knight's sword, not at the hands of a low-born churl." He smiled, showing white teeth. "If your steel can penetrate my armour!"

As Sir Andrew stepped forward, a press of the people pushed him back. "No, Sir Andrew," Sim said. "We should kill this creature who has murdered so many of our women."

"I am best suited," Sir Andrew protested.

"You killed the redcap," Sim reminded. "We don't want it said that men from the Wardlaw Valley men needed outsiders to fight for them."

"I shall kill him," a saturnine man claimed. He stepped forward, swinging his flail as he had done a thousand times to thrash grain.

De Soulis lifted his sword, caught the hinge of the flail, twisted, and ripped the weapon from his attacker's hand. Before the man could move, de Soulis thrust into his throat and withdrew.

"Who's next?" de Soulis asked. "Or will you all run away, now?"

Two men advanced side by side, prodding with their long spears. De Soulis waited until they committed themselves, allowing the spearheads to land on his body, then calmly chopped the spears in half and killed each man.

"Neither steel nor rope can harm me," de Soulis gloated. "There is nothing you can do to hurt me."

Sir Andrew pushed forward. "You are a murderer, Sir Hugo, and a disgrace to the knightly code. Now make you ready to fight."

"I am ready, Sir Andrew." de Soulis suddenly looked very old and experienced. A shaft of sunlight highlighted his white surcoat with its three horizontal red lines and the bar sinister. "I gave you good cheer and hospitality, as a good knight should. You are the false knight, Sir Andrew, not I."

The people formed a circle, standing on the recumbent stones and watching as de Soulis and Sir Andrew tested each other, advancing, striking, parrying, and withdrawing. Sir Andrew knew at once that de Soulis was an expert. He handled his sword with a skill Andrew knew he did not possess and used tricks beyond anything Andrew had learned.

"We had to fight in the Templars," de Soulis informed him casually. "We fought the Saracens daily, or we died. I could kill you with ease." He laughed, high-pitched. "But I'll kill you slowly, Sir Knight, so that the churls will witness the death of their deliverer."

He lunged, halted as Andrew parried, altered the direction of his attack, and sliced at Andrew's leg.

"Too slow, young knight!" de Soulis gloated, withdrawing a step. "The commons are not smiling now."

Andrew fought the pain as blood wept from his wound. "If you were a Templar, Sir Hugo, you must be in your dotage."

De Soulis laughed, feinted, withdrew, and feinted again, then lunged and thrust his sword into Sir Andrew's arm.

Andrew knew he would have to strike quickly, or the loss of blood would weaken him.

Distract him. Use his vanity.

"You look young for a man of sixty," Sir Andrew said. "And you fight like a man half your age."

"Sixty?" de Soulis laughed again, throwing back his head. "I was past fifty when I left Acre, Sir Andrew. I was an old man even then."

Sir Andrew parried his next thrust, feeling the power behind de Soulis's sword. "How do you manage to keep your youth? Is it the young blood you drink?"

Sir Andrew realised a green mist had emerged from the ground, concealing the common people. He and de Soulis were alone save for Lady Marjory, who stood at the edge of the haze, watching with a slight smile.

"No, Sir Andrew. I drank the blood because I enjoyed the taste. Better than the finest wine. My familiar, Robin, needed human blood, not me." He swung for Andrew's leg, smiling when Andrew parried desperately. "Herbs and potions, Sir Andrew. Lady Marjory and I drank herbs and potions to prolong our lives." He thrust again, and Andrew parried desperately.

"You're learning, Sir Andrew. I could have taught you to be a passing fair knight."

"Passing fair?" Andrew leaned on his sword, panting as the blood flowed from the wounds on his arm and leg. He took a deep breath, knowing he had only strength for one last attack.

Is this where it ends? Will all my training and hope end by a rogue knight in the middle of a sodden moor?

"What ails you, Sir Andrew? Does defeat at the hands of an old man not suit your desires?" When de Soulis threw back his head to laugh, Andrew grabbed his opportunity and sprang forward, using his sword like a lance.

Surprised, de Soulis had no time to parry. Andrew's blade took him full in the throat.

"By Saint Bride and the power of the Lord!"

Andrew put all his force behind the stroke, combining the blessed blade with the name of God. The point emerged with a fountain of blood at the back of de Soulis's neck.

"I have a double blessed sword, Sir Hugo," Andrew shouted. "All your crafts are useless against the blessing of Holy Church!"

De Soulis died instantly as Andrew pitched forward over his body to land heavily, gasping with weakness from the loss of blood. He lay on the grass, unable to rise as Lady Marjory watched. The green mist thinned for an instant, so he saw the common people gravely watching with Sim leaning on his spear, his scarred face concerned.

"He's dead!" a dark-haired woman shouted. "Sir Andrew has vanquished de Soulis!"

The people ran forward as Andrew pushed himself upright, staggering for balance. For an instant, he was back in hell with those pig-faced men and the young warrior who looked so much like himself. The warrior wore drab clothing and stared at him as if searching for help.

"What do you want to know?" Sir Andrew asked.

The green mist thickened, and Sir Andrew saw they were no longer in hell, but in Caercorbie's dungeons, with the vaulted roof above and de Soulis alive and laughing. Yet it was not de Soulis but another man with the same evil emitting from him.

"What do you want?" Sir Andrew saw the desperation in the warrior's face. Suddenly he understood. "I know!" he said, "I can help!"

The mist faded away, and he was back on the Thirteen

Stane Rig with Sim watching, de Soulis's body before him and the crowd roaring imprecations.

"Boil him!" a woman shouted. "Turn him into soup!"

Somebody had carried the metal trough from Caercorbie, and now the people set it up in the middle of the ridge.

"Boil him!" they chanted. "Turn him into soup!"

Eager hands had ripped doors from the castle and transported them across the causeway. Men built a fire while the women stripped the chainmail and clothes from de Soulis's body.

"Boil him! Turn him into soup!"

"He's old!" somebody shouted, and Sir Andrew saw it was true. In death, de Soulis's youthful appearance slid away until he was an old grey man with sunken cheeks and wrinkled muscles.

The herbs only worked in life, Sir Andrew realised. *They gave the appearance of youth while the reality aged.*

"Water!" a woman shouted. "Boil him in bog water as he deserves!"

Men brought handfuls of brown, peaty water from the bog and slowly filled the trough until the women deemed there was enough.

My work is incomplete. Sir Andrew struggled with blood loss and the confusion inside his head. *What must I do before I am finished here?*

"Tip him in!" the women shouted and toppled de Soulis's naked corpse into the trough. "Boil him to soup!"

Sir Andrew watched as two crows circled above the recumbent stones.

~

Eleanor's heart pounded as she stood before the altar of St Bride's Church. The atmosphere seemed to press down on her as if God and his angels were watching through disapproving eyes.

It was years since Eleanor had been in church, for the horrors of war had scoured away much of her faith. Now every step seemed an ordeal, and the building stretched before her to the gloomy depths. Selecting a pew, she sat on the polished wood and wondered what to say.

I cannot remember how to pray.

"I need help," Eleanor spoke aloud, with her words echoing in the cavernous interior. She looked up at the closer of the two stained glass windows and saw it depicted a knight fighting a dragon. Although Eleanor had passed the building a hundred times during the past few months, she had never studied the details of the stained glass. Sitting on the hard pew, she concentrated on the window, realising that the knight was not St George, but Sir Andrew Douglas, with the coat of arms plain on his shield.

"Well met, Sir Andrew," Eleanor said. "I wonder what you would say if you saw me here."

"He would be grateful to be recognised." The voice boomed from the shadows, and the minister emerged. "I haven't seen you in here before."

Eleanor started. "I haven't visited before," she admitted.

"You are always welcome." The minister sat on the pew two rows in front of Eleanor. "People normally visit the kirk when they are worried or in trouble," he was an elderly man with deep-set eyes, "and you seem troubled."

Eleanor stirred uncomfortably. "Perhaps so, Minister."

"Do you wish to talk about it?" His smile was gentle. "Either here or somewhere quieter." The minister allowed the question to linger for a moment. "Or would you prefer me to leave you alone with Sir Andrew Douglas and Saint Bride." He indicated the second stained glass window.

"Saint Bride?" Eleanor repeated the name.

"Sir Andrew swore by Saint Bride," the minister said. "The original church was built in Sir Andrew's memory and dedicated to his family saint."

Eleanor nodded without seeking details. "May I ask you a favour?" Eleanor asked.

"If it is in my power," the minister asked.

"Could you bless me?" Eleanor nearly whispered the words.

"Of course," the minister smiled. "Do you want a general blessing, or is there something specific in your mind?"

"Something specific," Eleanor admitted, wondering how much she could reveal to a Church of Scotland minister.

"Do you want to tell me?" the minister asked.

Eleanor took a deep breath as her heartbeat increased further. "I think I might be possessed," she said.

The minister looked surprised. "I did not expect to hear that," he admitted. "What makes you think something possesses you?"

"I have strange dreams and sometimes see crows that don't exist." Eleanor knew her words sounded weak. She could not tell the whole story.

"Ah." The minister nodded and suddenly frowned. "Mrs Machrie, isn't it? From Anton's Walls?"

"That's right," Eleanor admitted.

The minister smiled. "You were a nurse during the late war, I believe."

"I was," Eleanor said.

"You'll have seen some terrible things," the minister continued. "Enough to give anybody nightmares."

Eleanor grabbed at the straw. "I hope you are correct, Minister, but can you bless me anyway for my peace of mind?"

The minister smiled gently. "Of course, Mrs Machrie. Come with me to the font."

Eleanor braced herself, half expecting to feel something when the minister dabbed her with water and intoned the sacred words. The water was cold on her forehead.

"Is that it?" she asked when he finished.

"That's you blessed," the minister confirmed. "Come back if the dreams continue." He shook his head. "Tell me, Mrs Machrie, what you thought possessed you?"

"A redcap," Eleanor said unguardedly.

"A redcap? A powrie?" the minister said. "They haven't been heard of for a few hundred years."

Eleanor flinched. "A what? What did you call it, Minister?"

"A powrie. That's the other name for a redcap."

"Oh, dear God in heaven!" Eleanor stepped back. "We've suspected the wrong man!"

"I beg your pardon?" the minister asked, but Eleanor had run from the church.

CHAPTER 28

ANDREW HAD NEVER SEEN A MORE terrible sight than the
yelling mob surrounding the trough, poking sticks at the
contents. The murky water slowly bubbled and boiled,
dissolving de Soulis's body into a greasy mess in which white
bones floated.

The mob laughed, jeering at the end of their tormentor, yet
Sir Andrew sensed the underlying grief. The laughter was
high-pitched, nearly hysterical, as people grieved their missing
and murdered children.

The woman whose daughter hung in the dungeon dipped a
wooden cog into the trough. "You drank my daughter," she said,
"and now I will drink you!" She swallowed a mouthful of the
de Soulis soup. "Like chicken," she said, laughing through her
tears. "Or maybe pork."

Another woman stepped forward, using de Soule's helmet
as a drinking vessel. "I lost a daughter and a fine brave son to
this monster," she said and drank deeply. "You taste better than
you acted, de Soulis!"

Sir Andrew saw women in tears and men cursing at the

liquid remains of the man who had tormented them for so long. He felt his strength draining yet believed his wounds were not sufficiently serious to kill him. Cleaning his sword, he slid it into its scabbard and looked around.

I have to finish this quest by killing Lady Marjory, yet I swore a sacred oath never to hurt a woman. If I leave her, she may begin the horror again, but I will lose my knightly honour if I kill her.

Sir Andrew realised the noise had diminished. When he looked up, the green mist had returned, and Lady Marjory was watching him.

Lady Marjory smiled. "You have killed my brother and his familiar, Sir Knight, but you have not killed me."

Andrew looked around at the people. They were dim shapes at the edge of the mist, concentrating on the trough and ignoring him and Lady Marjory.

"They cannot see me," Lady Marjory said. "I have ensured that you and I are alone, Andrew."

"Have you used your crafts to put an enchantment on me?" Andrew asked.

"I have," Lady Marjory told him, with a smile he knew very well.

"What have you done to me?" Andrew asked.

"Weakened you," Lady Marjory told him. She stepped closer, moving with her habitual gliding motion. "You are a passing good knight, Sir Andrew." She smiled down at him as he crumpled to the ground. "But your knightly skills are no match for my craft." Lady Marjory straddled his body, smiling.

"You are dying, Sir Knight, and nobody knows you are here. Your faithful hound is now part of the pack, hunting in the hills; your hawk is soaring, searching for the wild birds of the moorland and I, your lady, have already chosen another mate."

Sir Andrew tried to push himself upright. "I am not dead yet," he said. Lady Marjory stepped back and waved her hand. A fail dyke rose, a green barrier between the knight and the commons. Sir Andrew heard the music and used the dyke as a lever to stand. The recumbent stones were sleeping sentinels in the gloom. He saw Lady Marjory smiling at him, and other figures emerged from the mist. One was a man, tall and dressed in a drab uniform but with the face and bearing of a warrior. Sir Andrew and the stranger looked at each other, recognising a bond but neither knowing what it was.

We've met before, Sir Andrew realised. *We've met in hell. I know you, my strangely attired companion.*

The second man was the elderly priest who had blessed him in the forest clearing. He carried his ornate Bible and a rough-hewn wooden cross while benevolent concern filled his eyes. The priest lifted the cross above his head and spoke in that strange language that Andrew had not understood but now heard clearly.

It is Brythonic, Sir Andrew said. *The language people spoke in this area before the Angles and Saxons first invaded.*

The third man was the minstrel, who played a soft tune on his harp.

Lady Marjory laughed, her voice harsh. "You cannot save him," she mocked. "I poisoned the edge of Hugo's sword, and by now, the venom is deep within his body."

"You speak truth," the minstrel said. "We cannot save Sir Andrew. His duty is done, and he will be remembered as long as men speak of chivalry and knightly valour." He strummed his harp, so the golden music eased across the clearing. "Nor can you save yourself, my lady."

"Nobody can see me," Lady Marjory gloated. "I will walk through the churls, find another knight and show him how to call a redcap from the pits."

"We can see you," the minstrel said and ran his fingers across the golden strings of his harp once more. The music increased, thinning the mist, so the dull green lightened, and vague figures appeared clustered around the trough.

Lady Marjory put a hand inside her green smock, removed a small bottle and threw it on the ground. Green smoke gushed out, forming a barrier around her.

The minstrel smiled and strummed his harp again, altering the green mist to a faded gold that closed around Lady Marjory like a mantle. She ran, clawing at the haze to see her path, and stepped into the bogland surrounding the ridge.

"You are in the Deep Syke," the minstrel told her. "Once it grips you, there is no escape."

"Help me!" Lady Marjory yelled. "I am a lady of gentle blood." She floundered on, with every step taking her deeper into the mire. "I am Lady Marjory de Soulis! I cannot die like this!"

I must help a lady in distress.

Sir Andrew stepped forward, staggered, recovered, and stretched a hand towards Lady Marjory. The priest shook his head and held the cross between them.

"Your eyes deceive you, Sir Andrew. That is no lady. The thing within her devoured any humanity many years ago. Let the Deep Syke take it."

The minstrel eased Sir Andrew aside and stepped onto the causeway, watching Lady Marjory as she struggled. Lady Marjory's youth melted away, revealing an aged woman with a deeply lined face and a withered body.

"No!" Lady Marjory shouted. "I cannot die. I will be back."

"I will be waiting when you do," the minstrel said, sitting on the causeway. He played a soft tune on his harp, with his fingers gliding across the strings and the notes golden across the moor. He watched the mud close over Lady Marjory's head, with a few bubbles rising to show where she had been.

"I'll be waiting," the harper repeated softly.

As Sir Andrew crumpled to the damp ground, the priest knelt over him, murmuring. He pressed his Bible against Andrew's wounds.

"You are dying, my young friend," the priest said. "You died fighting evil, and the gates of heaven are open for you." He said a prayer. "Rest easy now, for the goodness in your spirit will remain."

"Who is that man?" Andrew pointed to the warrior in drab khaki. "I have seen him before."

"He will continue your fight," the priest told him. "Your spirit will enter him when you depart."

"My spirit will live on?"

The priest nodded. "The spirit of good can never die," he said. "Close your eyes now, Andrew. We will ensure you have a burial as befits a crusader."

"A knight can ask no more than to die fighting for the right," Sir Andrew said.

The minstrel joined them with the harp under his arm. "Has he gone?"

"He has gone," the priest agreed.

The tall man in the drab uniform nodded with sudden understanding.

"I remember you," he said.

"You'll see us later," the minstrel said and began to sing.

"As I was walking all alane,
I heard twa corbies making a mane;
The tane unto the t'other say,
Where sall we gan and dine today?"

~

"Tom!" Eleanor ran into the outhouse that Thomas had converted into a workroom. "Tom, I know who the redcap is!" She pulled him away from a lathe. "Listen, Tom!"

"Calm down, sister-of-mine!" Thomas took hold of her shoulders. "Calm down and tell me the whole story."

"It's Robert Powrie," Eleanor said. "Powrie is another name for a redcap!"

"Powrie is a common enough name," Thomas said. "Start from the beginning."

Taking a deep breath, Eleanor related most of her experiences in the church. She did not mention her fears about demonic possession.

"Well, now," Thomas said when she finished. "That makes sense. We know Robert Powrie is charming, and Lady Fiona herself told me he was a troublemaker."

"And he knows Sir Hugh," Eleanor nearly shouted.

"They are old friends, according to Lady Fiona," Thomas said.

"What are we going to do, Tom?" Eleanor asked.

Thomas stepped back from his workbench. "*We're* not going to do anything, Eleanor. *I* am going to look inside Robert's house. I might not find anything, but it's worth a try."

"Be careful, Tom," Eleanor said. "More than your life is at stake here."

Thomas forced a smile. "I know, Eleanor. Something else is troubling you."

"No." Eleanor shook her head in emphatic denial. "I'm fine. When will you visit Robert Powrie's house?"

Thomas considered for a moment. "I'd like to go there tonight," he said. "I wish I could arrange a diversion to get him out of the house."

Eleanor's heartbeat increased. "I can do that," she said. "It's not right that you should take all the risks." The music coursed through her head.

"Ce fut en mai
Au douz tens gai
Que la saisons est bele,
Main me levai."

"How are you going to do that?" Thomas asked.

Eleanor gave her new harsh laugh. "Trust me, Thomas. I know how to lure Mr Powrie!" She laughed again, with excitement overpowering her nervousness as she anticipated the night ahead.

∽

"Sir Andrew is dead." The cry spread from person to person. "The good knight has died."

"Alas, for shame, he died while we feasted."

The commons left the metal trough and crowded around Sir Andrew's body. Nobody mentioned the fail dyke. "How did he die?" a woman asked. "He was sore wounded, but not grievously."

"Necromancy and foul deeds," the minstrel said. "The creatures poisoned Sir Hugo's sword."

Ellen of Netherhope cradled her belly. "Sir Andrew will live on through his son," she said. "I will bring him up to be a man like his father."

The minstrel nodded. "What will you call him?"

"Andrew Thomas," the woman said.

"Andrew Thomas Armstrong," the minstrel approved. "That is a man's name. He will breed a race of men, virile and brave like his father, and beautiful, strong women like his mother."

Ellen of Netherhope nodded. "I will bring him up as a warrior."

"Enough!" Sim took charge. "Let the dead look after the dead. We will bury Sir Andrew later. "I want Caercorbie Castle slaked. Level it to the ground so not a vestige remains. I want even the name forgotten, and neither man nor woman will speak of this place again. Let the grass grow over the thirteen stones, and the name of the ridge shall be expunged from our memory. Henceforth it is the Druid's Ridge."

One man lifted a crossbow, fitted a bolt, and fired at the two crows that watched from the battlements. The bolt hissed wide, and the crows lifted their wings and flapped slowly away.

CHAPTER 29

Robert Powrie looked puzzled as he strode along the High Street. "I got your note," he said, smiling.

"If you didn't," Eleanor told him, "you would not be here."

She stood outside the Wardlaw Inn, wearing her second-best dress under a smart coat and hat. "Shall we go inside? I've booked a table for two, and it would be a shame to waste it."

Sharon ushered them to a table. "I've put you beside the window, Mrs Machrie," she said. "It's the best seat in the hotel."

"Thank you, Sharon," Eleanor replied. She heard the music inside her head and allowed herself to drift closer to Powrie as they sat down, with her leg inadvertently brushing against his.

"I was surprised to read your note," Powrie said. "Your brother and I are no longer on the best of terms."

"Thomas is big enough and ugly enough to look after himself," Eleanor said lightly. "I thought you and I jogged along rather well the last time we met."

"I thought so, too," Powrie agreed.

Eleanor moved her foot, touching Powrie's. "Tell me about

yourself, Robert. You are a man of great influence in Newbigging, aren't you?" She looked up as Sharon placed menus in front of them. "Thank you, Sharon."

"No." Powrie laughed. "I'm only a building contractor."

"You did a good job at Anton's Walls," Eleanor said. "Thomas said he'd never seen as much work done as well in such a short time." She smiled into his eyes. "It was almost like magic."

Powrie shook his head. "No magic. Only graft and knowing what we are doing."

Eleanor probed further. "It seemed like magic to us," she said. "As if you called on some hidden powers." She held his gaze, trying to see inside his head. She let that idea grow while they selected their meal.

Powrie took the initiative when Sharon walked away. "Why did you want to see me?" he asked.

"Initially, to apologise for Thomas's behaviour." Eleanor had expected the question. "The war affected him, you see, and he can be a little hot-headed at times."

"He was upset," Powrie said and smiled. "It was worth the punch if it meant I meet you alone."

Eleanor met his smile. "I heard you were charming," she said and laughed.

That's not my laugh.

The music returned, increasing in volume inside her head.

"Ce fut en mai
Au douz tens gai
Que la saisons est bele,
Main me levai."

Powrie looked bewildered when Eleanor began to hum the song and then sang the words, still holding his gaze.

"I haven't heard that song for a long time," Powrie said.

"You remember it, though, don't you?" Eleanor asked. "When did you last hear it?" She sang the second verse, watching Powrie's reaction.

"En un vergier
Clos d'aiglentier
Oi une viele;
La vi dancier
Un chevalier
Et une damoisele."

"Many years ago," Powrie said.

"Who sang it?" Eleanor asked, leaning forward across the table.

"A lady I knew." Powrie's smile transformed into something else as light dawned behind his eyes.

"Was her name Marjory?" Eleanor asked. The two books that mentioned Lady de Soulis had only used her title, but the name slipped from Eleanor's tongue without effort.

"Yes, it was." Powrie half rose from his seat.

"Marjory de Soulis," Eleanor said and completed the song. "Six centuries ago, and just a few moments." She smiled. "I'm back, Robert or Robin, if you prefer!"

Powrie's face changed, broadened, with his nose becoming short and broad, his eyes altering colour to a deep red and his mouth narrowing to a slit armed with a double row of sharp teeth.

The music strengthened, and Eleanor felt a surge of power. With a little concentration, she saw Powrie's features change back to normal.

"Now we both recognise who we are," Eleanor said, "you can help me."

Powrie smiled. "What can I do for you, my Lady?"

"Tell me why I can't gain complete control. I am within this body, yet the owner repels me repeatedly." Eleanor frowned. "I can feel her struggling even as I speak."

Powrie chewed his underdone steak, blood dribbling from the corners of his mouth. "That knight, Andrew Douglas, stands guard with his twice-blessed sword."

Eleanor nodded. "He gave us far too much trouble. If we remove him, can we return in full?"

"Yes," Powrie gave a simple reply.

The music increased in volume inside Eleanor's head. "I wonder if Lady Janet Douglas would like her ancestor back at Maintree?"

Powrie smiled. "I am sure she would," he said. "You already know the lady, and removing the knight will open the gate once more. Rather than the odd stray infant, we can drain the entire valley."

"I'll write to Lady Janet this evening," Eleanor said.

Powrie's smile broadened. "You can do better than that," he told her. "Use the telephone."

"Lady Janet has such a thing, but we don't," Eleanor told him.

"The hotel does." Powrie's smile broadened.

∽

Thomas checked the street, aware that people could be looking out of their windows. Although it was only nine in the evening, Newbigging was quiet, for the inhabitants rose before dawn, worked hard, and returned home early. The street was empty as Thomas casually walked past Robert Powrie's house.

I hope Eleanor is safe with Powrie. I'll be as quick as possible.

Powrie's house was at the end of a terrace, with a lane at the side. Thomas stepped into the lane, glanced around, and climbed over the wall.

That's the easy part done.

Thomas remained still for a few moments and then padded to the back door.

The door was locked, and the windows closed, but Thomas was in no mood for subtleties. Lifting a rock from the garden, he smashed a pane in one of the lower windows, slipped an arm inside, slid the catch open and dragged up the lower half.

Thomas found Powrie's house untidy, with the bed unmade and a pile of clothes strewn over the floor. Powrie used the second bedroom as a store for his considerable collection of tools, which he maintained in good condition. Thomas found nothing untoward in either of the two bedrooms, while Powrie did not appear to have used the living room for weeks.

Powrie lives in the kitchen and the bedroom, Thomas told himself. *I hope this is not another washout.* He checked his watch, thinking of Eleanor alone with Powrie, told himself she was a grown woman and used to handling men, and continued to search.

The kitchen was in a worse mess than the bedroom, with a pile of unwashed dishes in the sink and a litter of crumbs on the work surfaces and the floor.

Is Powrie trying to attract vermin? Thomas asked, shaking his head. However, a dirty house did not mean Powrie was a redcap. With his hope fading, he noted the half-dozen empty wine bottles on the table, remembered Powrie's liking for red wine and grunted.

Maybe he's innocent, and I'm wasting my time.

Thomas opened the pantry door and stepped inside. The pantry was shallower than he expected, with the walls on two shelves empty and the third stacked with bottles of red wine.

Thomas frowned. *None of these bottles has a label,* he realised and saw two full demijohns at the back. *Does Powrie make wine?*

On an impulse, Thomas lifted down the closest demijohn to inspect the contents. Removing the cork, he dipped a finger into the wine.

That's not wine. That's blood!

Blood! Robert Pirie drinks blood.

Thomas stood still for a moment as the implications hit him. Eleanor was correct, and Powrie was the redcap, living amongst them like an ordinary man.

That's the threesome; Sir Hugh, Lady Fiona, and Robert Powrie. Now I'll have to rescue Eleanor before the creature attacks her.

As Thomas replaced the demijohn, he saw a button at the back of the pantry. Unable to resist the temptation, he pushed to see a door open on the side wall.

I thought this place was too small.

Striking a match, Thomas stepped through the door. The faint light gleamed on something white lying on the floor and reflected on a pair of gleaming red eyes.

"Jesus!" Thomas blasphemed, stepped back, assumed a fighting crouch, and prepared to defend himself. The match flickered and died, leaving him in the silent dark. He struck another, saw a stubby candle on a shelf and lit the wick, shielding the infant flame with his hand until it grew and spread yellow light.

"Dear God," Thomas said out loud as he looked around the hidden room. The walls were of bare plaster, painted red, the same as the ceiling and floor. Standing against the far wall was the most hideous statue that Thomas had ever seen, a hermaphroditic human with wings and the head and feet of a goat. Its right hand was raised, with two fingers pointing upward, and obscure esoteric symbols decorated the body. The eyes were of precious rubies, reflecting the candlelight.

"Dear God save us all," Thomas breathed. "What is that thing?" He stared at it for a few seconds, shocked by the blasphemy, and then realised the room contained other horrors.

A red blanket hung from two nails on the left. With one eye on the hideous statue on the back wall, Thomas unhooked the blanket and stepped back when a skeleton grinned at him.

"You'll be Hugo de Soulis," Thomas murmured. "Robert Powrie must have carried you here." He grunted when he saw the red splashes on de Soulis's bones and the sticky pool at his feet.

"Blood," Thomas said. "I presume that Powrie has been performing some disgusting rite here." He stepped back. "Well, Sir Hugo, Powrie, Sir Hugh, the amorous Lady Fiona, and Uncle Tom Cobley and all, your pranks won't work. We'll stop this great evil from returning."

Eleanor is alone with this creature! Thomas replaced the blanket, gave the statue a soldier's farewell, "Goodbye and bugger you," and swiftly left the house.

～

"Where shall we bury him?" Sim asked as the people crowded around Sir Andrew's dead body. "Here?" He indicated the grassy Thirteen Stane Rig. "Or should we transport him back to Maintree?"

"Neither," the minstrel instructed. "After we've slaked Caercorbie, we will bury Sir Andrew beneath the dungeons. He will keep guard."

The priest nodded. "Sir Andrew wished to go on crusade yet abandoned his hopes to help rid us of a great evil. We will bury him as befits a crusader." He hardly raised his voice, yet everybody present heard him. "For as long as Sir Andrew Douglas lies undisturbed, the evil cannot return. He is the Guardian of the Dark Slap." He waited for the murmur of approval to die down and held up a hand. "Furthermore, I will petition the crown to build a church in the Wardlaw Valley dedicated to St Bride, Sir Andrew's favoured saint."

The people murmured their agreement, hefted their tools, and marched purposefully towards Caercorbie, determined to destroy the castle and remove even the memory of the great evil from the land.

CHAPTER 30

"You were right," Thomas said. "Robert Powrie is Redcap."

Eleanor nodded, fighting the music that still echoed through her head. She felt confused, with a mixture of emotions and images battling for supremacy.

They sat in a nearly empty Dryfe Inn, with the rain pattering against the window.

"I know," Eleanor said.

Who am I? Am I me, or am I this thing inside me fighting for control? She forced a smile. "I have something to tell you, Tom."

"What's that, sister-of-mine?"

How can I tell him I might be possessed? The war has already damaged him; how will he react?

"Is it true?" Martin stamped to their table before Eleanor could speak. "Tell me it's not true."

"Is what true?" Thomas asked.

"Sharon at the Wardlaw told me that a Lady Janet Douglas is going to take away Sir Andrew Douglas's corpse."

"It's the first I heard of it," Thomas said.

"It's true." Eleanor felt sick at the admission.

"Why?" Martin faced Eleanor across the width of the table.

What can I say? The music grew louder inside Eleanor's head. She looked up. "I don't want to live on top of a grave," she said and gave her new, loud laugh. "Anyway, Sir Andrew has been away long enough. He should be home where he belongs."

Martin grunted. "It's a damned fool idea," he said. "One that leaves the area, and you in particular, open to all sorts of dangers."

"Why did you do that, Eleanor?" Thomas asked.

Eleanor's resistance crumbled as the music deafened her.

"Ce fut en mai
Au douz tens gai
Que la saisons est bele,
Main me levai."

"As I said," Eleanor replied, hardly recognising her voice, "I've had enough of living with a corpse in the house. Maybe you like it, Thomas, but I don't. Now, if you'll excuse me," she rose, "I'll see you at the car, Thomas."

"That's not like her," Thomas said as Eleanor swept away. "I don't know what's got into her."

Martin stared into his tankard for a long minute before he replied. "I might know," he said. "And it's not good." When he looked at Thomas, his eyes were old and very wise. "Have you noticed any changes in your sister lately?"

"What do you mean, Martin? She's a woman. She changes every few minutes." Thomas used humour to deflect the question. "She's worried, Martin. Sometimes she seems like a different person. I thought it was the strain of looking after me after the war."

"I think it's something else," Martin said, "something spiritual."

"Ah, the redcap thing," Thomas told Martin about Powrie. "Eleanor visited the church as well," he said. "The first time since 1917."

"1917?"

"She was a nurse for the wounded after Passchendaele," Thomas said. "After what she saw then, she lost all faith."

Martin sighed. "War is the devil's game." He stood up. "You'd better join your sister, Captain Armstrong before she does something even sillier if that were possible."

~

Eleanor stood over the skeleton, removed the ring from her hand and slid it onto the left signet finger of Sir Andrew.

"You're going home," she said. "You're going back to your family where you belong."

Sir Andrew lay still, but Eleanor felt something flutter inside her. Once again, she visualised the knight as a vibrant young man, smiling down on her.

He was naked, with a display of smooth muscles, an overdeveloped right arm with which he wielded his sword, and the grin of a conqueror.

"Come to me," Eleanor invited. "Come to me, my gallant young knight."

"Ce fut en mai
Au douz tens gai
Que la saisons est bele."

She laughed again, knowing she had inveigled him and was

entirely in charge. Reaching out, she pulled him closer, smiling. "You are mine again, Andrew Douglas of Maintree!"

The years drained away. Lady Marjory smiled through Eleanor's eyes, inhabited Eleanor's body, and spoke with Eleanor's voice. "The world sees me as Eleanor Armstrong," she said. "Very well, I shall be that woman until Sir Andrew is removed, and then I shall take over once more."

Lady Marjory's laughter filled the cellar.

"The guests are arriving," Thomas shouted down the stairs. "Are you ready, sister-of-mine?"

"Ready," Eleanor replied. "I am surprised there is so much interest in an ancient skeleton."

Thomas thrust his head through the open door. "There's not much else happening in the Wardlaw Valley, is there? Come on, Eleanor, Lady Janet is halfway down the slap, with the hearse following her, splashing through the puddles."

"Is it raining?" Eleanor asked.

"Aye, God is weeping on the just and the unjust, the holy and the unholy, and Deepsyke Moor."

By the time Eleanor mounted the steps, Lady Janet had arrived at the front door, with Sir Hugh Cummings and Lady Fiona pushing along the slap a few hundred yards away.

"Time to act the good hosts," Thomas murmured. "Thank goodness they're staying at the Wardlaw and not here."

Eleanor smiled. "Come on, Tom. You don't want a skeleton in our cupboard any more than I do."

The minister took Eleanor aside. "Are you all right, Mrs Machrie?"

Eleanor nodded. "I'll be better when the remains have gone."

"That's understandable," the minister said. "I'll be as quick as I can." He supervised Sir Andrew's removal into a coffin and gave a short prayer.

"Where did all these people come from?" Eleanor wondered as she looked at the increasing crowd.

"All over," Thomas replied. "I think somebody's held Newbigging upside down and shaken all the people out."

Eleanor studied the crowd, with Martin standing at the front with his arms folded and a flat cap pulled over his forehead. The minister stood beside him, holding his Bible close to his chest. Robert Pirie was at the back, trying to talk to an uncomfortable-looking Sharon.

"That's us," Lady Janet said after a surprisingly smooth operation. "Thank you for your hospitality, Mrs Machrie, and for allowing my ancestor to go home."

Eleanor smiled, fighting the music. "He deserves to be with his family." She tried to ignore Martin's worried face as Thomas wrapped an arm around her shoulders.

"It'll be over soon, sister-of-mine."

"Ce fut en mai

Au douz tens gai."

Oh no, my deluded young fool, it's only beginning.

Eleanor stood outside Anton's Walls as the hearse carried away the earthly remains of Sir Andrew Douglas. Thomas removed his hat as the heavy black car splashed over the track, with the puddles already spreading and deepening.

Fitting weather for a final farewell. Godspeed, Sir Andrew.

"It seems strange to fuss over a man who died centuries ago," Thomas said. "In the war, we could see a hundred deaths in a day, or thousands if there was a push on. We buried them without ceremony, or not at all."

"I know," Eleanor said. "Human life is cheap in wartime when evil takes over." She lifted a hand in farewell. "Fare ye well, Sir Andrew. You're going home at last."

She watched the two crows follow the hearse, cawing as if in triumph. The music crashed into her head.

"Ce fut en mai
Au douz tens gai
Que la saisons est bele,
Main me levai."

We are free!

"At least we'll have the house to ourselves now," Thomas said. "No unwelcome guests in the basement." He paused for a moment. "Not that Sir Andrew was ever unwelcome."

Anton's Walls already felt different with Sir Andrew away. Eleanor felt a new tension, and sensations that had once been weak were now stronger. She heard the French song echoing inside her head, sang a few words and slipped down to the basement. The old grave gaped open, with Sir Andrew's sword leaning against the wall.

"Did you keep the sword?" Eleanor asked as her heartbeat increased. "I wanted to send everything back to Maintree."

"I did," Thomas said. "I thought we should have something to remember him by."

"I don't think we should have parted the knight from his sword." Eleanor wondered at the worry building within her.

"He won't need it anymore," Thomas said. "I'll fill in the grave tomorrow and relay the floor."

Eleanor nodded. "I'll stay here for a while."

"Saying your goodbyes." Thomas smiled. "I'll see you when you're ready. Be careful, Eleanor. Don't fall in the grave."

Eleanor stood alone in the cellar, allowing the atmosphere to envelop her. She heard the whisper of the wind outside the house and sensed the soft movement of people all around.

"Are you there?" Eleanor asked. "Is somebody there?"

As if in reply, the electric light bulb flickered, faded, and died, leaving her in darkness.

"Thomas?" Eleanor shouted.

She heard a flutter that could only be a bird, stumbled to the wall and fumbled for the candles she had placed there in case of an emergency. Scratching a match, she applied it to the candle wick and waited as the yellow glow pooled light around the cellar.

"How did you get in?"

The candlelight reflected from the eyes of two crows, who stood at the head of the old grave.

"Get out!" Eleanor shouted. "Go on! Get out!"

The crows stood as they were, watching her through intelligent, bright eyes.

"You're not here," Eleanor said as a fierce elation replaced her initial fear. "Are you?"

The crows did not reply.

"What do you want?" Eleanor asked as something surged through her. She laughed, that loud, wild laugh that was familiar yet so unlike her usual laugh it shocked her.

"What's happening to me?"

The answer seeped inside her, warm and welcome.

"I have you."

Eleanor knew she had spoken the words, yet she did not recognise the voice.

"I am Lady Marjory!" She laughed again. "The knight has gone, and we are free to reclaim Caercorbie."

∾

Thomas stopped at the top of the stairs, aware something was wrong but unsure what. He turned around, blinking, when something unseen brushed against him.

"What the hell?" Thomas shouted a challenge and swore when the lights flickered and died.

That must be a fuse. I've fuse wire in the cellar.

Retracing his steps, Thomas fumbled for the door. "Eleanor!" he shouted. "I'll be there to fix the fuse in a minute!"

Opening the door, he stepped inside the cellar. "Eleanor?"

Candlelight flickered from the far corner of the room, revealing three people.

"Who the hell are you?"

∽

Thomas stepped into the German dugout, holding his revolver. "Achtung!" he barked the only German word he knew. "You are all my prisoners!"

Rather than three or four scared men, a dozen Prussian Guards loomed from the dark, three with rifles and bayonets and the others with clubs, knives, and other weapons. Thomas swore, crouched, and fired at the nearest man. He saw his bullet hit square in the man's chest, knocking him back against two of his colleagues.

"Borderers!" Thomas roared for support from his men.

Intelligence had reported a weak company of Bavarians held this section of the German trench, not the Prussian guard.

"Borderers!" Thomas yelled.

A six-foot Prussian lunged at him with a bayonet, teeth bared in a snarl. Thomas shot him in the head, seeing the man's skull dissolve in a porridge of brains, bone, and blood. The other Prussians came toward him, with one thrusting a bayonet into his leg.

Even as Thomas yelled, he saw a bright light at the back of the dugout and wondered if it was some devilish new Hun weapon.

∽

The three figures were indistinct, half obscured by a green mist. Thomas flapped a hand in front of his face in a vain attempt to clear the murk.

"Eleanor! Where are you?"

"Here, Thomas." A woman stepped closer, with the mist clinging to her. "Here I am."

Thomas peered into the gloom. "Are you Eleanor?" He knew something was wrong. The woman looked like Eleanor, but it was not her. "Who the hell are you?"

"You know who I am," the woman said. "I am your sister, Eleanor."

"Who is with you? How did they get past me?" Thomas stepped closer and coughed as he breathed the green mist. "Gas!"

~

The Prussians surrounded him, big men, half-seen in the gloom. Thomas realised the dugout was unusual, being built of dressed stone with slabs on the ground. He fired his revolver, with the report lost as the Prussians lunged at him. They had donned gas masks, looking inhuman in the dark, like creatures from one of Eleanor's Gothic novels.

"Gas!" Thomas shouted to warn his men and fired again. The bullets did not affect the Prussians, who merged into two men and one woman, looming through the green haze.

"What devilment is this?" Thomas asked.

The bright light changed shape, solidifying into a man.

"I've seen you before," Thomas said, gasping. "Are you British or German?"

The man stepped closer, with the green mist clinging to his chain mail. The knight shouted something to Thomas, but the words were indistinct.

The woman who looked like Eleanor extended her right hand to touch Thomas on the forehead. Her fingers burned, pressing through the flesh and into the bone. When Thomas lifted his hand to fend her off, the two men held him tight.

"Sir Hugh!" Thomas grated. "Robert Pirie!"

The demons have returned, except they've taken over Eleanor rather than Lady Fiona.

"Release my sister!" Thomas ordered. "Take me, but release Eleanor!"

The woman laughed. "I am Eleanor!" she said.

Thomas struggled with the men holding him. They were big and strong, but he had not survived four years of war without learning how to fight. Suddenly relaxing, Thomas slipped down, wriggled free of their grip, and threw a powerful punch that landed square on Robert Powrie's jaw. He knew it was a good blow even before it landed, yet Pirie did not flinch.

Powrie laughed, and his face changed into a malformed thing with a slit mouth, distended nostrils, and red eyes while his arms grew longer, with hooked talons at the end of thin fingers. A red cap, dripping with blood, perched on his head.

"Redcap!" Thomas said and punched again, uselessly.

"Here for your blood and your soul." Redcap's voice grated like gravel under a badly oiled farm gate.

"You'll get neither!" Thomas roared and leapt on him, fastening both hands around the creature's throat.

~

The leading Prussian swung a studded club at Thomas, breaking the skin on his temple and knocking him to the ground. Thomas lay there, momentarily stunned, as the other Prussians gathered around. When one poised a bayonet, Thomas grabbed him by the throat.

"By God, I'll take at least one of you with me!"

Thomas felt the Prussian's throat constrict under his hands and yelled as the bayonets thudded into him. He saw a hearse approaching him, bouncing through the mist. *There's Old Man Death with the door wide open; this is the end, killed in a rough house in a Hun dugout.*

The knight loomed above Thomas. "The sword!" he said. "Use the sword!"

A huge Prussian lifted his bayonet and poised it above Thomas's stomach, ready for the final thrust, until the knight stood between them with his shield held high.

"Sir!" Sergeant Kilner burst into the dugout with a section at his back. They found Thomas with his hands around a Prussian throat, bleeding from half a dozen bayonet wounds and laughing insanely.

"Thank the knight," Thomas said. "Thank the knight." He watched as the Borderers dispatched the Prussians in seconds and laughed again, refusing to relinquish his grip on the Prussian's throat.

"The knight saved me!" Thomas said. "The knight saved me!"

Kilner sighed. "The captain's gone," he said. "Totally doolally."

~

The knight lunged from the gloom, shouting. "Use the sword!" he said.

Thomas felt a jolt inside him as the memories returned. "The sword?" He gasped. He had removed the sword from Sir Andrew's grave before sending him to Maintree House.

Redcap ensured neither rope nor steel could kill Sir Hugo, but Sir Andrew had the sword double blessed.

The mist thickened as Eleanor, and the two creatures closed on Thomas. He punched and kicked, with his blows having no effect. The thing in Eleanor's guise watched, smiling until Thomas fell and rolled across the flagstones. He saw the sword, a bright gleam against the dullness of the mist.

"The sword!" Sir Andrew repeated as Thomas gripped the hilt. He felt the power surge through him.

Eleanor was intoning that nearly tuneless French song.

"Ce fut en mai
Au douz tens gai
Que la saisons est bele."

Her eyes were dark, bottomless pits stretching forever, her mouth open, lips full, red, and inviting. Behind her, there was nothing human about Powrie; he was a redcap with snarling pointed teeth and long, hooked claws.

"Cummings!" Thomas roared, holding the sword two-handed. "Are you there?"

"I have him," the creature who had been Cummings replied.

Thomas saw what appeared to be a young man, smooth-skinned, with a faint smile on his face and dressed like a four-teenth-century knight. He stood behind Powrie.

"Neither steel nor rope can hurt me!" the apparition said.

The Prussians were back, with the hearse parked, waiting and death waiting. Thomas hefted his sword and lunged, thrusting clumsily.

"Not like that!" Sir Andrew appeared close by, fair-haired, blue-eyed, and terribly young. He merged with Thomas, two warriors combining their fighting skills, and Thomas felt new strength coursing through him.

"By Saint Bride!" he roared, and the French music faded

although Eleanor continued to sing. More music eased into the cellar, the golden notes of a harp penetrating the murk.

Pirie leapt at him faster than Thomas believed possible, yet he parried with his sword, feeling the thrill of contact jar his arms as Sir Andrew whispered swift instructions in his ear.

Pirie snarled, spitting blood until Thomas twisted sideways, feinted left, and thrust his blade deep into the creature's stomach.

"Rip!" Sir Andrew ordered. Thomas pulled the sword sideways.

"Twice blessed!" Thomas shouted. "By St Bride!"

"Say the Lord's name!" Sir Andrew ordered.

"In the name of the Lord!" Thomas roared.

Pirie collapsed, writhing, with his face twisted in hate. De Soulis was next to attack.

"Lay the blade on him with the Lord's name!"

Thomas did not dispute Sir Andrew's advice. Rather than thrust, he altered the angle of his sword and placed the flat against de Soulis's face. "In the name of the Lord!"

De Soulis recoiled, screaming, and Thomas followed up, pressing the blessed steel against the handsome face, aware that Eleanor was pointing an elegantly manicured nail at him as she sang her song. The words coiled around him, distracting, weakening his resolve.

"Come to me, Thomas," Eleanor said, and he saw her alter into another woman, voluptuous, smiling with an open mouth, hungry for him.

"Lady Marjory!" Thomas recognised the siren and fought his temptation as he pressed the sword all the harder.

De Soulis crumpled to the ground, with his face altering. Sir Hugh Cummings lay on the flags, unconscious, as Thomas faced Eleanor.

She stood with her legs apart and hands on her hips, smiling, changing into every woman he had ever known. He remembered each one, from the dark-haired little French girl in the estaminet[1] behind Albert to the sympathetic Lady Fiona.

"Come to me, Thomas," the siren invited. "Don't you want me?"

The music coiled around him, beguiling, intoxicating, and dulling his senses.

"The sword!" Sir Andrew's stern voice commanded, breaking through the melody.

Thomas fought away the tendrils of pleasure as he felt the sword vibrate in his hand. The woman had changed to Eleanor, with her wide hazel eyes, but he knew the image was false. Turning the sword, he placed the flat of the blade against her face and pressed hard.

"Oh, dear God, I hope I am doing the right thing."

The woman screamed and backed away, with Thomas following, pressing the blade, feeling the power seep from the blessed steel into the evil that had infested his sister.

The music increased as Thomas pushed the flat of the blade against Eleanor's face, hating himself as his sister screamed, and then she fell limp; the music died, and Thomas collapsed on the stone-flagged floor.

CHAPTER 31

THOMAS GASPED as he lay on the cold slabs.

"Thomas!" Martin put a hand on his shoulder. "Are you all right?"

Thomas pushed himself upright and released the sword.

"I think I am," he replied, looking around. The electricity had come back on, adding harsh light. Eleanor lay at his feet, curled in a foetal ball.

"Eleanor?" Thomas knelt at her side. "Eleanor?"

"She'll be alright in a moment," Martin said. "She has too much natural goodness in her to succumb to evil." He smiled. "The double blessing in the sword augmented the blessing the minister gave her."

"What happened?" Thomas asked. "I saw a knight."

"Sir Andrew Douglas," Martin told him. "Your ancestor."

"My ancestor?" Thomas helped Eleanor to her feet.

Martin was smiling. "Sir Andrew was an unmarried knight," he explained, "and unmarried knights, like single men in barracks, don't grow into plaster saints."[1]

"I'll tell Kipling you approve of his verse," Thomas said.

"Ellen Armstrong of Netherhope carried Sir Andrew's child." Martin was smiling. "Your very distant ancestor and how you got your surname."

Thomas smiled. "Well done, Sir Andrew and Ellen." He remembered the fourth person in the cellar. "How is Sir Hugh?"

"Here." Cummings looked confused. "Where am I? I had a terrible nightmare."

"It was real," Eleanor told him, holding onto Thomas's arm. "Take me upstairs, Thomas. I need some air."

Thomas started when he saw the hearse parked outside Anton's Walls, with Lady Janet standing at the side. She looked oddly at Thomas.

"You made good time to get back here," Lady Janet said.

"I've never been away," Thomas said.

"We saw you on the track," Lady Janet told him. "You stood in front of a large flood and waved us back."

"The Deep Syke." Thomas remembered his images. "The hearse would have sunk in there."

"You were like a sentry guarding the slap," Lady Janet said semi-humorously. She nodded to Martin, who looked nearly respectable in a sober dark grey suit. "Mr Crozier told me Sir Andrew's story, and I have decided he should remain here."

"Here?" Eleanor said.

"After six hundred years," Lady Janet said, "Sir Andrew belongs here more than at Maintree. He should continue to guard the slap, with Captain Armstrong helping him."

Martin nodded. "We'll build a small graveyard beside the slap at Blackhouse Tower and put on a plaque explaining the reason."

Lady Fiona smiled, stepping beside Thomas. "The estate will help pay for it," she said. "After all, de Soulis was our ancestor."

Lady Janet sighed. "For all these years, we thought the crows were guarding our house; now we know they were watching in case another Douglas came to disturb Caercorbie."

Eleanor nodded. "They were uncanny birds. I hope they've gone for good." She lowered her voice. "How are you, Tom? How are the flashbacks?"

Thomas considered for a moment. "I think they've gone," he said. "I relived the worst, the one that tipped me over the edge. I saw the hearse and the knight, and now it's in the past."

Lady Fiona leaned over and squeezed his arm.

Eleanor watched, smiling. She knew her brother had recovered, and she was home at Anton's Walls, where she belonged, without a single crow to be seen.

Martin chuckled and strummed a small harp.

BACKGROUND NOTE

I based this little story on a well-known legend of Hermitage Castle in Liddesdale, deep in the Scottish Borders. According to one version of the tale, Sir William de Soulis kidnapped children and took them to Hermitage Castle for some diabolical practices. Helping Sir William was his evil familiar, a particularly nasty little demon known as Robin Redcap. The redcap used his powers to grant de Soulis invulnerability from rope or steel, so neither a blade nor a hangman's rope could harm him. In return, Robin Redcap demanded blood.

When the supply of children dried up, de Soulis kidnapped adults. The people of Liddesdale requested permission from the king, Robert the First, to remove de Soulis.

"Soulis!" King Robert replied. "Go and boil him in brew!" King Robert retorted, so the people of Liddesdale took him at his word. Snatching de Soulis, they wrapped him in a convenient sheet of lead as rope would not hold him. Presumably, the people obtained the lead from the castle roof. The people dragged de Soulis to a nearby stone circle named the Nine

Stane Rig, boiled a cauldron of water, threw him in and drank him.

And that was the end of the wicked Lord Soulis.

In reality, William de Soulis was a self-seeking traitor who joined a plot to murder or depose King Robert. The king had him arrested and sentenced him to life imprisonment in Dumbarton Castle. There is more about the legend in Jack Strange's book *Strange Tales of Scotland*.

Helen Susan Swift

APPENDIX ONE: THE TWA CORBIES

This is one version of a traditional Border song.

As I was walking all alane,
I heard twa corbies making a mane;
The tane unto the t'other say,
"Where sall we gan and dine today?"

"In behint yon auld fail dyke,
I wot there lies a new-slain knight;
And naebody kens that he lies there,
But his hawk, his hound, and lady fair.

"His hound is to the hunting gane,
His hawk, to fetch the wild-fowl hame,
His lady's ta'en another mate,
Sa we may mak our dinner sweet.

"Ye'll sit on his white hause-bane,
And I'll pick out his bonny blue een:
Wi' ae lock o' his gowden hair,
We'll theek our nest when it grows bare.

"Mony a one for him makes mane,
But nane sall ken where he is gane;
O'er his white banes, when they are bare
The wind sall blaw for evermair."

APPENDIX TWO: CE FUT EN MAI:
FRENCH LOVE SONG

"Ce fut en mai
Au douz tens gai
Que la saisons est bele,
Main me levai,
Joer m'alai
Lez une fontenele.

En un vergier
Clos d'aiglentier
Oi une viele;
La vi dancier
Un chevalier
Et une damoisele.

Cors orent gent
Et avenant
Et molt très bien dançoient ;
En acolant
Et en baisant
Molt biau se deduisoient.

Au chief du tor,
En un destor,
Doi et doi s'en aloient ;
Le jeu d'amor
Desus la flor
A lor plaisir faisoient.

J'alai avant
Molt redoutant
Que mus d'aus ne me voie,
Maz et pensant
Et desirrant
D'avoir ausi grant joie.

Lors vi lever
Un de lor per
De si loing com j'estoie
Por apeler
Et demander
Qui sui ni que queroie.

J'alai vers aus,
Dis lor mes maus,
Que une dame amoie,
A cui loiaus
Sanz estre faus
Tot mon vivant seroie,

Por cui plus trai
Peine et esmai
Que dire ne porroie.
Et bien le sai,
Que je morrai,
S'ele ne mi ravoie.

Tot belement
Et doucement
Chascuns d'aus me ravoie.
Et dient tant
Que Dieus briement
M'envoit de celi joie

Por qui je sent
Paine et torment :
Et je lor en rendoie
Merci molt grant
Et en plorant
A Dé les comandoie."

~

"It happened in May,
when skies are gay
And green the plains and mountains,
At break of day
I rose to play
Beside a little fountain.

In the garden close
where shone the rose
I heard a fiddle played; then
A handsome knight
that charmed my sight,
Was dancing with a maiden.

Both fair of face,
They turned with grace,
To tread their May-time measure;
The flowering place,
Their close embrace,
Their kisses brought them pleasure.

But shortly they,
Had slipped away,
And strolled among the bowers.
To ease their heart,
Each played the part
In love's games on the flowers.

I crept ahead,
All chilled with dread,
Lest someone there should see me.
Bemused and sad
Because I had
No joy like theirs to please me.

Then one of those
I'd seen there rose
And from afar off speaking,
He questioned me,
Who I might be,
And what I came there seeking.

I stepped their way
To sadly say
How long I'd loved a lady,
Who all my days
My heart obeys,
Full faithfully and steady.

Though still I bore
A grief so sore
In losing one so lovely,
That surely I
Would come to die
Unless she deigned to love me.

With wisdom rare,
With tactful air
They counseled and relieved me.
They said their prayer
That God might spare
Some joy in love that grieved me.

Where all my gain
Was loss and pain
So I in turn extended
My thanks sincere,
With many a tear,
And them to God commended."

Moniot d'Arras, (fl. 1213 – 1239) who composed this song, was a trouvere musician. This poem is his best remembered work.

NOTES

PRELUDE

1. A Mazurka is a lively Polish dance. In the First World War, some officers used the term to describe a hectic fight or another piece of excitement.

CHAPTER 1

1. Burn – a stream.
2. Laverock – the lark. Whaup – the curlew.
3. Stooriefeet – dirty feet. Some Border settlements used the name for incomers who arrived with the stoor – dirt – of travelling on their feet.

CHAPTER 4

1. Slap – usually a pass through hills. In this case, a route over bogland.

CHAPTER 5

1. Crazy, mad, from the name of a sanatorium in Bombay (now Mumbai).

CHAPTER 8

1. Palfrey – a horse for recreational riding as opposed to a charger, a warhorse.
2. Outremer – the Holy Land, once Christian but invaded and conquered by Islamic armies. The Crusades were campaigns to return the Holy Land to Christian rule.

CHAPTER 10

1. In this instance, a neuk means an obscure corner or lurking place, a hidden part of the river.

CHAPTER 11

1. The Angels of Mons – according to legend, during the Battle of Mons in 1914, a host of angels intervened to help the British. Although the story was a fiction invented by a London journalist, many people, even serving soldiers, came to believe it.

CHAPTER 12

1. Whaup – the bird otherwise known as a curlew.

CHAPTER 15

1. St Bride was the saint to whom James of Douglas prayed. The Good Sir James was one of King Robert the First's most trusted knights. St Bride was an Irish saint of the fifth century who began life as a slave and ended as abbess of Kildare. There are other saints of the same name, including a pre-Celtic Brigit, the goddess daughter of Dagda, lord of the Earth, but it is unlikely that James of Douglas or Sir Andrew would invoke a pagan goddess.

CHAPTER 16

1. I found no reference to this behaviour related to de Soulis, but Walter Comyn of Badenoch was supposed to have enjoyed such extravagances.

CHAPTER 17

1. A shell from a field gun, from the noise they made immediately before they exploded.
2. The burst of a heavy German shell, such as a 5.9 inch.
3. Vielle - a medieval stringed instrument similar to a violin.

CHAPTER 18

1. Doolally – mad, insane. The name is soldier's slang taken from a sanatorium in Bombay.
2. Toonies- townies, people who live in towns and cities rather than in the countryside.

CHAPTER 20

1. A sack of knitted wool, khaki coloured and about 45 centimetres long. Men used them for storing items of equipment and, when rolled up, as a cap during trench raids or in cold weather.

CHAPTER 21

1. The town of Albert was hotly contested during the German offensive of March 1918.

CHAPTER 22

1. Burn the water – a method of nighttime poaching by using lights to attract fish.
2. The Columban, Celtic or Culdee Church was predominant in Scotland before Queen Margaret and her son, David the First, encouraged the spread of Roman Catholicism.
3. The priest would speak in Gaelic or Brythonic, the languages of the Celtic peoples of Scotland.

CHAPTER 23

1. Quillons – the crossguard of the sword.

CHAPTER 25

1. The English gave Douglas Castle the name Castle Perilous because it was impossible to hold. Every time they garrisoned the caste, Sir James of Douglas, the Black Douglas, recaptured it.
2. Yett – gate made of interlacing iron bars common on Border towers and castles.

CHAPTER 30

1. A café-cum-pub in French villages where soldiers relaxed away from the front.

CHAPTER 31

1. "We aren't no thin red 'eroes, nor we aren't no black-guards too,
   But single men in barricks, most remarkable like you;
   An' if sometimes our conduck isn't all your fancy paints;
   Why, single men in barricks don't grow into plaster saints."
   "Tommy" by Rudyard Kipling.

ABOUT THE AUTHOR

Born in Edinburgh and bred in the Scottish countryside, Helen Susan Swift currently lives in the north-east of the country. Happily married, she works two jobs as well as writing in a variety of genres. Her interests include folklore and history, as well as hill-walking, nature and football, following Aberdeen FC and Ayr United.

She grew up visiting castles and stories, which gave her books a slight quirk when compared to others of the genres in which she writes. It is foibles and cares of people that interest her, the impact of image over reality and the realisation of the true depth of love rather than the shallow desire for material advantage.

∾

To learn more about Helen Susan Swift and discover more Next Chapter authors, visit our website at www.nextchapter.pub.

Guardian Of The Dark Slap
ISBN: 978-4-82416-875-7

Published by
Next Chapter
2-5-6 SANNO
SANNO BRIDGE
143-0023 Ota-Ku, Tokyo
+818035793528

14th February 2023

Ingram Content Group UK Ltd.
Milton Keynes UK
UKHW040637190323
418778UK00003B/53

9 784824 168757